IN YOUR FACE

IN YOUR FACE

A Novel

SCARLETT THOMAS

KATE'S MYSTERY BOOKS

JUSTIN, CHARLES & CO., PUBLISHERS

BOSTON

FIRST U.S. EDITION 2004

Originally published in the United Kingdom by Hodder & Stoughton, a division of Hodder Headline PLC.

This is a work of fiction. All characters and events portrayed in this work are either fictitious or are used fictitiously.

Library of Congress Cataloging-in-Publication Data is available.

ISBN 1-932122-08-1

Published in the United States by Kate's Mystery Books, an imprint of Justin, Charles & Co., Publishers, 20 Park Plaza, Boston, Massachusetts 02116 www.justincharlesbook.com

Distributed by National Book Network, Lanham, Maryland www.nbnbooks.com

10 9 8 7 6 5 4 3 2 1

PRINTED IN THE UNITED STATES OF AMERICA

For my mother, Francesca

ACKNOWLEDGMENTS

Thanks to John Rhodes (the Calculating Boy) and Bob Chase for those little snippets of stuff. Thanks to Kate: recognise anywhere? Big thanks to Kirsty. Thanks to Tom for always getting me up in the morning, changing the cats' water, and just being fab.

The secret of philosophy may not be to know oneself, nor to know where one is going, but rather to know where the other is going; not to dream oneself, but rather to dream what others dream; not be believe oneself but rather to believe in those who do not believe.

Jean Baudrillard

IN YOUR FACE

PROLOGUE: JULY 1987

THE OUTBUILDING IN WHICH THE GIRLS SHOWERED after Games was cold: cold for July, and almost empty by now. The girl stood alone under the hot water, watching a small grey moth batter itself against the curtain, becoming almost transparent as the water buffeted and eventually broke its wings. She regarded this curious suicide with only slight interest and began shaving her legs.

Her new Swatch — all the girls had them — glistened in the water, slightly greasy now that she had rubbed baby oil into her legs (Becky had told her that it kept the moisture locked in). It was gone six o'clock. Three hours later, just before lights-out, she would be on a bus into the local town. If she was caught she would probably be expelled. Big deal.

The tall grey brick building stood lazily, casting lugubrious shadows over a park near the centre of town. The girl liked this bit of the journey; off the bus, across the park past the crowds of students, academics, cyclists and lovers, past the police station and down the path until she came to the bridge. Then the short cut: over the bridge and through the hedge, across the cricket pitch and up the three stone steps, past the old stone-clad wall and in through the prefects' door.

Inside, the hall was quiet, just like the girl's own school. It had a similar smell: mahogany polish, dust and antique wood. Here and there, the odd wispy remains of a cigarette carried in on a blazer or in someone's hair. Coconut oil.

There was still the same end-of-term feeling that permeated her own school. The day after tomorrow the corridor would be full of trunks and overcoats, Mummies and Daddies. She had to make the most of tonight.

The girl made her way up the semicircular staircase, haunted, apparently, by the White Lady, whose picture, a sombre, Gothicy thing, hung at its foot. The girl took one look at it before she hurried up the stairs and through a labyrinth of corridors until she turned into the most haunted corridor, Maids', where servants used to have their quarters, and where the upper-sixth study bedrooms were now situated.

As the heavy door closed behind her the girl smelt the familiar smell that only existed in this part of the school: fresh cigarette smoke, beer, boys' sweat. The end-of-term feeling was ripe up here and the upper-sixth boys, unsupervised at the best of times, were running riot. *Sign of the Times*, the latest Prince album, blasted out of one of the rooms. It reminded the girl of Camden on summer weekends. It reminded the girl of the Spring term; losing her virginity. *This.*

She reached the seventh door on the left — *his* — and tapped gently before walking in. His friend, a smaller boy with glasses, raised his Budweiser bottle and whistled slowly under his breath. They all knew what they were here for. It had been talked about, planned. It was her fantasy, and no one else knew.

Elsewhere in the grey building a boy began his Servant Duty, a popular punishment that had been imposed on him by a prefect after he was caught using the wrong telephone to beg his mother to collect him early. At least he would be home soon, he thought as he knocked on the first door of the Maids' corridor; being here was driving him mad.

A red-faced boy opened the door and the sound of his TV blared out through it.

"What the fuck are you doing up here, turd?" he asked.

"I will be your servant and do whatever you want." The younger boy bit his lip as humiliation fluttered in his body.

"Piss off," said the older boy. "I'm busy. But if you come back later I might be able to think of something — like cleaning the toilets, perhaps."

"Ha ha," said the boy, and walked off down the corridor, stopping at every door and repeating the words as soon as each one was opened.

He didn't recognise the sound coming from the seventh room, and since no one answered his knock he thought he'd better not go in. He was about to turn away when one of the rougher boys came falling, drunk, out of his room and shoved heavily against him, pushing him onto the door which swung open, leaving the boy half in and half out of the dark, humid room.

He looked: but he shouldn't be seeing *this*. Three of them: the head boy, the prefect (the one who had set his punishment) and that rich girl from Saint Helena's. A threesome; two boys doing it to one girl.

The boy had just heard the last of her sentence as the door had opened. ". . . do whatever you want." The girl's words. Then, as he shut his eyes, wishing he hadn't seen anything, one of the boys: "You little shit." And all along, Prince, singing the nonsense lyrics of "Starfish and Coffee."

He turned and ran.

CHAPTER ONE

TO DREAM WHAT
OTHERS DREAM

THE ENVELOPE SAT THERE ON MY DESK: white and thin. *Lily Pascale*, it said on the front in the spidery writing that was so familiar now. I knew what was inside it, but I couldn't face opening it yet. There was some other mail which I dealt with instead, trying to prove to the envelope that it didn't bother me. The short Summer term was over, but there were still things to be done.

My office looked like a car boot sale, and I half expected some old ladies to turn up any minute to pick over the remains. I was supposed to have cleared everything out by now, but, being me, I'd left it until the last possible minute. My mother, on whom I had been relying for lifts to and from work, and who luckily also worked at the university, had been waiting in the corridor for the last half an hour while I regularly reassured her that I would only be another minute. Only I could be this disorganised. I was a hoarder, too, which didn't help. As well as all my *film noir* posters and old horror stills, my walls were still covered in slightly gory postcards and weird murder cuttings sent by friends who thought I would find them amusing. I'd specialised in crime fiction during my MA, and I taught it here as part of the English Literature degree. People who knew this were often surprised when they met me. Apparently I didn't seem like that kind of girl.

The local press cuttings from my noticeboard (*Lily scoops £20,000 reward! Lecturer saves students in dramatic moors rescue. Twenty-five-year-old crime fiction lecturer solves mystery which baffled police!*) had been the first to come down. Because of my passion for crime fiction, and also because I was in the wrong place at the wrong time, I'd been famous for about fifteen minutes. Just not in the way I might have hoped.

Before moving back to Devon to live with my mother and teach at the university I'd been an actress in London. Then I'd wanted my fame to come with glitter, glamour and pancake. But life's a funny thing and instead it had come, however briefly, with dead bodies, criminals and police chases. At my most famous I'd received some intriguing but vulgar offers to "sell my story" to the thinner women's magazines. In the local press I had been compared to Sherlock Holmes, which flattered me, and Miss Marple, which didn't. One of them, in a bizarre oversight, had even called me Lily Savage. Now I was just me again.

It took me ten more minutes to pull everything down from the walls and roll the Blu-Tack into a little ball, which I kept, because there's never any around when you need it, and then there was only my in-tray left to deal with. The problem was, I hadn't cleared it for weeks. There was probably a plastic tray under there somewhere, but you wouldn't be able to tell what colour it was. I started methodically, but it was too depressing, discovering all the lunches I was supposed to have attended and notes I should have replied to. In the end I just threw all the remaining bits of paper, strange invoices and unreadable memos into the big box of marking I was taking home and stood up to go.

"At last," said Mum, when I emerged.

"Sorry," I said, grinning as she slipped the prospectus she'd been looking at back on the table. We walked to the end of the corridor and both fumbled for our alarm keys. keys. Because of me, we were going to be the last out.

"Oh, hang up," I said, putting the box on the floor, turning around and breaking into a run.

I'd left the envelope on the desk.

* * *

The phone in my office began to ring as soon as I opened the door.

"Lily Pascale," I said into the mouthpiece. "Department of English and American Studies."

"Lily, thank God you're still there." The voice sounded breathless and desperate, but I couldn't quite place it. "It's Jess. Jess Mallone."

"Jess! God, I didn't recognise your voice. How are you?" Jess had been a friend once, or, more accurately, a fair-weather friend. We'd lost touch *during* university, never mind afterwards, and I couldn't imagine why she would want to phone now.

"Not very good, I'm afraid."

"What's wrong?"

"Look, Lily. I am so sorry to have to bother you like this . . ."

"No, it's fine, Jess. Calm down and tell me what's happened."

"It's a bit complicated. It's . . . Oh, shit. There were these . . . Oh, God. I don't know where to start."

"Look," I said, glancing at my watch. "The caretakers are about to throw me out of this building. Do you have a number I can call you back on?"

"Yes," she stammered. "Will you call me soon? It's just . . . I don't want to sound overdramatic or anything but I am *totally* petrified."

I scribbled down the number Jess gave me and ran back down the hall, slipping the envelope into my jeans pocket as I went. Mum looked a bit annoyed until she noticed the expression on my face.

"Is everything all right?" she asked.

"I'm not sure," I said, shaking my head in bewilderment. "Let's go home and I'll tell you about it on the way."

We walked out into the heat and over to the car, into which I immediately placed my box, which I was sure had grown heavier in my absence.

"Thanks for waiting," I said, while Mum unlocked the passenger door. "This shouldn't be for much longer, you know."

"When's the new car going to be ready?"

"Soon, I think. Couple of weeks, the man said."

Because of the reward, and for the first time since I could remember, I actually had money in my bank account and all my credit cards had been paid off. Thus the new car. This summer was also going to include house-hunting; something to rent, by the sea, I thought.

A few months ago I would never have imagined settling in Devon again, near my mother, but the idea appealed to me much more now. I loved my new job, and since I had become acting Head of Literature (a post which would expire this summer when they found a replacement), my career prospects were looking good.

"Who was on the phone before?" Mum asked, smoothing her hand through her red hair as we pulled away.

"Oh, the *phone call*," I said, remembering the wretched tone of Jess's voice. "That was really strange." I looked in the pocket of my jeans for the phone number I had written down. Good. It was still there. "Do you remember Jess?" I asked, looking at the number and trying to work out which part of London it was from. *691.* South, I thought.

"Jess who?"

"Jess Mallone," I said. Mum looked blank. "You remember John from university?"

"Oh, yes. He came to stay for the weekend and brought that girl."

"Yes, that was Jess. She was on the journalism course."

"Oh, I see. So what did she want?"

"I'm not sure," I said. "I think she's in some sort of trouble. She said she was terrified about something." I shook my head. "I don't know why she phoned me, though. I haven't spoken to her in years."

The rest of the journey was taken up debating Mum's recent work dilemma: should a man be allowed on Women's Studies? I laughed and said that most men didn't need to be taught how to study women, but received a withering look for that. Mum still hadn't decided by the time we reached Mawlish, but seemed to be erring on the side of no. I agreed with her. There had to be something dodgy about a man like that.

The sun was still shining relentlessly as we walked through the door of the cottage. Dropping the cardboard box full of marking in the cupboard in the hallway, I went straight through to my bedroom. The weather was trying to tempt me back outside, but I had two important things to do and I imagined both would take some time.

The phone rang for a while before Jess picked it up.

"Hello," she said uncertainly. It sounded like she'd been crying.

"Hi, Jess, it's Lily. Sorry I couldn't speak to you before, it's just . . ."

"It's all right," she said weakly. She paused for a moment, as if unsure about where to start. "I heard about you solving that murder."

"Did you?" I was surprised. "How?"

"My mother saw a piece about you in the *Bristol Evening News*."

"Goodness. I didn't realise my fame had spread so far."

My ironic tone was lost on Jess. She coughed and then sighed.

"I'm in a lot of trouble," she said, adding enigmatically, "I think."

"What's happened?" I asked, still baffled.

Jess started telling what sounded like her life story; a long preamble to what I hoped would be the point to all this. She began where our short-lived friendship had left off, talking about how she had got a 2:1 at university and then been taken on by a newspaper as a cub reporter. A lucrative job offer had tempted her to go into DTP for some big stationary firm. Since leaving that job she had become a successful freelance journalist — which she loved. I remembered that Jess had been devastatingly attractive when I knew her, and I wondered if she'd changed. Everyone had noticed it: her pale green eyes and cliff-edge-straight blonde hair. She was pale all over and frighteningly, starkly thin.

Everyone at university had called her the Ice Queen, and although we'd all claimed not to know what John saw in her, it was painfully obvious that he saw what we all couldn't help but see: a gorgeous, almost ghostly young woman on a mission to succeed; the kind of person that made you feel big and ungainly no matter how small you were. I remembered trying to explain that to someone, arguing that to make someone feel big was sometimes worse than making them feel small, but they couldn't really see it.

The thing that had always haunted me about Jess was her scar, which I only saw once, by accident, the weekend she stayed here at the cottage. It was triangular and bright white, like three miniature strip lights cutting across her waist. She'd always covered it quite well, never wearing crop-tops or bikinis, but I had seen it when she came out of the shower after we'd all been to the beach. I imagined there was a story behind it but I'd been too polite and embarrassed to ask what. There had been a rumour, some time in the first year, that she was attacked. She never talked about it, but for a couple of weeks she wore her Ray-Bans in seminars.

As she carried on talking I toyed for the second time that day with the envelope that was lying by me, still unopened, on the bed. It seemed that Jess was now living with a boyfriend called Tyler and had been very happy until yesterday when her world had, as she put it, collapsed.

"So what happened?" I asked again, reaching for a cigarette and a notebook — two items I always needed when I was on the phone.

"Have you been watching the news?"

"Um . . ." I thought for a minute. "Not recently, no. Why?"

"The murders of the three women in London. Have you heard about them?"

"No. Sorry, it's been the end of term and . . ."

"It's all my fault." Jess started to cry again.

"Why? How? What do you mean, it's all your fault?"

Jess blew her nose noisily. "You know I said I've been free-lancing? Well, I did a story about them — the women that were killed — for a magazine, about their experiences of being stalked. It was published yesterday, then they were all found dead. I never thought —" She stopped abruptly, like she didn't know what to say next.

"What?" I asked gently.

"Nothing. I just can't believe this has happened. The police are going to be round here soon. What am I going to tell them?" Jess gulped and took a deep breath. "Fuck."

She even swore glamorously.

"*Fuck,*" she said again, with more emphasis.

I put my cigarette out. "Do you know anything about what happened?"

"No. Well, yes, partly. But it's just all too complicated." She paused. "I know you think it's strange that I'm phoning you after all these years, and I know I wasn't a very good friend at university, but . . . you're probably the only friend I have left."

Considering that I had completely forgotten her until she phoned, it sounded like she was in a pretty bad situation.

"What about John?" I asked.

"I can't go running back to him," she said, slightly bitterly. "Please say you'll help."

"I would," I said slowly, "but I don't really understand what you want me to do. I mean, what are you asking, exactly?"

"You've got to help me work out what's going on here. It's all fucked up and I don't know how to make sense of anything any more. You caught that other murderer. You've just got to try and help me work out who did this before it fucks up my life completely."

"But I can't, I mean, that was just luck . . ."

"Look. I know some stuff. I just can't tell the police right now. I need to get it all straight in my head before I do."

"Okay. Well, I'm quite a good listener, I suppose."

"Can you come soon?" she asked quickly, catching me off guard.

"*Come?* To London? But I thought you said —"

"Please, Lily. I'll pay your train fare and everything. Please?"

"Well, if you haven't got anyone else . . . I suppose I can try and find some time." I looked at the envelope one more time and wrote Jess's address down on my notebook. "But I think I've got a wedding to go to."

CHAPTER TWO

BAD THINGS

THE WEDDING INVITATION, once I'd summoned up the courage to take it out of its envelope, didn't come as any great surprise. The slightly too Gothic typeface didn't make it look any better: I was being asked to attend the marriage of my best friend and colleague, Fenn Baker, and a first-year student, Bronwyn Young. Along with the invitation was a note from Fenn asking me to meet him tomorrow afternoon in the city for coffee. I sighed and walked up to the bathroom for a much-needed bath, and undressed in front of the mirror.

My dark brown curls tumbled down onto my shoulders as I removed my hair from the clip that had secured it all day. Watching myself in the mirror while the water filled the bath, I was pleased to note that my teenage jealousy of girls like Jess who were thinner and paler than me had evaporated several years ago, and that I actually quite liked my reflection now. Men did too; frequently the wrong ones.

Like Fenn. Stupid, stupid Fenn. I couldn't help feeling angry about the whole situation: there was something so wrong about it all, about this wedding. It was taking place not because Fenn and Bronwyn were in love, but because she was pregnant. You really had to know Fenn to understand this. It was by no means the done thing, of course: it was the nineties, neither set of parents had forced his hand, and even Brownyn, according to Fenn, had been surprised when he'd popped the question.

In the last three months since the proposal we'd been over and over it. It had turned out that his own mother had been abandoned by his father before Fenn was born, and he'd never had the chance to get to know him. Fenn wouldn't have wished either his mother's experience or his own on anyone else. So he'd proposed for that reason; for an unborn child which, incidentally, plenty of people weren't certain was his.

Trying to rationalise with him, I'd pointed out that he could keep in touch with Bronwyn and the baby; that there was some middle ground between marriage and what his own father had done, but there was no way he was going to change his mind. It seemed naive to me; a way of putting off the inevitable. Fenn and Bronwyn were not going to be together for ever. They didn't love each other.

Turning the soap over in my hands I thought wistfully about all our stolen moments in which these conversations had taken place. We would meet in a bar or museum café in the city, and talk for a while about the books we were reading and art and philosophy and life. Then, inevitably, we would talk about *the baby* and its consequences, Fenn wringing his hands and wondering aloud how he had got into this whole mess.

The wedding was soon and I didn't want to think about it. Instead I thought for a while about Jess. Why had she phoned me? I had no idea what I would be able to do to help her. As I kept trying to tell people, apart from the aberration last term, I was only really into crime fiction — real murder turned my stomach.

How did you kill them?

You already know how I . . . Oh, I see, you want to hear it from me. Well, I stabbed the first one and strangled the third one. The middle one I pushed in front of a train. That's always been a fantasy of mine, the train thing. It's about power, I suppose.

I can remember the time when I changed: when I stopped being powerless and started being in control. It was on a train platform, in Cambridge I think. I had always been scared of someone pushing me over that line, you know, that yellow line that separates you from the track and ul-

*timately from the train. Woo, woo [imitates train whistling] — splat. I
just decided to become the person who pushes, rather than the person who
stands there waiting to be pushed. Then my life became easier. [Pauses.]
You do want to know about me, don't you? Not just the murders? I mean,
that's what this is all about, right?*

After my bath it was gone seven o'clock. I dried off my hair with a
towel and pulled on some new jeans and a loose vest top. It was
getting a bit cooler outside now, so I walked downstairs to my
room to find a cardigan. My half-Siamese cat, Maude, seemed to
be stalking something behind my bed, but as soon as she heard me
come in, she chirruped happily and trotted over, holding her small
grey face up to mine as I bent down to stroke her. Having greeted
me satisfactorily she went back to her hunt, which I guessed involved the pursuit of her favourite toy, a pale blue furry blob which
used to be a fish.

I put the invitation away in a drawer, not wanting to look at it
any more, and wandered through to the living room, where Mum,
my brother Nat, his girlfriend Beth and her twin brother Paul
were all noisily playing Scrabble.

"That is *not* a word," said Beth indignantly as I walked in.

"What's the word?" I asked, walking over to the only available
armchair and flopping down in it.

"Quacksalver," said Mum wearily. "Did you have a nice bath?"

"Yes, thanks," I said. "Quacksalver? That's too many letters,
surely?"

"Paul is trying to add *salver* to *quack*," said Beth. "Hello, by
the way."

"Oh yeah, hi, Lily," said Nat. "You're good with words. What
do you reckon?"

"It's some kind of fraud, isn't it?" I said, surprising myself
slightly but remembering the word from one of my more difficult
Sunday crosswords. "An impostor of some sort."

"That's what I said!" said Beth, her usually soft voice rising
with exasperation.

"No," I said, smiling. "The word; that's what it means."

"Ha!" said Paul and grinned at me. "Do you want to play?"

"I think I'll watch," I said. "It's been a long day."

"Aha," said Nat in a German accent. "She likes to *watch*."

"Stop it," said Mum. "You're disgusting."

"What do you mean?" said Nat teasingly, adding in the same accent: "Maybe it is just your imagination," which made everyone laugh.

I watched the game of Scrabble become more hysterical as people, particularly Nat, started trying to get away with ever more bizarre words. I expected that Nat, Beth and Paul had just finished band practice, since their group, The Immense Standing Timbers, was due to make a long-awaited local comeback. After a while I grew bored with their antics *(Of course Elvis is a word, he's the king of rock and roll!)* and flicked on the TV to watch the news.

The first headline made me go cold.

"Police are still looking for leads in what have been termed the *Magazine Murders*. Initial enquiries failed to provide any connection between the three victims — all women in their twenties whose bodies were discovered yesterday — until it was revealed that the women took part in a 'true life story' for *Smile!* magazine. The feature detailed the women's experiences of being stalked, which has led to speculation that the crime may have been committed by one of the stalkers connected to the story.

"We will now go over to our correspondent, Trevor Novell, who is at one of the crime scenes. Trevor, is it true that the police have recently uncovered evidence at this scene which conclusively links at least two of the killings?"

"Yes, Aamon, that's right. Behind me you can see thirty-eight Madison Gardens, the house in which Tam Hunter was strangled to death yesterday lunchtime. A knife has been found inside the house, and although police have not yet made an official statement the word is that the knife is believed to be the same one used to murder Sasha Brookes, whose body was found in a park in north-east London yesterday morning."

"Is there anything conclusive there to suggest a further link with the killing of Rebecca Marsh?"

"As you know, Rebecca Marsh was pushed in front of a train just after the morning rush hour yesterday. Reports first suggested she fell, until forensic investigators called to the scene found evidence of a struggle. Police are expecting this to be confirmed by the post-mortem. Remarkably, up to one hundred witnesses who were on the scene at the time have been unable to provide a complete description of the killer. Most people believe that Rebecca's death was the second in this spree and yes, most people do believe this to be the work of one man."

"Thank you, Trevor."

"Thank you, Aamon. Now back to the newsroom."

"This intriguing case has raised concerns about the need for anonymity in magazine publishing and calls are being made for the issue of the magazine, which was published yesterday, to be withdrawn from the shelves. W. H. Smith has already removed all its copies, but there have been no moves so far by the publisher actually to recall the issue."

Muting the volume, I turned away from the TV and looked at everyone else. Since the item was a day old, I thought the others might have heard other reports with more details.

"So what happened?" I asked.

"More or less what they said," said Mum. "I don't read *Smile!* Has anyone seen a copy?"

"I've got it," said Beth, pulling a thin, papery magazine out of her bag. As well as the suddenly infamous *I was stalked* headline were others: *I was held hostage by terrorists; My night with the aliens; Orgasm every time* and *Say goodbye to cellulite.*

"Let's have a look," said Nat, grabbing at the magazine.

"Oooh, can I see?" said Mum.

They flicked to the correct page, and everyone started trying to read it at the same time. I tried to get a look over Mum's shoulder, but all I managed to see were some blurred photos and unreadable text, hovering under Jess's byline. Nevertheless, seeing the magazine feature made the whole thing seem a bit too real. Jess had somehow made me agree to go to London, but there was no way I could get involved in this. I would phone her tomorrow and tell her I had other plans, or something. That would be the most sensible thing. And if she knew anything about these murders, she should be telling the police.

* * *

Did you enjoy it?

The only one I actually enjoyed was the third one — Tam. She wanted it — and she enjoyed it as well, you may not believe me but she really enjoyed . . . Sorry. You don't really want the details, do you? Oh, you do? Okay. [Lowers voice.] I was going to knife her as well. But I'd read this thing about the pleasure of suffocation, and I thought that this was probably going to be my only opportunity to try it.

The police think that if you're a spree killer you have a "signature," an MO — modus operandi — and that you do it the same way every time. But I don't get that, I mean, if you eat ice cream for the first time you don't just get one flavour, do you? You try them all. That's what I was doing.

With the strangulation — Tam — I just knocked at the door and walked right in. I started immediately, grabbing her hair and pulling her towards me. She screamed, which put me off at first. I kept thinking: what if someone hears? Anyway, after a while I got into it, the screaming, that is. Her eyes were wide and frightened, but excited, I think. What would I know? It excited me, anyway, just like I'd heard it would. I used the knife to cut some of her clothes off, holding her around the neck as I did. It took longer than I thought and I was exhausted afterwards. I just wanted the job done so I could leave and think about normal things. After all, I'm just a normal person, really.

When I woke up the next morning I felt unusually refreshed, my body reminding me that this was the holidays at last. I looked at the clock by my bed and saw that it was just after ten. I wasn't meeting Fenn until four, so I pottered about doing a bit of ironing and having a long bath until it was time for *Columbo*. My hair dried in the breeze from the window, and once Columbo had unmasked his man (it was the dentist), I took some clothes up to the bathroom and started to get ready.

Although I probably shouldn't have cared what I wore to see Fenn, now that he was *intended* for someone else, I still chose my clothes carefully. (He wanted to ask me something, the note had said, and I was both excited and apprehensive about what that might be.) My favourite jeans were a pair of blue 501s, very old and faded with frays on both back pockets and the beginnings of a hole on one knee. I teamed these with a white top which clung in all the right places and stuck my hair in a high ponytail. I kept my make-up minimal, as always, wearing just red lipstick and black mascara. I never wore eyeshadow; since I had one green eye and one blue. I found it difficult to select colours that didn't clash with one or both of them.

At a quarter to three I was ready and, not wanting to bother Mum for a lift, I took a cab from the village to the train station and arrived at The Tearooms in the city with ten minutes to spare.

CHAPTER THREE

ONE FOR THE ROAD

Would you describe yourself as a serial killer?

I told you. I'm just normal. [Laughs]. Anyway, it was a spree. Do you know what that is? Of course you do. I looked it up. I could have been a mass murderer, you know, if I had managed one more. To be a mass murderer you have to kill four: four or more victims killed within a short time-span. There is something that experts [laugh] call a "cooling-off period." Serial killers have a cooling-off period: a time to reflect on and enjoy your last murder before thinking about the next one. Spree killing is a series of sequential killings — but no more than three, remember — with no cooling-off period. [Laughs.] By the time I'd cooled off, I'd done what I needed to do. There was no need to kill any more.

The Tearooms was quite empty as I took my usual seat at a small round table by the window, which was open even though there was no breeze coming in. Watching a fly try to escape, I thought about this little café that I came to every time I was in the area. I liked it here for several reasons. They did wonderful espresso and little Italian cakes that you couldn't get anywhere else in the city, and this was the place Fenn and I always met up to have half innocent, half guilty coffees that I was sure he didn't tell Bronwyn about.

Wondering again what he wanted to ask me, I reminisced about the day, only a couple of months ago, when we had first met. I smiled when I remembered that he'd scared me in an empty class-room and I'd convinced myself he was a murderer; in fact he was an enigmatic literature lecturer, specialising in nineteenth-century fiction and romance (in books, of course, and almost with me).

A waitress came over, looking hot and flustered, and I ordered a double espresso and a slice of chocolate tart. Looking at my watch I saw that it had just gone four. A few moments later the small door to the café opened and there was Fenn, looking ha-rassed but gorgeous in old grey jeans and a white T-shirt. He hadn't shaved for a few days and his stubble brushed my cheek softly as he kissed me hello.

"You look delicious," I said as he put his sunglasses, car keys, mobile phone and cigarettes down on the table.

"Thank you," he said, sitting down and gesturing to the wait-ress for a cappuccino. "And you look ravishing, as always."

We always greeted each other in these sorts of terms, at least when we were alone (Bronwyn probably wouldn't understand), and although it was our standing joke, I certainly meant all the things I said. He was very good-looking. More than that, he was stylish. Fenn was the first man I'd ever met who really liked shop-ping for clothes and who could spend longer at cosmetics counters than I did, buying all kinds of new-fangled moisturisers and ex-pensive things for his skin. Sometimes people assumed he was gay and I often called him a fashion victim, but all the effort paid off. He was very sexy.

"Are you thinking dirty thoughts again?" he asked innocently, making me blush.

"You know I'm not capable of that," I said, slightly embar-rassed by the truth in this statement. I hadn't exactly been around the block and I still wasn't sure whether Fenn knew that.

"Hmm," he said, almost to himself. His cappuccino had arrived and he was absent-mindedly dropping brown sugar rocks into it.

"How's Bronwyn?"

"Fine." He shook his head and then looked deep into my eyes. "Am I doing the right thing, Lily?"

"I don't know," I said honestly. "You know it's not what I'd do, but then I'm not you."

"No."

We sat in silence for a few moments then I changed the subject, trying to cheer him up a bit.

"How were your second-year essays?" I asked, unable to think of any neutral topic other than work.

"Appalling, as usual," said Fenn, smiling. "I don't know what's wrong with that group."

"They had bad lecturers for most of the year," I said, slightly defensively. "Although that's no excuse. You wonder if some of these students forged their A-level certificates."

"I know. Although I wonder if they would be capable even of that." He sighed. "I'm just glad to have a bit of a break now term's finished."

"I would be as well," I said, "if it wasn't for the pile of essays, memos and God knows what else in my cupboard."

"In your *cupboard*. Out of sight, etcetera. *What* a good idea."

"I thought so."

"So did I," he said dramatically. "Last year."

"What happened last year?"

"I forgot about them until the day we went back. Then, reminded by fifty students that I was supposed to be giving them their essays back, I realised that I'd actually lost them." Fenn cleared his throat and looked at me innocently. "Forever."

"Forever?" I said. "What did you do with them?"

"I put them in a cupboard."

"Couldn't you just get them out of the cupboard?"

"I moved house in between." He burst out laughing and so did I. Fenn was a younger, more good-looking version of the proverbial mad professor; incredibly bright, but very, very disorganised and absent-minded. "They blew it up."

"What?" I said, between giggles.

"The house."

"You're joking."

"No, I'm serious. I told you, these things only happen to me. There's a supermarket there now."

"What did you tell the students?"

"I told them to get over it. Most of them throw their essays away once they get them back anyway."

"But how did they get marked?"

"Randomly."

"That's very naughty," I said.

"I couldn't see what difference it made," he said. "They were all going to get lower seconds anyway."

"Oh, well, that's all right then," I said, laughing and lighting a cigarette.

"You look serious," said Fenn after a few moments, breaking my thoughts.

"Just thinking about work still. My body knows it's the holidays but my brain doesn't. Sorry."

"That's all right." He smiled. "You've done a really good job this term, you know."

"Have I?"

"Oh yes. Everyone thinks so."

"Oh," I said, surprised and flattered. "Thanks."

"You need a break of some sort. A holiday."

"You're telling me. Thing is, I don't go on planes. I'm not altogether sure about boats and I don't have anyone to go with."

"Well, if I didn't have to get married I'd be more than happy to accompany you somewhere exotic."

"Hmm, somewhere we could go by train, like Bournemouth?"

"We'd get you in a plane somehow."

I sighed as a cool breeze found its way through the window and brushed my face.

"If you weren't getting married," I mused. I reached for a cigarette and so did Fenn, our hands and eyes meeting at the same moment, locked for all of two seconds. Too long for friends, not long enough for lovers.

He coughed uncomfortably. "But, of course, I *am* getting married."

"I know."

"You do understand what this means, don't you?"

"No," I said, slightly taken aback by something in his tone. "What?"

"We're not going to be able to do this any more." Fenn held

his hands out and looked sad. I wasn't entirely sure what he meant. One minute he was talking about taking me on a romantic holiday (I wished!), now this.

"Sorry?"

"*This.* I mean, we'll see each other at work and stuff, but I'm going to have to take my share of the childcare, you know, and . . ." He trailed off.

"And what? Bronwyn feels threatened?"

"In a word, yes." He sighed. "There's no easy way to say this." He lowered his eyes to the table, like he was embarrassed about what he was going to say. "We've agreed I shouldn't see you socially any more."

"You *are* joking," I said, trying to keep the disbelief and contempt out of my voice but not totally succeeding.

"No. It was a compromise. I mean, she wanted me to stop working with you as well, but I drew the line there." He laughed uncomfortably. "I don't think I'd be able to bear never seeing you again."

"So why the hell are you going along with it?"

"Don't be like that, Lily," he said quietly. "I've got to try and make this work."

"But at what cost? Losing a friend?"

"You're more than a friend, Lily," he said, taking my hand in his. "We both know that. So does Bronwyn, though. That's the problem."

"Then why . . ."

"I just have to do this. I know I'm putting our friendship on the line; God, I'm risking my own happiness over this, but I don't have any other choice. That baby needs a father."

"Yes, and what happens when you can't hack it any more? What happens when two years down the line you finally realise that you've made a mistake and leave? Won't that be worse?"

"We'll have to wait and see." He smiled ruefully. "Maybe it'll work out."

"Maybe? Fenn, if you're already saying *maybe* then this doesn't look good."

"I wish you'd be more supportive," he said, taking his hand away. "This is hard enough."

22

"You wish I'd be more supportive?"

"Yes."

"Even though I can see you're making the biggest mistake of your life? Marriage isn't a game, Fenn. I've had friends who've just rushed into things and regretted it. It's hard to get out once you're in, you know."

"I do know all this," he said quietly, his eyes cast down.

"I don't think you do. Marriage is really serious, you know. If you were in an accident or something, it would be Bronwyn who'd get to decide whether to let you have an operation or let the doctors turn off your life-support machine. If she thought you'd gone mad she could have you committed. You can't take this lightly. If it didn't work out, it would take months — maybe even years — to organise a divorce, and it would probably cost more than the wedding."

"This isn't about money. It's about giving a child a father."

"By giving its mother a husband? Come on, Fenn. Parents aren't necessarily expected to be married these days."

"In your opinion."

"Not just mine. Everyone thinks what you're doing is a bit mad."

"Well they can think what they like. It's my life."

"Is it? Maybe not for much longer."

"What's that supposed to mean?"

"It means I think you're signing your life away. Literally."

"Well, it's my choice."

"Like not seeing me any more. Is that your choice?"

"It's a choice I've got to make."

I sat there in silence for a moment. Then I snapped.

"You just can't see it, can you?" I said, my voice coming out choked and hissy. "You're telling me that you can't see me any more because *Bronwyn* says so, and then you're talking about making your own choices? You're not getting married, for goodness' sake, you're joining a bloody *cult*. I can't deal with this any more, Fenn."

Finding myself somehow up on my feet, the only thing I could do was grab my cigarettes and storm out, which I did, mumbling something inarticulate like *you know where I am if you* . . . as I went. As I walked quickly to the train station I wondered what I had been going to say. *If you* . . . change your mind? Unlikely. Want to marry me instead? Ridiculous. What, then?

I never did find out what he'd wanted to ask me, but by now I didn't care. I fumed all the way home on the train thinking, *what a bastard* in time with the sound of the train on the tracks. I imagined some list Bronwyn had made for Fenn: *Organise cake, Pick up wedding dress. Organise honeymoon, Tell Lily you're not allowed to see her any more.* What was the matter with these people?

By the time the cab delivered me home from Totnes station it was almost half past seven. I felt tired, grubby and pissed off and couldn't wait just to get inside and calm down. Never mind a holiday — I needed a hot cup of coffee and a quiet room to get my head back together.

As I paid the cabbie and walked towards the door I noticed two cars in the driveway along with Mum's. One, a yellow Mini, I knew belonged to Beth, but the other, a slightly rusty Beetle convertible, I'd never seen before. I assumed it belonged to one of Nat's friends.

Pushing the back door open and walking into the hallway, I could hear sounds of music and laughter coming from all over the house. Mum was sitting at the kitchen table with Sue, from whom most of the laughter seemed to be coming. Sue was Mum's work colleague and best friend. I knew the car hadn't been hers. She hated cars and never drove, having given up radical feminism in all but appearance in favour of eco-warriorhood.

As I walked in I almost sent Nat flying along with the three mugs of coffee he was holding.

"Watch out," he said good-naturedly, ducking around me and grinning.

"Sorry," I said acidly, still reeling from my run-in with Fenn.

Needing a cat to stroke, I looked around for signs of Maude, but I assumed she was taking refuge from the noise somewhere. I put the kettle on and walked through to my room, sitting with my head in my hands for a few minutes. I had a strong urge to go to bed. Then the kettle started whistling. Pulling myself up from the bed, I went back into the kitchen, determined to make my coffee and get out of there without becoming embroiled in any jolly conversations.

"Hello, Lily," said Sue, spoiling my plans. "You look well."

"Thanks," I said, searching in the cupboards for the coffee.

"Hello, darling," said Mum. "What are you looking for?"

"The coffee. I'm sure I bought some more the other day."

"I think Nat may have used the last of it," said Mum.

"Great," I said, slamming the cupboard door.

"I'll buy some more tomorrow," said Mum, instantly trying to pacify me. She hated it when I argued with Nat.

"Would you like some wine instead?" asked Sue. "We can open another bottle if you want."

"No thanks," I said. "I've had a long day. I'm just going to have a bath and go to bed, I think."

"Your mum's been telling me about her creative-writing group," said Sue. "It sounds fascinating."

"They're all absolutely mad," added Mum. "You'd be in fits if you met them."

"I'm sure," I said, managing a smile. After all, it wasn't their fault I'd had a crummy day. I was glad Mum had been going to this group; it seemed she was finally getting somewhere with the novel she'd been working on for years.

As I walked through towards the stairs I heard voices in the living room, chattering and giggling, and then above them all I heard Beth's voice.

"Is that you, Lily?" she shouted.

"Yes," I called back.

"Come and look at this," she said, adding, presumably to Nat, "I think we need another woman's opinion."

I walked into the living room and found Bronwyn sitting between Nat and Beth on the sofa, clutching a selection of bridal magazines and maternity-wear catalogues on her lap. Great. Just the person I didn't want to see. I couldn't complain, though — she was Beth's best friend. When I'd first met her she'd seemed like a transparency of herself, with the same kind of vacant paleness as Jess. Now she was blooming: her blonde bob looked sleek and shiny and her usually pallid cheeks glowed.

"What?" I asked.

"What's wrong?" asked Nat.

"Nothing. I was just on my way upstairs for a bath. What do you want?"

"What do you think of this swimsuit?" asked Beth, excitedly. "For the honeymoon, I mean."

"I'm not very good at things like that," I said, unable to think of anything I would like to look at less. "Why don't you ask Mum?"

"Don't worry about it," said Bronwyn quietly to Beth.

There was an uncomfortable silence for a few moments, but Beth didn't appear to pick up on the bad feeling in the room.

"We're all going wedding shopping tomorrow," she continued. "You should come, it'll be loads of fun. Bron's got everything except something blue."

"I can't," I said quickly, searching for an excuse. "I'm, um, going to London."

"London?" said Nat. "You could have told me."

"I didn't know until yesterday," I said truthfully. "One of my friends from university is in some trouble." I chose not to mention that the "trouble" was headline news. "She needs someone to help her out and —" I glanced at Bronwyn — "since I haven't got anything better to do for a couple of weeks I thought I'd go and stay with my father."

Beth looked slightly shocked at this obvious snub. Maybe I really wouldn't bother to come back for the wedding. That would show Fenn. Before I knew what I was doing, I'd packed my bags, had a bath and gone to bed, stopping only once to phone my father, Henri, to tell him to expect me tomorrow evening. I tried to phone Jess to tell her the good news but there was no reply. I assumed she was still desperate for me to come, so I resolved to phone her from the train tomorrow.

CHAPTER FOUR

APPENDIX

He's following You — Stalkers' Victims Tell Their Stories . . .
by Jess Mallone

Public concern about crime has never been greater as we approach the end of this century. Statistics show that women are more concerned about crime than men, which isn't a surprise, since we are five times more likely to be on the receiving end of a violent crime than a man. Reassuringly, further statistics indicate that you are more likely to be hit by a bus than suffer rape or an attack from a stranger. But there is an increasingly common form of crime which is perpetrated by strangers against women. It has happened to Madonna and Princess Diana. Could it happen to you?

Sasha, a 22-year-old fashion buyer from Hackney, has still not fully recovered from her ordeal at the hands of a stalker.

"I was eighteen at the time and working as a fashion designer's assistant in east London. On the way home one Friday night I became aware of someone following me. I started walking faster until I was almost running. I was really scared."

Sasha ran home, terrified. "I felt safe once I'd slammed the door behind me," she says. "I had a hot drink and went to bed, convinced that I had imagined everything."

But Sasha didn't realise that she was going to be pursued relentlessly by this man for the next six months.

"The next day I still had the feeling that I was being followed or watched, but every time I looked around there was no one there. I felt really stupid," she says. When she returned home there was a letter waiting for her.

When Sasha read the note she was nearly sick. "I am always watching you," it said. "Don't look behind you — I'll always be there."

She didn't call the police at the time, because she thought it was probably a silly prank. It gave her a real shock, though, and she made sure her doors and windows were always locked after that.

Ten days later the phone calls started. A man's voice, usually whispering things like "I can see you," or asking her, "What are you wearing under your skirt?" Again, she didn't think it was the right time to call the police. But when the phone started ringing almost all night, Sasha decided to take action. She phoned the telephone company and got them to trace the calls. What they found out terrified her. The calls were coming from the phone box facing her house. He really could see her.

Sasha started screening her calls after that, and luckily her stalker seemed to burn himself out.

Madeline Zeger, a clinical psychologist based at Harvard University, has been studying the motives of stalkers for over ten years. She explains: "These men — they are usually men — are selfish and intent on fulfilling their needs. They are committed to their obsession and typically very, very clever about what they do." Some victims are disturbed that a stalker finds out details about who they are and what they do, but Dr. Zeger points out that if a tabloid journalist can do it, then anyone can.

The psychological profile of these men is diverse, but studies have shown that they are likely to be white, middle-class and articulate with a stable family background, but possibly a difficult relationship with their mother. They are usually perfectionists and are very organised; they are collectors and hoarders, sometimes of pornography but usually of more mundane things, like football stickers or milk-bottle tops. Some work professionally but most tend to drift from career to career, sometimes choosing professions such as journalism in which their psychosis is institutionalised and they can be perceived as "normal."

Most stalkers are fairly harmless, and most incidents, however disturbing and inconvenient, are the result of what the stalker thinks is love for his victim. But sometimes their motives are more sinister, as Rebecca, 29, a photographer from Hertford, found out.

"I used to travel to work on the train, taking the same connection every day. There was a man who took the same train, and he always used to smile at me. We never spoke and I assumed he was just another commuter being friendly."

A week later Rebecca was just about to get into the bath when she heard the doorbell.

"Running to answer it in my dressing gown, I didn't even stop to think who it might be," says Rebecca. "When I opened it I couldn't believe what I saw — it was *him*, the man from the train, carrying a bunch of flowers."

Somehow, the man, calling himself Gregory, talked his way into Rebecca's flat and then refused to go. Rebecca was frightened, but there was nothing she could do. Even when she directly told him to leave, he didn't.

He stayed there for about an hour talking about himself. He had been watching Rebecca every day, he said, convinced that she would be the one to save him from himself. Rebecca started to panic when she realised that for all those months she had seen the man on the train he wasn't on his way to work — he was stalking her.

Suddenly he made his move and grabbed her, pulling her onto the sofa with him.

"All I can remember thinking was, 'This is it, I'm going to be raped,'" she says. "He was struggling to get my dressing gown off and became more and more aggressive, grabbing me everywhere and slapping me around the face. He told me that he was going to hurt me — to punish me for what I had done to him. I didn't understand what he was saying, but I knew he was serious. It's funny, but all through the attack I just kept thinking how stupid I had been to open the door without looking to see who it was first."

Luckily, "Gregory" didn't actually rape Rebecca. She did suffer a serious sexual assault, however, and is in counseling trying to work through her ordeal.

Francine Linker, a counsellor with the Rape Crisis Centre, says of the attack on Rebecca that: "In this situation victims often blame themselves, thinking that they were in the wrong place at the wrong time, that they shouldn't have opened the door, or whatever. But we have to be clear about this: the victim is *not* the one at fault."

Of course, not all stalkers are strangers and in a large number of cases, the victim is stalked by someone she knows. Tam, 30, an artist from south London, was relentlessly pursued by an ex-boyfriend, Stuart, who couldn't get over her.

"I kept telling him that it was over," says Tam. "But he begged me again and again to give him another chance. The problem was, I'd already given him all the chances he was going to get and I just wanted a clean break — to be able to get on with my life."

But Stuart wouldn't leave her alone.

"He turned up with gifts almost every day," she says. "When I ignored him in person he resorted to telephone calls. When I blocked out his number with call-screening he just changed his number or used call boxes." Although he never threatened Tam, Stuart made it almost impossible for her to lead a normal life. If she went on a date with a new man he would turn up and scream that she was being unfaithful to him. It ruined several new relationships, and caused her unbelievable stress. She didn't report these incidents to the police, since she believed there wouldn't be much they could actually do. So much for the new anti-stalking laws. Eventually Tam was forced to leave her home and get a new job.

"I felt like a fugitive," she says. "In one day I changed my life completely. I decided to play Stuart at his own game. I waited until a day when I knew he wouldn't be able to follow me and then took action. I had already sent off and changed my surname on my driving licence and lined up a new flat in my new name — by phone. While Stuart was in court I just moved, leaving no forwarding address or anything. It was as if I had disappeared off the face of the earth and I have to admit, it was very exciting. I know I am safe now, unless we happen to bump into each other, but hopefully he's over the whole thing by now."

Jocelyn James of the Action On Stalking Network gives this advice on coping with being the victim of a stalker. She says that you should consider the following:

- Stalking is illegal. You should report all incidents to your local police station. Get the police to file each complaint under the same case number so that you can prove there is a pattern of behaviour.
- Tell the stalker to stop. Do this in front of a witness, if possible, in writing. Keep a copy of the letter.
- Keep a journal with details of the behaviour. Note times, dates and locations and describe each incident in detail.
- Record harassing phone calls on a tape-based answering machine. Date and keep the tapes to use as evidence. Also keep any unwanted mail and any other physical evidence.
- Alert your friends, family, colleagues and neighbours and provide them with a picture or a description of the stalker.
- Get a mobile phone and programme in the number of the police so that you can call them quickly if there is a problem.
- Join a support group and share your worries with friends and family. Do not associate with people who trivialise your problem and most importantly . . .
- *Do not blame yourself.*

CHAPTER FIVE

THE MURDERER

I BOUGHT A COPY of the controversial *Smile!* magazine on the way to the station, from a village shop that was still stocking it; oblivious, it seemed, to the stir it was causing elsewhere. I was catching the two minutes past eleven train which would have me in London just after two. I wasn't sure whether to go and see Jess straight away or relax at Henri's first. I thought, briefly, that I could always forget about Jess and just have a short holiday with Henri, but my conscience wouldn't allow that. She'd been a friend once, and she needed my help.

The train, a huge, noisy InterCity, was bang on time and I scrambled on to first class, remembering someone telling me that you could upgrade at the weekend for hardly anything. I chose a comfortable-looking seat by the window and threw my mobile phone, my notebook, the book I was reading and *Smile!* magazine down on the little table in front of me. I couldn't help feeling excited, like a child on its first train journey. Since learning to drive I had always used the car for long trips, and so this was almost a new experience for me. The train made me anonymous: I could be anyone, going anywhere. I liked that.

As the train gathered speed out of the station I slowly began to feel the anger and hurt of yesterday floating away. I wouldn't say I was *relaxing* exactly; I was nervous about what I may or may not find in London and anxious about whether I would hit it off with Henri's new girlfriend. I got on well with my father, although I didn't see him as often as I would have liked. He and Mum had split quite amicably years ago when it seemed that he wanted a much more footloose lifestyle than marriage allowed.

Fenn may have thought marriage was some honourable heroic dreamworld but from my own parents I knew better. My father was a chain-smoking, wine-drinking French womaniser; my mother was a radical feminist. This hadn't made for the greatest match on earth, and they were much better friends now they were divorced. I sighed. Why did everything have to lead back to Fenn? I had to put him out of my mind somehow.

So I was going to immerse myself in helping a friend. That suited me. Deleting the word *Fenn* from my mind, I picked up the phone to call Jess. Her phone rang twice and then the answerphone came on. *You have reached the office of Jess Mallone. If it's urgent please call my mobile on 0440 222 314 otherwise please leave a message after the tone . . .*

"Hello?" I said to the machine, expecting Jess to pick up. She didn't. "Hello, this is Lily Pascale. Jess, I'm on my way. I don't know what time I'm going to arrive in London, so it's probably best if I come and see you tomorrow . . ."

"Hello?"

"Hello?" I was surprised to find that I was suddenly talking to a smooth-voiced man with a Scottish accent. I remembered what Jess had been telling me on the phone on Friday and took a guess. "Tyler?"

"This is Tyler Moss. To whom am I speaking?"

"Lily Pascale," I said. "Jess probably mentioned me to you."

"I seem to remember you from somewhere," said Tyler. "You caught a murderer."

"Something like that," I said, laughing. "I assume that Jess isn't in?"

"That's right," he said. "But she said you were probably coming to visit."

"Yes. Could you tell her I'll be round at about four tomorrow?"

"Yep. Sure thing."

"Great," I said.

I had barely got the contents of *Smile!* magazine when I started to feel sleepy. Maybe it was all those lipsticks and frozen-food adverts. I blinked and looked out of the window for a few moments, trying to wake myself up, soon becoming transfixed with the way the open blue river turned into marshland and then back into a river again before suddenly, after a short tunnel, becoming the sea; wide and wild and looking high-tideish and almost menacing. I shivered slightly but stared nevertheless, the proximity of the train track to the seafront providing the illusion that the train was actually travelling on the water.

We were approaching another tunnel and it was beginning to rain. There was a series of *whoosh* and *pitter-patter* noises outside and the sea suddenly had millions of little dimples. I turned from the window and back to the magazine, only getting two pages further before my phone started to ring. I cursed it in my head and hoped that none of my plans were being cancelled as I picked it up and pressed the receive button. It was my voicemail service, helpfully calling to inform me that I had one new message, which started to play immediately.

"Hello, Lily, it's Fenn. I need —"

And all of a sudden we were in the tunnel and it seemed I was going to have to wait to discover what it was that Fenn *needed*. Whatever it was, I suspected it wasn't going to involve an apology or a change of heart. *Stuff Fenn*, I thought silently. *Let him make his own mistakes.*

I read *Smile!* curiously, wondering where they got all the incredible stories. Soon I came to *the* story, and I read it carefully, trying to pick up on any details that might be important. Jess's name was at the top of the article, and in different places over the double-page spread were pictures of the women, each placed at an appropriate site. Sasha in a park, Rebecca on a train platform and Tam in her new house. They were all attractive women, all successful — and all *dead*. The thought made me feel sick. Who could do something like that?

Staring at the pictures, I wondered if the women had known each other: Sasha with her bubbly blonde hair and fake eyelashes; Rebecca with her raven hair and pale, drawn face and Tam with her curly red hair and catlike green eyes. They seemed too perfect, somehow, as a threesome. Very *Ballet Shoes*. I imagined that if they had hung around together they would each have worn a different-coloured ribbon. What would they be? Pink for Sasha, yellow for Rebecca and blue for Tam.

But they were dead. No ribbons, no anything any more. Flicking through the rest of the magazine, I wondered how much blame *Smile!* were taking for all this. The whole thing was like a kind of late twentieth century sideshow, all these real-life freaks and victims on display. It made me feel uncomfortable that people were willing to be a part of all of that: objectifying themselves, allowing themselves to be made much of — and for what? To prove to other people that *they* were the normal ones?

I wondered if the magazine had specified that Jess should find three women who all looked so different, and how many people she'd interviewed before she'd decided on these. The murders had taken place on the day of publication, which had me thinking. The killer must have planned; he (I assumed it had to be a he) must therefore have seen a copy of the magazine prior to publication. It was probably someone who worked for the magazine, I thought, or someone who knew Jess or one of the women really well.

My thoughts all faded into one another eventually, as I realised I was falling asleep. I yawned and let my head fall to one side, calmed by the movement of the train.

Could you describe for me, chronologically, what happened?

Yes. Do you mean on the actual day? Okay. I got the magazine, although I knew what was in it anyway. I just wanted to be able to remind myself what they looked like, and make some final plans. I was excited: I was on my way to London on a big dirty train.

[Laughs.] I read Smile! *magazine avidly, wondering where they got all those incredible stories. Soon I came back to the main story, and I read it carefully, trying to pick up on any details that might be useful. There were pictures of the girls, each placed at an appropriate site, Sasha in a park, Rebecca on a train platform and Tam in her new house. (See? See how it all falls into place?) They were all attractive women, and I felt my stomach lurch with a sick excitement as I remembered that soon they would be*

dead. I wondered if they knew each other: Sasha with her frizzy bleached hair and sluttish blue eyeshadow; Rebecca with her black, greasy hair and pale, deathlike face and that tease Tam with her stupid red hair and too-bright green eyes. They seemed too perfect, somehow, as a threesome.

I dreamt about them, on the train, listening to the clickety-click as my hunting knife danced in my bag.

There was a flash of forked lightning in the field outside, and I sat up sleepily and lit a cigarette.

Why do you call Tam a "tease"?

Like I said, she wanted it. It wasn't just that, though, she wanted me. I don't know if I've done mankind a favour or what [laughs]. I'll tell you what, though. That one would have shagged anything that moved. Even me when I was trying to strangle her. You probably think I imagined it. I suppose I could have done. You look excited, too, come to think of it. Maybe I'm imagining that.

As the train pulled into the station I woke up properly, excited to be back in London again. Walking from the train platform to the line of cabs outside I decided what I was going to do for the rest of the afternoon. The cab took me to Henri's house where I was planning to drop off my heavy bag. Luckily, my father was at Sunday lunch somewhere, so I put my bag in the living room along with a note explaining that I was *here*, but not quite here yet.

After a quick cup of coffee I let myself out by the front door and walked to Camden Road station. I was going to the spot I'd recognised from the photo in the magazine; to the site of the first murder. I was going to London Fields.

The rain and storms I had seen from the train didn't seem to have reached London yet, and I could feel the hot sticky air clinging to me uncomfortably as I waited on the deserted platform. I knew that the Sunday service wasn't very good on this line, but I wanted to use it nevertheless, since it would take me through Islington into Hackney. The train soon came and I got into the empty carriage and sat back to enjoy the ride.

I went straight to that park in Hackney. Not Victoria Park, the other one. There's a book about it. Oh, never mind. That's the way she walked to work, every morning at eight-fifteen.

I'd watched her the week before. Sashaying across the grass in her high heels and polyester suit. She looked like an office girl. I wanted to do it right then — the spontaneous kill — but it wouldn't have been the right time. I had to wait; I think you already know why. I waited under the viaduct for about half an hour reading the graffiti. Piss on my face, it said. Nice place, I thought. There were steel bins there, you know, the type that they always light fires in in the films.

She arrived shortly, swishing through the park, alone and seemingly unconcerned. I thought that was odd behaviour for someone who was stalked in a park, but you never know the way these young girls' minds work. There was a pub in the park so I walked around it and fell into step behind her. She knew I was there: first she could hear my footsteps, then my cough as I cleared my throat, and finally the warmth of my breath on her neck as I pressed my chest against her back and pulled her backwards.

She didn't have time to scream. I grabbed her hair and pulled her around to face me. Thinking about it now, I wonder why she didn't scream. Maybe she did. The rest of it happened in slow motion. She lost her footing as I spun her round, and she fell on the knife. Ha ha [laughs], she stabbed herself. She walked into the knife . . . And then I twisted it, just to make sure, hearing the rip of her nylon blouse and her soft breath turn to blood on my neck.

I kissed her hard on the lips as another commuter emerged from nowhere. Her screams fell-into my mouth silently. We were lovers in the park.

London Fields station was shut. I had known this would be the case on a Sunday, since I used to use this slightly pathetic line quite often when I lived in Islington. However I also knew the way to get around that problem — on the old trains at least. As my train — very old and rickety, thank goodness — approached the station I wondered whether my luck would be in. It all relied on the signal box just beyond the station: if it was red I would be in business, otherwise I would have to make a boring backward trek from Hackney Central.

Sensing the train slow to a halt and feeling very naughty indeed, I quietly unlatched the door and hopped off, remembering the way my ex-boyfriend Anthony and I used to do this whenever we visited his brother, who lived just off Mare Street. I grinned to myself as I felt the soles of my old Converse trainers hit the hot tarmac and my knees bend in response to the jump.

The station was deserted, of course, and I felt a cold ache in my stomach when I realised that the murderer had probably walked very close to here on his way to kill Sasha. Suddenly full of adrenaline and fear, I ran down the stairs and out into an alleyway, which was much darker and hotter than I remembered, and as deserted as the station had been. Graffiti hung off the concave red-brick walls and bits of corrugated iron and steel bins lay strewn about like abandoned props from some film about inner-city life that had been too depressing to make.

One day I'll go back to London Fields, I thought, remembering the novel I'd taught the second-years last term. I smiled at that, thinking it had sounded more romantic in the book, and walked on, suddenly wanting to emerge from this long dark tunnel and see some light.

Thinking to myself as I walked, I continued until I suddenly heard a set of footsteps swishing around on the dusty concrete, becoming faster the quicker I walked. I turned around abruptly, gasping, with no instinct about what to do next.

But of course there was no one there; the footsteps and the paranoia belonged only to me. I fumbled around in my pocket for a cigarette and lit it as a train thundered above my head.

There wasn't as much blood as I'd expected, which I suppose was a good thing. When she stopped struggling [coughs] I withdrew the knife and replaced it in my rucksack. I let the girl go and she slithered slowly to the ground, her red hands still holding in all the blood as she clutched her stomach.

The park was still as I walked away whistling and acting as though I were innocent. I walked back through the alley towards the station, where, as luck would have it, I could take a connection to the next place I was due to be. I washed my hands and went.

* * *

Emerging from the alleyway alongside a busy-looking pub. I felt comforted to see plenty of trendy people standing around outside, enjoying cool drinks in the heat. The park was just beyond, so I headed confidently past the crowd and onto the grey pathway running through the grass and started walking slowly, imagining what must have happened here.

As I walked I began to feel a sense of isolation once more as the jokes and laughter from the pub faded and grew distant. I wondered why Sasha had been walking here by herself; I didn't feel very comfortable doing it, and I had never been stalked. I wondered if she had been lured here.

Slowly I began to get an uneasy feeling. Not *fear* as such; more of an insecure feeling, a *what the hell am I doing here* feeling, right in the pit of my stomach. Why had I come? Why did I want to get involved in murder again when I hadn't enjoyed it that much the first time? Suddenly I wanted to be at home, not stuck in some deserted park in the middle of London. I had thought that coming here would be interesting but as I stood here looking around, it just seemed like a park to me. I could imagine what had happened with terrifying clarity, but I wasn't going to make any brilliant deductions like this.

Knowing that I couldn't do much until I'd seen Jess, I walked to the end of the path and onto Richmond Road, where I turned right to get back onto Mare Street. Why *was* I here? Jess wanted to talk, but we could have done that over the phone. In my mind I started to remember what it had felt like last time, working out what no one else could. There was something good about that feeling. *But this is not a crossword,* I told myself sternly. *This kind of thing should really be left to the professionals.* But I knew this wasn't going to stop me. I was here now, and I was interested.

CHAPTER SIX

JARGON

HENRI'S CAR WAS PARKED OUTSIDE the house when I returned and he greeted me at the door.

"Hello, Papa," I said, smiling broadly. "How are you?"

"Very well." He kissed me on both cheeks, and while he did so I registered his companion, an elegant Asian-looking woman in a pink shift dress and matching high heels. I assumed she was the new girlfriend. Her sleek hair was arranged in a neat French plait and I almost felt too intimidated by her tidiness to kiss her hello until she smiled warmly and came towards me.

"The mystery daughter," she said, kissing me three times. "Lily. It's a pleasure."

"This is Star," said Henri. "She'll be staying for a while."

"My flat's being decorated," she said, raising an eyebrow slightly. I raised my eyebrow too, wondering if Henri — heaven forbid — was finally getting serious with someone. Most of his girlfriends were half his age and lasted one evening only. Star seemed different in every way: sophisticated, grown-up and, pleasingly, older than me.

I carried my bag up to the spare room and stuck it on the bed. Pulling my mobile out of my pocket I plugged it in to charge up, not switching it on just yet (if anyone asked, I could just say I'd been in a very long tunnel, which wasn't strictly a lie).

When I emerged, I found myself being sucked downstairs like a Bisto Kid by one of my most favourite smells in the world, freshly brewed coffee, which was coming from the kitchen. Floating through into the sitting room, I collapsed in one of Henri's massive armchairs. I still felt a bit like I was moving; trains and long car journeys always had that effect on me. Star was stretched out on the sofa and smiled nicely when I sat down.

"You beautiful women relax," called Henri from the kitchen. "I will serve you in a moment with fine coffee and handmade cakes. *Merde.*"

There was a bang from the kitchen and I looked at Star and laughed as more and varied French curses tumbled through into the sitting room.

"Handmade cakes?" I asked her. "Surely Henri hasn't . . ."

"Good heavens, no!" she said laughing. "No, when he says *handmade* I think he means they hand-make them in the shop."

"Oh," I said, relieved that my father was still the same man (almost) that he always had been. He was a great cook, but cake-baking wasn't really his style. "So," I said, slightly nervously. "How did you meet?"

"It was at a conference," she explained. "I'm a doctor as well, and there was a group of us presenting papers on medical law. We were all staying at the same hotel and one night I was walking down the corridor when I heard, well, basically, what you can hear in the kitchen now. I called to him in French, to see if he would like some help — he had lost his little scoop in the ice-maker — and so he swore at me too, but I found it and we became the best of friends."

"How romantic," I said, giggling slightly at the thought of my father in a temper over a little ice scoop. "Are you French as well?"

"Mauritian," said Star. "But my first language is French."

"Is your name really Star?"

"No. It's Tarasvati. But most English people can't get to grips with that, so when I first came here, to go to university, I just used my nickname. Most people do that; it's what my family call me too, so I don't really mind."

"So you've been in England a while, then?"

"Oh, yes. After university I never really went back."

"Just like Henri," I said, smiling. "Do you . . . I mean, are you a practising doctor?"

"No," said Star, shaking her head. "I do research."

"What's your subject?"

"Treating psychopathy. An oxymoron I'm sure, but I'll wait for the results."

"Lock them up and throw away the key," said Henri good-naturedly, walking through with a tray piled high with cakes and three small espresso cups.

Star laughed. "I'm beginning to think that way myself," she said "You become a bit jaded after you've done as many interviews with them as I have."

"Yes, I can imagine," I said, remembering that my last run-in with a psychopath hadn't been a pretty sight.

"Anyway, I'm very intrigued by what *you* do," said Star, picking up a coffee cup and a large cake.

"What, teaching?"

"No, no." She shook her head. "I should have said what you *did*. The crime you solved."

"Maybe later? It's a bit of a long story."

"I'll hold you to that," she said, smiling. "I hear that your deductions were quite brilliant."

"What have you been telling her?" I asked Henri, embarrassed but touched.

"Me? Nothing," said Henri, holding his hands up.

"Anyway," said Star mysteriously. "I'd love to discuss the whole thing with you if you have time. Particularly your latest case."

Since I hadn't told either Henri or Star what I was really doing here I was more than surprised. Henri saw the look on my face.

"It's her *intuition*," he said, pronouncing the word in French and shaking his head in disbelief.

"A trick of the trade," said Star, smiling and offering me a delicate-looking cake. "*Secrets,* they're what I specialise in, I suppose."

"Well," I said, "in that case it should be me who picks your brain, to try and work out a way of living up to this reputation I've got."

I sipped my coffee slowly and finished off my cake. After a while Henri and Star slipped off into the kitchen to prepare dinner — apparently there were some people coming — while I lounged around in the chair, flicking through all the cable TV channels.

Eventually I caught the news and learnt that the police had some people "helping with their enquiries," although there were no actual suspects as yet. They were appealing for people who knew the victims to come forward, and asking for anyone who knew the identity of any of the stalkers from the story to do the same. I thought it was odd that they hadn't tracked down the stalkers yet. Meanwhile, the debate still raged about whether the magazine company should withdraw the issue. Current speculation suggested that they probably would, but that they would wait until they had sold enough issues first.

It was almost seven, and the dinner-party guests would be arriving at half past. I wandered into the kitchen to find Henri and Star locked in a particularly passionate embrace. I smiled and retreated, going to the bathroom instead for a much-needed shower. After peeling my clothes off my sticky body I stepped eagerly under the hot water. Looking around the bathroom I could see plenty of evidence to suggest that Star was a frequent house-guest here. Moisturiser, eye cream, Clinique skin freshener (which I was looking forward to trying) cotton wool pads (a pack of two hundred, half-used, which indicated either a lot of nail-varnish-removing or quite a few overnight stays since they were bought) and tampons.

I reached for an interesting-looking bottle of lemon gloss shampoo, glad that Henri's bathroom was finally civilised and now contained more than just Crabtree and Evelyn sandalwood soap (nice but samey) and scruffing lotion (men only).

The water was just right and I enjoyed the sensation of it tumbling down onto my head, flattening my hair and making my whole body tingle. I managed to find a deep conditioning treatment in the now overflowing bathroom cabinet and smoothed it over my hair as soon as I had switched the shower off. I toned, moisturised and massaged my skin a bit (I think it was *Smile!* magazine that said this was good for you) and then rinsed my hair. I pulled a towel around me, applied some make-up and walked to the spare room, where it took me only moments to slip on a little black dress I had bought for these sorts of occasions. Usually I let my hair dry naturally but tonight I blow-dried it, leaving only five minutes to have a cigarette before the guests arrived.

While I smoked, I thought. Wasn't there some message from Fenn on my mobile? I dialled the voicemail number and waited while the remote robot phone rang in the distance, wondering what he'd wanted: what he'd *needed*. Eventually it connected. *You have no messages*, it said. How peculiar. Maybe I'd dreamt it. Maybe he hadn't needed anything after all.

The doorbell went just as I stubbed out my cigarette. I walked down the stairs to find Henri, wearing chinos and a white cash-mere V-neck, greeting three smart-looking people: an elegant couple both wearing what looked like Armani and a young man in a casual suit. I smiled as I realised that the words *casual* and *suit* could only be combined within Henri's social circle. In Mum's world *casual* meant jeans covered in paint, and smart was just a clean version of casual — with the possibility of a long flowery skirt if the occasion demanded it.

When Henri was young he was possibly even more bohemian than Mum, and had been sent to England by his almost aristocratic parents to attempt to keep him from taking part in any revolutions. He wore his dark chestnut hair shoulder-length then as he did now, although now it was cut at Vidal Sassoon and had a grey streak framing either side of his face. I thought his blue eyes had become more grey recently, though, and lost some of their sparkle. Maybe Star would help bring it back.

I smiled at the guests and followed them into the sitting room. The couple were Lloyd Green and Lucy Cousins, a TV producer and artist respectively. I had met them before, a few years ago, and remembered that both were interesting characters. In their younger days she had achieved her first few minutes of fame by at-taching herself to a billboard to promote one of his projects. The young man wasn't familiar at all, and I looked at him for a moment before introducing myself, deciding that while he had what most people would call boyish good looks, I didn't find him in the least bit attractive. He looked like a rugby player, I thought; big, blond and tousled with a cheeky grin and dark hazel eyes.

"Cal," he said, holding out his hand. "Pleased to meet you."

"Hello," I said. "I'm —"

"*Lily.* I know. Henri has told me all about you."

"Has he?" I said, wondering why. Then I realised. I was being set up, albeit in a charming way. Cal, it seemed, was here to "make up the numbers."

"Cal," I said. "Short for . . . Callum?"

"Calvin," he said. "But everyone calls me Cal."

"Pleased to meet you," I said, thanking Star who handed me a glass of champagne. "What do you do?"

"I'm a creative. I work in advertising."

I looked around the room, feeling the cold dry bubbles of the champagne hit my head immediately as I realised that after such a long journey and my extra-curricular trip to Hackney I was not completely up to this. Rather embarrassingly, I just wanted to go to bed. The chattering of the others quickly became background noise as I wondered what Jess was going to tell me tomorrow. Something wasn't quite right about the conversation we'd had on Friday, and the prevailing questions still in my mind were ones I hoped to get some answers to: what did she know, and why didn't she want to tell anyone?

I was startled out of my thoughts by Cal touching me on the arm.

"Lucy was talking to you, Lily," he said.

"Sorry, Lucy," I said. "I was lost in thought. What were you saying?"

"We wondered what you thought of the *Excitement* exhibition," she said. "Cal's creative partner Jon is showing there. He's collected these crime scene photographs. They're really vile by all accounts, and *I* think they should be banned. We're interested to hear what you think."

"I don't really know," I said, feeling like I was on the spot and wondering what the *Excitement* exhibition was. "I'm not based in London any more, so I'm not very up to date with everything."

"Yes," said Henri, entering the room dramatically. "My only daughter has gone to live far away from her poor lonely father."

"Don't be so silly," said Star affectionately, rising from the arm of a chair that she had been perching on and inviting us into the small dining room to eat.

I was well into my pudding — some kind of mascarpone thing involving walnuts and cherries — before anyone mentioned my new-found infamy, and found I was rather too tired to want to become the centre of attention. Most of the meal had been spent debating the mysterious *Excitement* exhibition, the *Scene* series and censorship. On the issue of censorship, we were all agreed: it should be banned (boom-boom). But the idea of showing murder scenes as art was less easy to resolve. Personally I didn't object to reality as much as I did to fantasy: people getting pleasure from fictional slasher films was worse, I thought. I had voiced these opinions briefly and then drank rather a lot as the conversation moved from this to advertising to TV and then back to crime, which was where I came in.

"So we hear your life has become even more exciting since you moved to the country," said Lloyd, pushing his small bowl away and lighting a cigarette, prompting me, Star and Henri to do the same. "Got any good anecdotes for us?"

"Only the murder-mystery," I said, smiling. "But I'm sure you've heard it all already."

"You caught him red-handed, didn't you?" said Lucy. "That must have been dreadfully exciting."

"You caught a criminal?" said Cal, his eyes almost popping out of his head.

"A murderer," I corrected.

"This was quite recently, wasn't it?" asked Lloyd.

"Mmm."

"And apparently the girl that was murdered was your student?" asked Lucy.

"Yes, although I never knew her," I explained. "I joined the university in the week after the murder had taken place. Stupidly, I'd thought I could just ignore it all, but of course I ended up right in the thick of it."

"And this is what got you into amateur sleuthing?" asked Lloyd.

"Um, well, I'm not really *into* it. I mean, I only did it once."

"So it's not likely to become a hobby, then?" said Lucy, making everyone laugh.

"No," I said, almost meaning it.

"It must have been so exciting," said Cal. "Tell us more about the actual crime and everything."

"There isn't any more to tell, really," I said uncomfortably.

"I'm sure Lily's had enough of talking about it," said Star, coming to my rescue. I knew she probably understood. It *had* been exciting: exciting, terrifying and unpleasant. On TV they never mentioned that dealing with dead bodies and psychopaths gave you nightmares as well as glory, and that once you had a horrific image in your head you would never get rid of it; that when you dreamt you would always dream of *that*.

"I wonder what turns people into killers," said Cal thoughtfully, unsuccessfully waving some of the cigarette smoke away from his face.

"Their childhoods, I expect," said Lucy. "Just like everything else."

"That's not strictly true," said Star, downing the rest of the glass of wine she had been nursing. "Most of the patients on my research programme had quite stable backgrounds. Particularly the organised offenders."

"What are organised offenders?" asked Lloyd. "Is that, like, a *category?*"

"Yes. They're criminals who plan their crimes," said Star, smiling in a more sinister way than I had seen before. I suspected she liked her work a lot and was very good at it. She got up and fetched another bottle of wine from the rack. "Meticulously," she added when she returned to the table.

"Like on TV?" asked Henri, too excitedly, poking fun at his guests without them realising.

"Exactly," said Star.

"But aren't psychos, you know, *obviously* mad?" said Cal.

"No," she said. "Everyone just tells you that to stop you being frightened."

The smile came back.

"In fact," she continued, "really dangerous psychopaths appear quite normal. They usually have a partner, a job and a stable family background. They are calm and relaxed while they commit a crime. They are socially adept, and sometimes go to great lengths to acquire the trust of their victim, usually by impersonation."

"God," said Cal.

"I feel an installation coming on," said Lucy.

"I read somewhere that they're likely to be first-born sons," I said, stubbing my cigarette out in one of Henri's huge glass ashtrays. "Is there any truth in that?"

"Oh, yes," said Star. "That's one of the things I've been testing. I was surprised to find that it does seem to hold true in about . . ." she thought for a moment, "eighty per cent of the cases I've looked at."

"I used to think my patients were peculiar," said Henri proudly, "until I met Star."

Everyone laughed at that point, clearing the chilled atmosphere that had crept over the table. Henri was a fairly well-known psychiatrist working in Harley Street and had a growing number of celebrity patients, the identities of whom people were always trying to guess.

"He has an *astrologer* now," said Star provocatively.

"Mystic Meg!" said Lloyd.

"Patric Walker!" said Cal.

"Isn't he dead?" asked Lucy, looking confused.

"My lips shall remain . . . *closed*," said Henri, wrinkling his brow. "*Condamnée?*"

"Sealed," said Star, having, it seemed, taken over my job as translator. I thought that Henri actually wilfully suppressed a lot of the English language, since he had been in the country long enough to learn it several times over. Sometimes I thought he did it deliberately, to get attention and to keep his Frenchness alive.

"Poker!" he said suddenly, hitting the table drunkenly with the palms of both hands. "We must play poker. Fetch the cards, Lily."

"I don't gamble," said Cal, looking slightly afraid.

"I do!" said Lucy, looking excited.

I found a pack of cards in one of the drawers in the kitchen, and brought it through, playing with it and moving the cards about slightly as I walked back to the table.

"She's rigging them," said Lloyd, jokingly.

"I could well be," I said, all the wine making me mischievous. "But I bet you're a better poker cheat than me."

"I wish," said Lloyd.

"We'll see," I said, shuffling the cards slightly. "Shall we do an experiment?"

"Oooh, a card trick," said Lucy, clasping her hands together.

"You seem to be a woman of many talents," Cal said.

"We'll see," I said again.

I gave the deck to Lloyd and instructed him to cut it three times, making four piles of cards on the table.

"Right," I said. "We'll call the piles A, B, C and D."

"Okay," said Lloyd seriously.

"I want you to pick up pile A," I said, watching Lloyd's nicotine-stained hands shake slightly as he did so. "Take the three top cards from the pile and move them to the bottom. Then, dealing from the top of the pile, place one card onto pile B, one onto pile C and one onto pile D."

"This is very exciting," said Star. "Where did you learn all this?"

"My misspent youth," I said, smiling. "Right," I said to Lloyd. "Pick up pile B and repeat. Remember to take the top three cards and put them on the bottom, then deal the next three onto piles A, C and D."

"Does it matter what order I put the cards on the piles?" he asked. "I think I've forgotten which one is C."

"That one's C," I said, pointing as Lloyd carefully placed a card on top of the three remaining piles. "Now repeat with each pile left."

Everyone watched fascinated as Lloyd got into the rhythm of placing the three cards under the stack in his hand and then distributing three cards to the other piles. He looked up at me expectantly when he had finished.

"So you say you've never cheated at poker?"

"No," he said.

"Let's see, shall we," I said, lifting the top card from each pile. They were, of course, all aces. At this point, rather embarrassingly, everyone clapped.

"Thank you," I said.

"You see," said Henri. "My daughter is a genius."

I winced slightly, but I was glad all the same. I hadn't impressed my father this much since I learnt to walk.

Poker was abandoned in the end, in favour of coffee in the living room. I smoked a few too many cigarettes until I heard a clock strike twelve in the distance, and then I made my excuses and went to bed. Tomorrow was going to be a complicated day.

CHAPTER SEVEN

THE TRIANGLE

MY HANGOVER WOKE ME EARLY, demanding to be dealt with. When I tried to ignore it a brass band started playing in my head. I had to get up. Bleary-eyed and pale-faced, I stumbled downstairs in search of cigarettes and aspirin and bumped straight into Cal. What was he doing here? I looked at the clock in the hall and saw that it was past nine.

"Aren't you supposed to be at work?" I asked.

"Not till ten," he said. "Nobody creative starts work before ten."

"Oh," I said, and walked into the kitchen where I found a half-full packet of someone's Gitanes (I'd misplaced my own cigarettes) and a freshly brewed jug of coffee.

"I made you some coffee," said Cal, appearing in the doorway.

"Thanks," I said, politely. I usually drank milky hot chocolate in the mornings, but the state I was in, any liquid would do. I poured a cup and sat down at the now clear table and lit a cigarette, which had the curious effect of making me feel much better and much worse at the same time.

"You smoke too much," ventured Cal.

"I don't mean to be rude," I said, ignoring his observation, "but what are you still doing here?"

"I fell asleep on the sofa," he said. "I'm sorry if I gave you a fright."

"Has my father gone to work?"

"Yes, and Star's gone too." Seeing my expression he moved back towards the door. "I suppose I'd better be getting a move on as well."

"Good idea."

He stood by the door for a few moments, looking at me almost suspiciously. His blond hair was slicked back against his head with water, looking darker and less tousled than last night, and he'd had a shave.

"Can I call you?" he asked, having not got the message that I wanted him out of the house.

"It's a free country."

"I really found what you were saying last night fascinating, you know. I'd love to get to know you better."

I didn't know what to say. "Um . . ."

"You probably think I'm a bit boring," he cut in, "but I was behaving myself last night, you know, with your father being a client and everything."

"Henri's your client?"

"Yeah, didn't you know? I'm working with Lloyd's production company on some promotional stuff for him."

"Oh."

"Anyway," he said, un-propping himself from the doorway, "I'll give you a call sometime."

"I'll look forward to it," I said, as sarcastically as I could get away with without really offending him. It wasn't his fault I didn't find him attractive.

A few minutes later I heard the front door close and relaxed, alone in the house at last. I switched on the radio and made myself some bread and jam for breakfast which I ate slowly before going upstairs to get dressed. Something that Cal had said had made me think, so while I plaited my hair I stood almost endlessly by the phone, on hold to the British Rail information line. I needed to find out two things before I went out today.

An hour later I was back at London Fields station waiting for a train. The information line had confirmed both things I had wanted to know. Yes, London Fields and Hertford East were on the same line, and yes, there was a service running on weekdays at eight thirty-five which got into Hertford East at nine thirty-one. This meant that if the murderer had been travelling by train he would have been able to escape from the site of the first murder and get to the site of the second in just under an hour. I didn't know if this information would be of any use, but I filed it away nevertheless.

Another hot day was brewing as I paced up and down the platform, on which there were only three other people waiting. I suspected that at rush hour one would see quite a different picture, although probably not on this, the out-of-London side of the station. The train came and I hopped on gratefully, feeling spooked by the idea of standing on train platforms for too long. I was on my way to the site of the second murder, Hertford East, to get things in perspective before going to see Jess.

I had to change at Hackney Downs to get the connection to Hertford East and the whole journey took less than an hour. I remember sitting there reflecting on what I'd done, and what I was going to do. I had practised so many times. Up and down the same train line, timing it just right, watching them. It transpired that Rebecca didn't always take the same train, but that just made things easier. I knew what train she was getting on that Thursday because I booked her to come into London for an important photo shoot myself.

The train seemed to take forever, although in reality it was a little under an hour. When I got to Hertford East it was already quite hot so I stripped off the denim jacket I had been wearing and carried it, along with the other necessary items for today: my mobile phone, my notebook and an A-Z of London.

The station was busier than London Fields. A small sign had been placed near the stairs on the London-bound platform, asking for people travelling the previous Thursday to get in touch with a police incident room in London. I walked the length of the platform, train-spotterish, making small notes in my notebook. Why had no one seen the attack happen?

As soon as I felt I'd seen everything, I hopped on the next train back to Liverpool Street. Passing through London Fields again without stopping, I was able to see the park; almost as deserted as it had been on Sunday. Most parks in London filled up at any hint of sunshine. Not London Fields.

The train went fast and I arrived with plenty of time to grab a packet of sandwiches and a drink from a shop in the station. The next thing I had to do was take the tube to Surrey Quays; to Deptford, my least favourite place in the whole of London, but the home of both Jess and Tam nevertheless.

When I tried to phone Jess, I ended up speaking to Tyler again.

"Where is she?" I asked when he informed me she was out.

"Just . . . um, I've got some people here with me at the moment." He sounded uncomfortable.

"Will she be back this afternoon?"

"Let's hope so." He laughed. "You never can tell with Jess."

Tubes almost rivalled planes, for me, as the worst way to travel. I didn't mind so much when they were out in the open air, but there was something about being underground that really spooked me. Underground was where you went when you were dead, and death disturbed me a lot. I could have taken a cab, except that going over the river always got too expensive (although the thought of going underneath it was worse) and I was trying to keep on some kind of trail. On *trains*, because it had to have been like that. Opening my A-Z, I saw the shape I had drawn to link the three murder sites: a triangle, of course, and one which, my experience of driving in London told me, could not have been covered by car in the required time. Even in the middle of the night with only cabs and night buses to negotiate it would have been tough. But on a rush-hour morning? No way.

My notebook started to fill with doodles, diagrams and theories. I had read in some theory of crime book that prosecuting lawyers had to prove three things: motive, means and opportunity. This was therefore the main aim of any detective, and in order to prove the guilt of a suspect you had to provide evidence that there was enough of all three.

This was the scientific method, and it got my vote. Jess knew something, but not everything, otherwise she'd have gone straight to the police. She clearly thought I had some expertise in this area and although most of what I knew I'd read in books, I was going to try to be as useful as possible. Since I obviously had no idea who could have done this, or why, I was starting with *opportunity;* considering how the killer would have planned, travelled and so on. Maybe Jess would be able to provide some insight on the women and who may have wanted to kill them. Once we'd put our information together, maybe all I would have to do would be to convince her to talk to the police.

Surrey Quays was a colourless subterranean station, made more colourful only by the large numbers of tramps and drunks hanging around inside and out.

"Got a fag, love?" asked one of them, a large red-faced man in a purple hat standing just outside the exit.

"Er, yes," I was forced to say, being in the process of lighting one at that moment. I pulled one out of the thin packet and gave it to him.

"You are a *very* beautiful lady," he slurred, taking the cigarette and kissing my hand.

"Thank you," I said and walked off down Evelyn Street, smoking and thinking. The walk was depressing as the road became more and more deserted. There had been shops here once, I thought, but now all that remained were boarded-up shells and failed ventures, all firmly closed and uninviting. The other side of the road looked a bit more promising for a while, with a couple of launderettes and a fish and chip shop, until they too faded into nothing and I felt quite alone.

I reached Hertford East at nine thirty-one and saw her there on the platform opposite. Rebecca. These creative jobs start so late in the day, particularly for freelancers. Particularly when they are working for me.

She was standing alone, far from the other late commuters, which I thought was understandable in the circumstances. The train platform was busier than one might have thought, but then work hours are so flexible these days, don't you think?

I had to create a diversion. I couldn't be seen at this early stage. It was a firework. I lit it, dropped it in the bin by the stairs and then walked over to Rebecca; sweet Rebecca, who was, like all the others, looking for the train until . . . BANG. There were fireworks [laughs]. Everyone looked at the colours and those close to it jumped back as it went off. Everyone was looking the other way, so nobody saw when I walked up and gave her a hard push. She screamed, but by then I was gone. I didn't watch the fast train hit her but I heard it. There was a soft, muffled thump and a sharp crunch. That was the end of her.

After that I crossed platforms again and got on the next train back to Liverpool Street, via the lovely London Fields, where from the window of the train I could see the police, the body and the crowds. There was an ambulance there as well. Shutting the door after the horse had bolted. I waved, but no one saw me. [Coughs.]

The next thing I had to do was take the tube to Surrey Quays into the heart (if indeed it had one) of Deptford, my most favourite place in the whole of London and the home of my next victim.

The tube journey to Surrey Quays was quite awful. But I knew I had to keep it like this: on my mission, relentlessly and passionately on my mission. Unthinkable and untraceable. No one cares about people on trains.

I remember that there was a particularly disgusting gaggle of tramps — what is the collective noun for tramps? A murder *of tramps — outside the station. One of them, a man in a purple hat, asked me for a cigarette but I just told him I was a psycho killer and walked off down Evelyn Street, hearing my knife tumble around in my rucksack. The walk was a depressing one (just the type to put you in the mood for murder), and I grew excited as the busy road became more desolate and deserted. There may have been shops there once, but not any more. The other side of the road looked a bit more cheerful, with a couple of launderettes and a fish and chip shop, until they too decayed into nothing and I felt quite exhilarated.*

Tam's house was very close to Jess's block of flats, which I thought was a peculiar coincidence. Would Jess also have come here when she interviewed the women? Me, Jess, the murderer: had we all done it this way round? I shivered and continued walking.

Turning into Alloa Road made me feel safe again. There were proper shops here and a row of nice-looking Victorian houses. I found the turn-off for Madison Gardens and approached slowly, looking at everything as I went past. This was the only actual address they had given out on the news and I wanted to make sure I didn't miss any details.

Number thirty-eight was a large town house of the sort usually occupied by students, squatters or young professionals. My assumption that it was probably a house-share was further suggested by the fact that the front door itself wasn't blocked off by the police as it would probably have been if the house was solely Tam's. To further confirm my assumptions, the heavy sound of loud bass reggae notes started to seep out of the house and I realised that there must be someone in. I was confused. I'd thought Tam had lived alone, but the mind made funny connections sometimes, and since I wasn't sure why I'd assumed that I put the thought out of my mind. I was about to knock on the door when I heard the music stop as abruptly as it had started. The door opened and I found myself face to face with a big, scruffy, dreadlocked man.

"All right?" he said cheerfully, seemingly not in the least bit concerned to find a stranger hanging around in his garden. "You must be Rainbow. I saw you from the window. Joe said to come in and wait for him, he won't be long."

He leant on the wall just outside the front door and waited for me to go inside. I thought quickly for a moment, wondering who Rainbow was, and whether I could get away with impersonating her for long enough to get a look inside the house. Deciding that I didn't have anything to lose, I smiled and walked past the heavy-built man into the musty hallway, coughing as the smell of rising damp hit me. I didn't know if it was my imagination, but I got the impression that he had enjoyed making me push past him to get into the house, and was half sure that I'd felt his hand brush my chest as I did so.

"Sorry about the mess," he said, gesturing at all the police tape lying around in the corridor and grinning naughtily. "We're going to get in trouble for this, probably. The tape was meant to stay up around the door, but we had a bit of an accident." He paused, possibly enjoying the expression of semi-horror on my face. "Fucking Old Bill. Suppose you know what happened?"

"Uh, Joe didn't tell me much," I said carefully. "When's he due back?"

"Said he'd be about half an hour. I'm Dean, by the way."

"Pleased to meet you," I said, taking care not to walk too close to him. "So what *did* happen?"

"I suppose you never met her, you know, *Tam?*"

"No."

"She got strangled," said Dean, matter-of-factly. "In there."

He gestured at what I assumed must be the living-room door, which had recently been padlocked and had a big yellow police Restricted Entry sign on it.

"God," I said, not having to pretend to sound horrified. I felt a wave of something like nausea wash over me as I imagined some strange man knocking at the door and forcing his way in. "What happened, then?" I asked again, standing still and wondering why Dean didn't seem very concerned that someone had been strangled in his living room.

"Dunno," he said, shaking his head. "Fucking weird, though. *Fucking* weird."

He turned away from the door and walked the length of the damp corridor to a large kitchen from which smells of long-forgotten washing-up and burnt garlic came.

"Cup of tea?"

"Yes, please," I said, wondering if I should ask for coffee until I thought about my character and decided that someone called Rainbow probably drank tea: *herb* tea, to be more specific, of which there were at least ten packets in the overflowing cupboard that Dean now opened.

I sat down at the kitchen table, a round yellow Formica thing that looked as if it had come straight out of an early seventies sitcom. I put my notebook, A-Z and mobile phone down on the table in front of me, not particularly feeling like someone called Rainbow but knowing that I would have to try to convince Dean that I was her. I used to belong to a theatre company when I lived in Islington so I just hoped my acting skills would get me through this.

Dean switched on the kettle and then reached into his pocket and drew out a packet of kingsize Rizlas and proceeded to fill one of them with Golden Virginia, which he then topped up with large, crumbled bits of sticky black cannabis. Hoping he wasn't going to offer any to me (doubting Rainbow and me would agree on drugs), I lit a cigarette instead.

"This is the first day the police haven't been in here," said Dean, licking the thin gummed strip at the top of the cigarette paper and using both his expert forefingers to roll up the thick cigarette and then smooth down the wet join. He rubbed his construction up and down absent-mindedly.

"If you're going to stay here," he said slowly, eventually lighting his joint and drawing deeply on it, "you'd better keep your gear out of sight. The police presence here is, like, *visible.*"

"Yeah, I can imagine."

Looking at my watch I saw that ten minutes had already passed since I arrived. I was going to have to get some information out of Dean now and then leave, quickly, before either Joe or the real Rainbow got here. I would have to put off actually searching the house until another time, although it was hard to see when or how this would be possible. I considered engineering a theft of Dean's keys but thought better of that.

"I bet you're all really upset," I said coaxingly. "It must be awful."

"No one's surprised, if that's what you mean. Tam's had it coming for a long time."

"Why?" I asked, shocked at his attitude. Surely no one deserved *that.* I felt my shoulders tense as more nausea flooded me. I couldn't imagine what it would be like to live with such unsympathetic people. *Poor Tam,* I thought.

"She owed a lot of people," said Dean, shrugging his shoulders. "Big. That was why she . . ."

"What?"

"Hasn't Joe told you *any* of this?" he asked, looking at me curiously with one eye creased into a caricature baffled squint.

"No."

"She used to do art, at Goldsmith's, until she got in with some of the more, um, *hardcore* students."

Dean paused there and poured boiling water into two mugs. The aroma of cloves and fruit instantly filled the room. He offered the joint to me but I shook my head and raised an eyebrow, making a mumbled excuse about it being too early and trying to cut down. He brewed the tea and placed a chipped and grubby blue mug in front of me, deliberately brushing my shoulder with his hand as he walked back over to the sink, making me shiver with both revulsion and embarrassment. I looked at the insipid purple fluid inside the mug and gingerly took a sip from it. It was fruity indeed, but rather weak and dishwatery and I wondered whether I would get away with leaving all of it.

"Hardcore?" I repeated, replacing the mug on the table.

"Yeah. Bondage. *Art.*" Dean snorted, and although I vaguely knew what he was talking about I was too bewildered to respond before he started talking again.

"She stopped going to college in the end and tried to raise money for some bloody installation she was planning; live body-piercing in Islington or some place like that. No one liked her, you know. She never bothered with paying rent; never stumped up for all the fucking drugs she took. All she ever seemed to do was hang around with these dodgy blokes. I never wanted to know what was going on, if you know what I mean, so I never asked. And then, of course . . ." he held his hands out — "*this.*"

"Do you think one of these blokes murdered her?"

"Not if what the papers are saying is true. But then I wouldn't know."

"What have the police been making of it?" I asked. "Have you all been interviewed?"

"Yeah," said Dean sleepily. "But if you ask me it's all better just left alone. Fucking forget about it, that's what I reckon."

"Don't you think whoever did it needs locking up?"

"Yeah," he said, smiling poisonously. "But then so does half of London."

"Do you think it was the stalker, that ex-boyfriend Stuart?" I said, forgetting for a moment that I wasn't supposed to know anything about this and inwardly cursing myself for coming out of character so easily.

"Stalker?" he said, laughing nastily. "Yeah, right. She would have loved that. I've never seen this Stuart bloke, but I suppose all that could have gone on before she moved in here. But I don't think it's got anything to do with it. She was, you know, *asking* for it. Maybe they'll find out about the other two poor cows, I don't know. Maybe the bloke who killed Tam was different. Maybe it was an accident. Know what I'm saying?"

"Not really," I said, feeling my pulse race. "What *are* you saying?"

Dean cleared his throat and pulled another Rizla out of his pocket. I got the feeling he was enjoying this; that he enjoyed *power* and the performance possibilities it gave him. I knew a little about this sort of domestic set-up from my own days as a student in north London, and I had a feeling that the real Rainbow, whenever she appeared, would probably end up sleeping with Dean — in a *free love* kind of way, of course. He was arrogant, perplexingly blasé (although that was probably the drugs) and pretended to know *everything*. From the size of the block of cannabis that he removed from his pocket I guessed he was some sort of dealer. I didn't like him at all, and wished he would cut to the chase and tell me something useful.

He was about to start talking again when my mobile rang. I swore under my breath and picked it up. The caller display told me that it was Fenn, phoning from his home number. I felt my heart dance in my chest, and the thought of a friendly voice invading the cold atmosphere in this house was almost enough to make me take the call, but I needed to hear what Dean was going to say next. I calmly pressed the answer button and then the end button, cutting Fenn off as he was saying *hello*.

I turned expectantly to Dean, but he walked out of the room suddenly, looking at his watch as if he had something important to do. I looked daggers at my phone, wishing I'd had the sense to switch it off before coming in here. Then I would have had two pieces of information: one from Fenn on my voicemail (where had the other message gone, anyway?) and one from Dean, who now appeared to be making a phone call himself in the hallway.

It was clear that I wasn't going to get any more out of him, and, fearing the arrival of Joe and Rainbow, I decided now was the time to leave. But just as I was about to walk out of the kitchen, a word from Dean's conversation made me stop and listen.

"Jess Mallone?" he said again. "No, mate, I don't know her . . . Yeah, *well* weird. I know that Tyler vaguely. You could try him, I suppose . . . Wouldn't bother if I was you. Don't know really, too stuck-up . . . I think it was all through him . . . Anyway, I'll see you later with that stuff. Yeah, mate, cheers . . ."

Realising Dean was about to hang up, and hearing voices coming from outside. I walked briskly past him, mumbling something about going to the shops as I went. I got out of the front door as quickly as I could, pushing past a couple coming in, and ran all the way back to Evelyn Street. I stopped and pulled myself together briefly, and then, with my mind still doing cartwheels, I turned into Rainsborough Avenue, to the flats, to see if I could get some answers from Jess.

It was a good job I'd done my own research because it turned out that Tam lived with a load of students and I had to get it right: the time that she would be there alone. I'd watched for a week or so, but there never seemed to be a pattern to any of their movements. In, out. The same ones, different ones. I didn't even know who lived there and who didn't. In the event I just had to watch and hope.

At one point I saw someone I knew very well. What were they doing in there? Clandestine. Doing something bad. I chuckled to myself [laughs]. That just made it so much better. I knew my plan was going to work. When I was almost sure they were all out, I made my approach. I knocked on the door and she opened it. You know the rest.

What did you do then?

After I'd finished with Tam I left quickly, not wanting to be seen. I don't remember passing anyone in the street, except for one of Tam's housemates, some bloke with dreadlocks who seemed too stoned to notice me. I walked fast, knowing I'd almost finished now. I crossed Evelyn Street and walked towards the block of flats just beyond. I had a present for someone: a small piece of T-shirt, covered in blood.

Chapter Eight

Bleak House

THE BLOCK OF FLATS in which Jess lived was run-down and uncared-for, the gravel façade providing a cold welcome which seemed more like a goodbye than a hello. It took me a while to find the main door to get in; I had expected a grand lobby of some sort (never having been in this kind of tower block before) but there was none. Instead, the entrance was to be found hiding around the back of the building, to all intents and purposes a side door, which was propped open with a brick.

I stood looking at the doorway for a while, trying to work out the meaning of the brick, when a tall, balding man emerged from the entrance, almost knocking me over and then apologising furtively as he helped me pick up the things I'd dropped.

"I take it the security system isn't working?" I guessed, gesturing at the brick, and then at a grubby off-white panel by the door, which I had just concluded was intended to work with some kind of gadget to open the door (like in SF films but less *glossy*).

"Typically," said the man.

"Does it do this a lot?"

"After there's been a break-in," he said. "Which is quite often, I suppose."

We stood there for a moment looking at the brick. Then the man turned to me and smiled.

"Here's what happens," he said. "Someone breaks in, by shattering the glass and climbing through, right? Then the alarm goes off, but by the time the police bother to come and see what's going on he's long gone, or more likely sitting in his flat, pissed, wondering what he did with his magnetic key . . ."

"Magnetic what?"

"One of these," said the man, holding out a white oblong matchbox-sized piece of plastic. "Anyway, any break-in overrides the system and then it doesn't work for a while. Last time it took them three months to mend it, and then that only lasted for a couple of weeks before someone else smashed the window. When the system isn't working we have to prop everything open, or no one can get in."

"Isn't that dangerous?" I asked.

"Not considering the kind of people that live in there, no."

"Out of interest," I said, just as he turned away, "when was the last break-in?"

"Last week sometime," he said uncertainly. "I'm not sure. Wednesday. Thursday. I'm sure it wasn't before that because I was showing our new flatmate how to use the magnetic key when she moved in, which would have been Tuesday."

"Thanks," I said.

"No problem."

Inside, the smell was overpowering, like piss in an ashtray. I still couldn't believe they were living like this. It didn't seem right. The walls inside were buttercup, or something. I suppose it doesn't matter what they were, but all at once I was reminded of something from long ago. Somewhere I used to live: an institution. Does that surprise you? Of course, the smell was different. No bloody furniture polish here, obviously. There was no furniture, or none you could polish. Just sterile walls, doorways. Piss.

I walked up the stairs opposite the front door, feeling the dark and gloomy ambience grow thick and caustic as I went. The red handrail was sticky under my fingers. I probably left traces of the girls' blood there, and I imagined it mingling with all the other stuff on the rail: sick, spunk. I know — and you may wrinkle your nose, fair enough. But you've got to believe how nasty those stairs were. I could see the car park through these thin slivers of window; some girl walking across looking earnest and slightly lost.

By the time I reached the second floor the lights had packed up and there were no more windows. Now, this was probably the hottest day of the year and the rubbish chute was just down from where I was standing. The smell . . . I don't even think I can describe it. Flies. There were lots of flies: bluebottles, mainly; too fat and concussed to fly, just fizzing away on the floor like little black Alka Seltzers. I trod on one and watched its insides spill out on the floor. Sorry. I just couldn't help remembering that. On the day of so many new experiences, this was another one. I'd never managed to actually squash a bluebottle before.

I entered the ground-floor lobby and walked up the staircase quickly, disliking the smell and the murky blackness that I found myself submerged in. I couldn't believe that something as simple as replacing a light bulb should cause problems on a staircase like this. How many council workers *would* it take to change a light bulb?

Once I reached the third floor I was pleased to see that there were windows again and with hazy hot beams of June sunshine coming through, filtered twice: by the glass and then the layer of dust on the glass. Heavy London sunshine. I looked out of the window briefly and saw the top of the canopy over the front door, unpainted and covered with Tesco own-brand crisp packets, sweet wrappers, a porn magazine (*Razzle*) and a football.

Once out of the stairwell, I was confronted with another door of the same type as the front door, requiring the same magnetic key. For visitors, there was a buzzer like the one downstairs. However, this couldn't have been working either, since the door was propped open with a thick white sock.

The floor. It's strange what you remember, isn't it? I walked through the door and down the corridor. It was long; longer than any corridor I'd ever seen and the floor was covered with the strangest industrial floor covering. It was plastic, of course, and that kind of Bourbon-biscuit brown that you get in factories and schools. But it was the bumps that got to me: the little nodule things on the floor. My shoes squeaked as I walked along, deeper and deeper under the intense orange light. Like . . . [pauses] Orpheus. Like Orpheus into the underworld I went, feeling, mainly because of the lighting, that I was coming down with a strange virus, and forgetting that the outside world, with its sunshine and sticky children, ever existed.

CHAPTER NINE

STARFISH AND COFFEE

JESS AND TYLER'S FLAT was right at the end of a very long, orangey corridor. I was having trouble picturing why Jess would want to live somewhere like this: she had always seemed so *together* at university. Beyond all the Ice Queen stuff had lurked something more powerful, we'd all known that. The designer labels, the clipped voice and her car, a black BMW, had all confirmed the rumours about her father: he was a millionaire. And therein lay my confusion. What would the girl with everything possibly be doing living in Deptford, in a block of flats like this?

Shaking away my doubts with a flick of my hair, I turned off my mobile and knocked hard at the door. I wondered what kind of state Jess would be in. Poor thing; when I'd known her the most she'd ever had to contend with was the odd chipped nail or missed half-hour at the gym. And there had been the attack, of course, but had that ever really happened?

Eventually the door opened and I found myself face to face with two policemen who appeared to be leaving. Beyond them stood a man: Tyler, I assumed, wearing Adidas tracksuit bottoms and no shirt. One of the policemen handed a teacup to him and mumbled something like, "Thank you for your time."

"We'll be in touch, Mr Moss," said the other policeman, flipping shut a small black notebook. "And if you could tell Miss Mallone to contact us as soon as possible we would be very grateful."

He turned towards me and smiled a smile which he probably thought was *searching*.

"Unless of course this is Jessica Mallone herself?"

"Oh, no," I said, smiling back and raising my hands in a show of innocence. "I'm, um, well, no one really."

"No one really," said the policeman slowly and deliberately. "Do you have a name?"

"No. I mean yes, of course." I blushed slightly at my own inarticulacy. "Lily Pascale. I was friends with Jess at university. I've just come round to see how she is."

"You'll be lucky," said the policeman. "If we could have a few moments of your time?"

"Sure," I said, wondering why on earth they would want to talk to me.

At the policemen's insistence I entered the flat and walked up the three small stairs to what must have been the living room, in which a familiar but forgotten pop song drifted softly out of a stereo in the corner, as if the volume had been turned down for the benefit of the policemen. I was struck, briefly, by the studio-ish qualities of the space, with its bare floors and blank or half-finished canvases. I wondered whether Tyler was an artist, throwing him the briefest of glances just to see whether he looked like one.

"So," asked the first policeman, opening his notebook. "When did you last see Jess?"

"Um, about three or four years ago."

"I thought you said you were friends?"

"We are," I said. "Or were. We spoke on the phone."

"When did you last speak to her?"

"Friday."

"And how did she sound to you?"

I paused for a moment, as I realised something wasn't right here. "Where is Jess?"

"She's gone away," said Tyler meaningfully, his Scottish accent unplaceable and seeming too broad for the south, too affected for the north. He looked at the policemen. "Maybe you'd have more

luck if you were actually out there looking for this bloke." He
looked from them to me, wide-eyed and pissed off. "Can you believe they think Jess had something to do with all this?"

"You think she was involved somehow?"

"For the record, we don't have enough information to suspect
anyone yet," said the moustached policeman tiredly, as if he'd had
a hard time from Tyler already. "We just want to find her. We don't
want to accuse her — we just want her to help with our enquiries."

"Oh."

"Did she tell you where she was going?" asked the other policeman.

"No," I said. "She gave me the impression she would be here.
I mean, I've come all the way from Devon to see her and —"

"Aren't you satisfied yet?" cut in Tyler, regarding the policeman. "*No one* knows where she is."

"Okay," said the policeman, sighing and handing me a business
card with the Metropolitan Police logo on it. "If you remember
anything, or if she does get in touch with you, maybe you could call
us on this number."

"So where is Jess?" I asked, once the policemen had gone and Tyler
had made some coffee. "Has she really gone away?"

"What? Sure. Of course she has," he said, setting the mug
down on the hard floor between the edge of the sofa and a canvas
propped up against it. Since the police left he had become a good
deal less animated. The atmosphere in the flat had become cold as
Tyler seemed visibly to brood; I assumed about Jess.

He walked in and stood by the window contemplating the
south London scene outside. I sipped my coffee: it was very strong,
black and hot. The music continued to drift out of the speakers but
other than that the flat was oddly silent.

"I can go if you want to be on your own," I ventured, speaking
to Tyler's back. "This must all be a bit . . ." I trailed off. A bit what?
None of the words seemed right. His girlfriend had run off, there
was a murder enquiry going on and he seemed to be stuck bang in
the middle of it. Jess had implied to me on the phone that she knew
something. Now she was gone. What would have made her want
to disappear?

"Yeah," he said.

"You do know why Jess called me, don't you?"

"Yeah. I think you said on the phone."

"So . . ." I began, waiting for him to take the cue and jump in. He didn't. "So I'm not sure what to do."

"What about?"

"Well, the murders," I said. "Jess wanted my help. She wanted me to help her work out what could have happened with these murders. She practically begged me to come, and I got the impression she thought she might be in trouble or something."

Tyler stayed silent.

"So here I am," I continued. "I mean, should I just forget about it or . . ."

"No," he said, turning around suddenly. His hands were gripping his coffee mug too tightly and they were becoming red. "No," he repeated. "Jess wants you to do it. Um . . . Look, did she tell you about her suspicions?"

"No. She didn't tell me anything very much, just that she'd done this story about three women and then they ended up murdered." I noticed Tyler wince when I mentioned the three women. "Anyway," I continued, "that's why I'm here. But it's going to be hard to discuss everything if she's gone away."

"Well," said Tyler, sitting down on the chair in front of me. "I suppose I'll have to do. Fire away."

"Well," I started, "what were these suspicions?"

"She didn't tell you anything?"

"No."

"Okay. Now, she mentioned to me . . . In fact she *told* me to tell you that she thought someone at the magazine could have been involved."

"Great," I said enthusiastically, thinking that this was an obvious place to look anyway but not wanting Tyler's sullenness to return. "Any names?"

"Sorry, no."

"Did she tell you where she was going?" I asked, realising that if Jess had told Tyler to pass on this information, she hadn't simply disappeared; this had all been very deliberate.

"No."

"Mmm," I said, thinking.

"There was one thing she told me was important, though," said Tyler, leaning forward on the sofa and letting his eyes widen conspiratorially. "Do you want to know what it is?"

"Yes," I said, playing the game and not adding the word *obviously*.

"Right. It's a bit of a riddle, I'm afraid," he said, scratching his head. "She said . . . she said that it was Peeping Tom who did it."

"Peeping Tom?" I asked. "Is that some sort of nickname for someone, or something?"

"I don't know. That's all she said."

"But surely . . ."

"What?"

I was going to point out that if Jess knew who did it, why hadn't she just told the police and left them to get on with it, but I knew that this wouldn't go down too well. So instead, I just said: "Nothing," and then, "Thanks."

My patience was running out and I didn't trust Tyler at all. It wasn't just the moodiness, it was something underneath: beyond his heavy-set, good-looking appearance, beneath his dark brown hair and school-uniform-blue eyes lurked *something*.

"Where does Jess keep all her files?" I asked.

"Come on through," said Tyler, getting up from the sofa. "I'll show you."

I followed him through the door to the living room and up three more steps past what smelt like a bathroom, and a big double bedroom. Finally, after going round a corner and down a small passage, we came upon what must surely have been the most secluded room in the flat.

"This was her study," he said, and with the smallest smile, he turned and left me to it.

The room was dark and slightly musty; only a thin shaving of light penetrated it from a small window over which a makeshift curtain had been loosely pulled. I flicked on the light and walked further inside, pulling the insubstantial door behind me. The room was cluttered and lived-in. Books and videos were stacked haphazardly in about ten piles against the wall to my left and although there were several shelves along the wall to my right, these held only ornaments and trinkets, along with the small Sony stereo system that I recognised from the flat John and Jess shared when we were at university.

In a jumbled pile next to the stereo lay a selection of CDs, which ranged in genre from rock to soul to house, several of which, the more brightly coloured ones, had the word *Ibiza* in their titles. Here and there amid the pile were the anomalies most people my age would recognise: The Waterboys album (with *"The Whole of the Moon"* on it), The Blow Monkeys, Lloyd Cole, the Smiths and, right at the bottom, the Spice Girls.

In a separate space on the shelf was a distinct and obviously more precious collection of CDs, linked, it seemed, by the artist who at the time was most definitely known as Prince: *The Black Album, Controversy, 1999, Purple Rain, Around the World in a Day* (my favourite), *For You, Lovesexy, Parade, Dirty Mind* — they were almost all here; the absence of the not-so-good nineties albums more than made up for by the presence of the obscurer eighties ones. This was a true fan. Jess wasn't the only one, clearly. The album Tyler was playing in the living room, now turned up almost to full volume, I finally recognised as *Sign of the Times*.

Jess's desk sat at the far end of the room, facing a wall on which posters of current TV heart-throbs were pinned: someone whose name I couldn't remember from one of the Australian soaps and several members of the cast from *Friends*, among others. I shook my head and giggled silently, remembering that when we were at university everyone thought she was being ironic, when in fact she was just (as one of our friends cuttingly put it) deeply shallow. Her desk supported other objects in line with this view: a fluffy pink pencil case, a Horses and Ponies calendar, two copies of *Smash Hits*, the *Hip and Thigh Diet* and a Teletubbies mug filled almost to the brim with mouldy, undrunk tea.

I glanced at her diary, which lay on the right of the desk, still left open on last week. The words *Smile! story out today* were written in red pen under the date Thursday 19 June. That was the day the murders were committed, I remembered with a shiver: last Thursday, the day before Jess had phoned. I scanned the next few days, turning the page and noting the way she marked everything in there — days in advance, clearly. I imagined she wouldn't make it to the *lunch with Mark*, pencilled in for tomorrow, or the *party at number 16* for tonight. I was surprised to see that this appointment, the one I made from the train yesterday for four o'clock today, was not there. Maybe she had been in too much of a state to remember to write it down.

A computer, a big, expensive-looking Apple Mac (again, from Jess's student days) stood in the middle of the desk, its beige casing grubby and its screen sheathed with a thin film of dust. I pressed the On button on the keyboard and sprang back as the machine chimed the characteristic *dong* which had been set far too loud. I looked guiltily over my shoulder to see if Tyler was about to burst through the door and then relaxed. He hadn't heard anything, and, more to the point, it shouldn't matter even if he had. I was only doing what his girlfriend had asked me to do, just not in quite the way I'd planned.

While I waited for the machine to fire itself up I scanned the rest of the desk. An uneaten Milky Way sat next to the mouldy tea and beneath both these objects lay a pile of pink, blue and yellow envelope files. Removing the mug and the Milky Way I looked at the first file — *Revenge* it said on the front. Inside I saw several drafts of what was clearly another magazine feature, in which three women, this time Mary, Jean and Kari, talked about their experiences of revenge. The whole thing seemed to follow the same format as the piece on stalking, and the slightly battered copy of *Smile!* magazine that I found at the back of the file confirmed my thoughts. It had been another feature for the magazine, appearing in the March 1997 edition.

The next folder, a grey one, contained some notes on a feature called *My Adoption Hell* for *Stella* magazine. A photocopy revealed that this feature had been written over a year before, appearing in May 1996. I picked up the other two files, expecting to find the same thing: research for articles, and the articles themselves. Instead I found something quite different.

The first file I picked up, the yellow one, was labelled *In*, and contained two sheets of paper. Both had the words *Commission Form* at the top and both were signed by the same woman: Kathi Trimbull from *Smile!*. The first included the brief for the *Revenge* piece and the second outlined the *Stalking* one. The *Stalking* brief read as follows:

Dear Jess,

Good to speak to you on the phone yesterday. As I told you then, we would love to commission the *Stalking* feature to appear in the "Real Life" section of the magazine.

The style of "Real Life" is a bit like a monthly magazine — longer and more reflective than the standard *Smile!* feature. You should adopt an in-depth approach and you can include your own views if you want.

We will need three different, identified case studies — people who are prepared to be named and photographed. If any of them lost weight or suffered any kind of physical deterioration as a result of their ordeals, then any snaps they may have would be great because then we can do a before/after kind of thing.

The two case histories you mentioned are ideal. The third should possibly be something less sinister — maybe an example of someone who was stalked by an ex-boyfriend or something.

Deal with each of the case histories in turn and intersperse with expert comment. I can give you the numbers of some experts if you are stuck. Madeline Zeger (an American psychologist) has been helpful in the past. Also look into societies that are specifically about stalking and see what kind of comment you can get from them.

Please include the age and job of everyone mentioned, and, as you already know, get most of the detail out in the form of direct quotes.

Please file between 1500 and 1700 words. If you go slightly over, don't worry.

Speak to you soon,
Kathi

There was nothing else in the folder (I suspected any commission form from *Stella* had long since been misplaced).

The second folder, labelled *Out*, contained the evidence for what the first folder suggested. Contrary to what Jess had told me on the phone, it seemed that she was not a very successful freelance journalist at all. The *Out* folder bulged with copies of letters she had written to magazines, offering to write features for them, and stapled to each one was a rejection letter. I flicked through and saw a lot of familiar names: *Cosmopolitan, Elle, Vogue, Independent on Sunday, Minx, Daily Mail, News of the World* and bizarrely, *Motorcycle Monthly* and *Christian Week*. I put the folders back down where I had found them, feeling like I'd found something I hadn't wanted to see; something more personal than dirty underwear or dust on a door frame. I'd found evidence of Jess's failure, and that didn't make me happy.

Sighing, I sat down in front of the computer with a feeling that there was something missing. I drummed my fingers on the desk for a few moments before I could work out what it was. But of course — it was the *Stalking* file. I assumed that if Jess had one for the *Revenge* piece, then she would have done the same thing for her following commissions (however few of them there seemed to be). She was the type of person, it seemed, who filed religiously: the room may have been untidy, but that didn't mean it wasn't organised. The Prince archive, the rejection letters and now, clicking on the hard-drive icon on her computer, it seemed her computer files were also meticulously arranged. So where was the research on the *Stalking* feature?

Thinking that the information had to be here somewhere, I set about looking through Jess's computer files. A folder named *Jess* opened to reveal several sub-folders: *Personal, Features Ideas, Features, Admin* and *Finance*. I clicked on *Features* which opened to reveal two new folders: *Revenge* and *Stalking*. I opened the *Stalking* folder and found several files, all of which I opened and read. Each file was a new draft of the piece, which wasn't very useful to me. What I wanted to find were the research details: the contact numbers and addresses of the women and some more background information on why they had been selected. I found it interesting that there were always three case studies in these things, as if one person's experience could be written off as unique and two people's as coincidence. I pondered on this as I searched all the other files, finding nothing until I opened the *Personal* folder and found a folder within it called *Correspondence*.

There, finally, I found everything I wanted to know, the information being contained in numerous letters and, more frequently, faxes to Kathi Trimbull, the features editor of *Smile!* magazine. I printed out most of the correspondence, including a fax giving the addresses and phone numbers of the three women from the *Stalking* feature. I had about seven pieces of thin printer-paper all together, which I stacked and folded once and slipped neatly among the pages of my A-Z, for some reason not wanting Tyler to know exactly what I'd taken.

He was still standing in what seemed to be his favourite spot by the window when I emerged. There was something softer about him; instead of holding himself erect he was slightly hunched, and his hands, which had been balled into fists before, now hung loosely by his sides.

"Find anything?" he asked.

"Not really," I said. "Just some stuff, you know."

He turned to face me: his eyes looked red.

"This is such a mess," he said softly.

"I know."

"You will do your best to find out what happened, won't you?"

"Of course. Tyler?"

"What?"

"Do you really not know where Jess went?"

"Yes," he said, sounding sincere. "I really don't know. She just went. She left a note, in case I was worried. Then she phoned to tell me she was all right."

"Can I see the note?"

"The note? Uh, I suppose so. I'll just go and get it."

Tyler left the room and was gone for three or four minutes. When he returned he was holding, a small Post-It note with just one sentence written on it. *Goodbye. Back sometime.* The note seemed to have been hurriedly written; Jess's normal handwriting had shrunk and become less readable.

"What does *sometime* mean?" I asked.

"You tell me. But you know Jess, she'll wait until it's all blown over and then come back. She won't be too far away, you can be sure of that."

"When she spoke to me on the phone she said it was all her fault," I said. "Do you know what she might have meant."

Tyler looked up. He seemed surprised — more than surprised. His first couple of words came out in a stammer. "She said *what?*"

"That it was her fault. What did she mean?"

"I don't know," he said, managing to collect himself but leaving me thinking, *What are you hiding?* I didn't ask this, of course, noticing him looking pointedly at his watch and thinking I'd better get a move on. There was so much more I wanted to know, but, fearing another mood swing, decided I'd better cut my losses and go, I added the goodbye note to the files I already had and left.

I managed to hail a cab after walking down Rainsborough Avenue for about five minutes and arrived back at Henri's, hot, sticky and tired out at seven o'clock.

Chapter Ten

Everything is False

IT APPEARED THAT HENRI had some late clients, so I got in to find Star sitting alone at the kitchen table reading the *Guardian* Media section.

"Hi," I said, dumping my things down on the coffee table in the living room and walking through. "Anything in the news?"

"Oh, more violence on TV — *Teletubbies*," said Star wearily, with a slightly cynical smile. "Did you have a good day?"

"I'm not sure," I said. "If I did it probably won't become clear until much later."

Star laughed at this. "You're up to something, aren't you?" she said, putting down the newspaper. She pushed her chair back and stood up slowly, walking gracefully over to the kettle and switching it on. "Coffee?"

"Oh, yes thanks."

"Someone phoned for you at lunchtime," she said. "A man with a sexy voice and a funny name. It began with an F. I told him to try your mobile."

"Fenn," I said, putting my head in my hands. As I did so a fragment of excitement began to twist through me — until I suppressed it. It would have been nice to be pursued by him, but not when he was getting married in four days' time.

"Boyfriend?" asked Star.

"No," I said. "But very nearly. One of us had a lucky escape, I'm just not sure which one."

"Oh?"

"It's a very long story. I'm sure you don't want to be bored by it."

"It'll make a nice change from my psychopaths," she said, making them sound (or was it just me?) almost cute.

So I told her the whole story, over one and then two strong coffees and about half a packet of cigarettes: the day I met Fenn in a deserted classroom at the university where we both taught literature; his innocent charm ("Very sexy," said Star), his slightly anarchistic humour; his too long hair and deep blue eyes; his Ph.D. project on heroism in literature; his charisma and finally our blossoming romance, which stopped blossoming on May the first precisely, when I'd found out about his accidental fatherhood of someone else's child.

"So what's the problem?" asked Star.

"He's marrying her," I said. "Bronwyn — one of his *students*. I mean, he thinks it's a good enough reason that she's pregnant, and of course she swears he's the father, but . . ."

"You don't think so?"

"I'm not sure. She's a nice girl, but a bit desperate. I'm sure there's a story there, underneath, but it's just that no one knows what it is — and no one seems particularly interested in finding out. Of course I could be in Devon sniffing around myself, but I don't think anyone would thank me for that. And I wouldn't want to be known as a bitter, jealous wedding-wrecker."

"I can see that," she said, smiling at my turn of phrase. "So let me guess: you're here to take your mind off it all?"

"Yep. But don't tell Henri."

Star smiled in complicity. "Of course not. And to take your mind off things even further, what do you say to opening one of your father's prized Bordeaux and getting down to discussing what I really want to know?"

"What's that?" I asked, confused.

"Whatever it is you're up to."

"Ah, yes," I said, sighing as I briefly recapped my day in my head. "Although I'm not sure what there is to tell."

Nevertheless, half an hour and a bottle of wine later we were happily settled in the living room with bits of paper all over the sofa and me recounting my day and Star occasionally saying things like *Aha!* in a slightly disconcerting way.

"Please don't say you know the answer already," I groaned after a few more *aha*s and a couple of *I knew it*s.

"You're worried that I will become the Dupin to your . . . What was his name?"

"Oh, he wasn't important enough to have one," I said, smiling because she'd hit the nail on the head, and wondering whether she managed to pull this mind-reading trick on her pet psychopaths. "The Holmes to my Watson, perhaps."

"Well I don't think there's any chance of that," said Star, giggling and pouring the remainder of the wine into my glass. "*You* are obviously the one with a gift for these things. Although I have to say these mysteries fascinate me. I love all the stories and novels. Henri thinks I'm mad and says I should get enough of 'that sort of thing' at work."

"It's *safe danger*, though, don't you think? Crime fiction. It's the one way people can get a thrill without getting one, if you know what I mean."

"The thrill of the hyper-real," she said. "You should read Baudrillard. One of the psychopaths rates him quite highly."

I laughed. "I will."

"It's interesting, isn't it," she mused, "that you've managed to convert your love of crime fiction into such a worthwhile hobby."

"I'm not sure my mother would see it that way," I said. "As *worthwhile*, I mean. She thinks it's all terribly dangerous."

"Mmm," said Star distractedly, "I suppose so."

"We'll just have to hope it happens like in the books."

"Yes. Solve it and escape unhurt and everything."

"Exactly. Anyway, that's what I was talking about earlier, when I said that all this would have some great meaning later on." I gestured at the pieces of paper on which we had, with the help of the alcohol, been constructing complex scenarios complete with Venn diagrams in order to try to understand what I'd already found out. "Once I find the final thrilling clue in the last chapter, and all that."

"Yes, that's the way it always seems to happen," said Star. "In the library, usually."

"And here was me thinking that life didn't imitate fiction," I said.

The evening continued in the same fashion, interrupted eventually by Henri making a grand entrance at about ten o'clock, demanding wine, kisses from his "two favourite ladies" and something to eat, which Star went off to rustle up in the kitchen. I watched TV with him for a while and read some of the paper until it became clear that the happy couple wanted to be alone, and I retired to my room with a large glass of water (in case of hangover) and an interesting-looking thriller I'd borrowed from Star.

Once I got to my room, though, I found it hard to concentrate on the book, as my thoughts became invaded with images of murder: a knife dripping with fresh blood; a train hitting a young woman's body and then the murderer's bloody, sweaty hands urging the life out of another woman. Why?

I felt guilty, suddenly, for treating it all as a game. Maybe I had read too many books. In fiction it was all so much *fun* — the "cosy" village murders were just conundrums to be solved like riddles. It was possible for people to like crime fiction without actually engaging with the violence: no one *really* died.

Disturbed, I went over and over my day in my head. How could Jess have just disappeared? I couldn't work out what she was playing at and why she would have wanted to go. But most of all I wondered what would have linked the three women, Sasha, Rebecca and Tam. Had they been stalked by the same man, or was there something else?

Waking up early on Tuesday morning — for me — which meant nine-ish, I jumped out of bed feeling enthusiastic about what I was going to achieve that day. I didn't know quite what was going to be on my agenda; my first task was to set one. My confusion of last night had cleared somewhat and the jumble of information I had was beginning to unravel in my mind.

My brain, even though it hadn't woken up properly, was therefore going like a twister, whizzing from idea to idea almost too quickly for my still sleepy body to keep up. But there were too many questions; even more now I'd had a chance to sleep on it all. I needed to find out how Jess had known the three victims, what had connected them and who the "blokes" were that Tam had been involved with. Tyler had been surprised that Jess had thought it was her fault. Why was that? And also, where *was* Jess?

I walked into the kitchen and put a pan of milk on the stove for my hot chocolate, peeping out of the window to confirm what I suspected: it was going to be another scorcher. I poured the milk into my cup just before it started to boil, adding a generous tablespoon of Henri's organic hot chocolate powder, which was the very best I'd ever tasted. Tearing a lump from yesterday's baguette, I sat down at the table with the intention of scanning the papers for information on the murders. However I was soon distracted by a thin sheet of notepaper with my name on it held down (in case there was any kind of breeze, which seemed unlikely) by a vase of flowers.

I opened it up to find it was from Star.

Some advice:
  1) Start with the victims,
  2) Assume that everything you know is false.
     Good luck
     Star xxx

The note made my heart beat fast. I found it spooky, for some reason, as if I'd been crept up on by a well-meaning practical joker. Then, more rationally, I decided it was sweet: I liked Star a lot and she was trying to help.

She was, of course, right about starting with the victims — although I also had to follow up the Peeping Tom lead, which I'd forgotten to tell her about last night, and which I didn't understand. I knew there was a film called *Peeping Tom*, and even that it was one of the many films I should have watched at university, but that didn't mean I'd seen it. I also knew that the phrase meant voyeur, but that didn't help me much either. The idea of someone spying or peeping at something they shouldn't led me right back to the idea of the stalkers and the theory that was currently doing the rounds in the papers. So the stalker or stalkers did it. Surprise, surprise; at least if that's what Jess had meant, which I doubted.

I pondered for a while on the idea that everything I knew was false, making a mental note to ask Star exactly what she meant later on. Did she know something I didn't, or was this just a radical new method of deduction? Either way, initial experimentation with this technique (I am not me, etc.) proved that philosophical reasoning was possibly not the way to go with this problem. I finished my breakfast in a continuing haze of ideas, plans and *what-I-must-do-nexts* until I short-circuited somewhat, lit a cigarette and walked into the living room with the papers to see if I could catch the news on TV.

The main story on *London Today* was Jess's disappearance. It seemed that regardless of Tyler's protestations of her innocence, the police were desperately trying to get in touch with her, to, as they put it, eliminate her from their enquiries. The papers described in more detail what the police were hoping to get from Jess: they needed information on the three stalkers. It appeared that the trail had gone cold on all three of them, and since they were the three biggest suspects, the police must have felt very frustrated. Back on the news, speculation about the magazine was continuing. The publishers still hadn't withdrawn the issue, seemingly milking the hyped sales for all they were worth.

Peeping Tom. *It was Peeping Tom who did it.* Much as I still doubted the accuracy of these words, it was about time I got a look at the film to see if there was anything of relevance in it. This should have been simple, but I must have phoned twenty video rental shops in the area before I gave up. Of these, about eleven had never heard of the film; five claimed that it had been deleted and four others suggested I try the BFI, which I did next.

The woman on the end of the phone was very helpful and gave me a choice of several libraries, which made me initially enthusiastic about getting hold of the film. However, when I got through to the biggest library I was informed that it was only available on 16 mm and not on video. I couldn't believe it. Why was it so hard to get hold of such a well-known film?

Not knowing where else I could possibly try, I gave up on that line of enquiry for a while and went back to thinking about Jess and her disappearance. Tyler hadn't been much use in explaining why she would have wanted to leave, and it didn't seem that there would be any close friends to ask — she'd said she didn't have any. I sighed.

Trying to find her myself would probably be a waste of time. Since she hadn't told anyone where she was going, she obviously didn't want to be found, and if anyone was going to find her, it would be the police. They had much more sophisticated techniques than I did, and going on the trail of missing persons wasn't my area of expertise. And she could just come back of her own accord.

I took my cup through to the kitchen and rinsed it before going back to the telephone and dialing another central London number. I wanted to make an appointment to visit the offices of *Smile!* magazine — to see who Jess had been in touch with there and what they knew. If Jess did turn up I wanted to have some useful information for her, and besides, I was intrigued.

"Hello, Heart and Lomax," sang a voice after the phone had rung exactly twice.

"Hello," I said uncertainly. "I was trying to get in touch with *Smile!* magazine . . ."

"Features or advertising."

"Um, features, I suppose."

I waited while the switchboard made the connection for me, wondering what Heart and Lomax was, until my thoughts were interrupted by a surly-sounding "Features."

"Hello," I said, clearing my throat. "My name's Lily Pascale. I spoke to someone once a couple of months ago . . . um, someone wanted to do a feature on me."

I'd decided this was the best way of introducing myself, since *Smile!* had been one of the more persistent bidders for my story at the time. They'd been quite perplexed that I hadn't wanted to talk to them. I would have been more willing had they been the *Observer.*

"Lily *Pascale?*" repeated the woman sternly. "I don't remember you. What was the story?"

"Oh, I found out who murdered a girl — Stephanie Duncan — in Devon in Ap —"

"Oh, yes," said the woman more warmly. "I remember you; apparently you were very reluctant. So you've decided to go public?"

"Not exactly. I was actually wondering whether I could talk to you about Jess Mallone."

"Jess?" She sounded surprised. "Go on."

"She's an old friend of mine from university. Last week she called and asked for my help. She seemed to have some information about the murders but needed someone to help her make sense of it. I think she felt guilty about the fact that she'd done the story and felt responsible in some way." I realised I wasn't getting to the point. "But I've got a problem."

"She's disappeared," said the woman dramatically.

"Yes. I came all the way down to see her but she'd gone by the time I got here. I've managed to get some information from her flat and everything —"

"Does she still want you to investigate?" she interrupted excitedly, drawing out the word *investigate* like a piece of bubblegum. "I mean, have you been in contact with her?"

"No, I've no idea where she is. I was going to give up and go home but her boyfriend, Tyler, insisted she wanted me to carry on."

"Does *he* know where she is?"

"No. Or if he does, he isn't saying."

"Has he been in touch with her?"

"He said something about a phone call, but he didn't say what was said."

"Goodness," said the woman. "So, how can we help you?"

"I wanted to ask some questions. Since I can't ask Jess I thought it would be best to get in touch with you."

"More questions," she sighed. "We've had the police in all week. Well, fire away, I've got five minutes. What do you want to know?"

"Oh, lots of things really," I said, actually not knowing at all what I wanted to ask. I hadn't been prepared to do this over the phone. "I'm not sure I caught your name."

"Kathi," she said. "Kathi Trimbull, Features Editor."

"Oh, right," I said. "I saw your name on some of Jess's stuff. Look, I don't want to be a pain, but I wondered if I could come in and see you."

"Come in?" she asked somewhat incredulously. "You want to come here?"

"Yes. If that's not a problem."

"Oh, no, it's not a problem . . . It's just, well, we get used to doing everything by fax and phone. I was rather expecting you to fax a list of questions."

"I could do that if you want," I said. "But I'd rather come over."

"Okay. Well, I don't see why not. Just not today because we've got a deadline, and possibly not tomorrow either, because we've got an editorial meeting. Um, what about Thursday?" I heard the sound of diary pages being flicked on the other end of the phone. "Oh, it looks like I'm free for lunch, so if you came just before that I could show you around and then we'll go out somewhere. That'll give me another chance to persuade you to go public with your story."

"I'm not sure how much luck you'll have," I said, laughing. "But that sounds fine."

"Great. Thursday, then," said Kathi, and put the phone down.

Feeling slightly disappointed that I was going to have to wait until Thursday, I decided that now would be as good a time as any to do some proper research on Rebecca and Sasha, as I had their addresses. I grabbed a bag and my cigarettes and left the house without any further ado. The sun hit my face immediately and I was forced to go in again for sunglasses.

Back outside the air was thick with heat and vibrations: distant voices, kids playing in a garden down the road and a huge bumble-bee on Henri's hedge. I wiped my brow which was already becoming sticky and walked towards the tube station.

[Silence. Sounds of sighing and shuffling around.]

Sit down, it's all right. No one's coming.

Sorry.

Okay, let's backtrack a little. Tell me about your childhood.

All right.

I was born in London and went to school there, an inner-city primary school full of weird teachers and even stranger kids. I was the normal one, then. Anyway, my dad — he's dead now — suddenly got a big promotion when I was about seven. I left my school and the whole family moved out of the area, to some place up North, where my father was working as a developer in a soft drinks factory.

*After that I didn't see Dad so much, but Mum did her best to com-
pensate, even though I didn't really mind. I spent all my time testing
these new drinks they were manufacturing: banana milkshakes, fruit
squashes and strange purple and blue things which didn't really have a
flavour. My mother used to make a fuss. "Don't give him all that artificial stuff, darling," I remember her saying to my father again and again.
But his attitude was that if it was good enough for all the other kids, "it's
good enough for my boy," and that was the end of that.*

*It must have been all those chemicals that made me such a hyperac-
tive child, come to think of it. I had a strange condition, diagnosed when
I was about eight and a half — I can't remember what the doctor called
it. I remember being told to cut down on sweets and fizzy drinks, but Dad
didn't really have anything to do with fizzy drinks: they were all still. So
I carried on drinking those.*

*I was going to a new prep school which seemed leagues away from my
school in London. When I was nine I started getting into slightly weirder
stuff, I suppose. Well, you would probably call it weird. I had this friend
called Jonathan who was a bit of a tearaway. He was the second-newest
boy in the school and the two of us were drawn together. All the others had
known each other since they were about four and we were real outsiders.*

*I suppose it was because we were outsiders that we acted as such. We
both become obsessed with comics and would trawl the local shop for them
every Saturday morning, and frequently on weekday afternoons when we
were bunking off as well. It was easier for me to bunk off than it was for
Jonathan: I had a note from the doctors saying that I was allowed to leave
the room whenever I had those violent feelings. Oh — did I forget to say
that my hyperactivity was violent?*

*So I would calmly leave the classroom whenever I felt like it — fre-
quently when the teacher asked me a difficult question — and walk into
town, to the park, or the comic shop or whatever. Sometimes, if it was after lunchtime (I would have a carton of drink in my lunch box), I would
get these urges that I have never had before or since. Urges to kill and
have sex at the same time — do you know what I mean? Actually, that
isn't quite accurate. It was more that the idea of killing, of wringing
something to death with my bare hands, gave me a hard-on. I remember
not being embarrassed about that, my miniature cock sticking up in my
school trousers like a little stump. So I wasn't embarrassed at all — quite
the contrary, I would walk, or rather strut, about the small market town*

with my Transformers bag and my Star Wars lunch box, with my little
stump sticking straight out in front of me as I bowled along the streets,
swearing at people who were in my way and pulling faces or spitting at
old ladies, fantasising about what Judge Dredd or Captain America
would do next.

Anyway, I'd been going in the comic shop, Exotique, I think it was
called, for about two years when the manager, a guy called Rick, asked me
if I wanted to see some other stuff, more special stuff, he said. Actually, it's
not strictly true that he approached me. I'd been badgering him for a
while by then about more violent, hardcore comics that I had been read-
ing about; ones that were imported from America — ones I knew he'd
have. I couldn't believe it when he said he'd sell them to me.

The intensifying heat of the late June sun made my journey slower,
breathier and sweatier than it may ordinarily have been. It wouldn't
have been any better had I brought the car, since leafy, shaded
parking spots were hard to come by in London, but since I was a
habitual driver I had grown used to carrying more stuff than hard-
ened public-transport users who seemed, I had observed on the
tube to Liverpool Street, to be able to get by with just a paperback
stuck in a pocket. I looked at my rucksack and sighed. Inside was a
large notebook, *Smile!* magazine (the controversial issue), a camera, a Dictaphone, a map of the South-East, my A–Z, the notes
from Jess's computer, my mobile phone and a cardigan in case it
was colder on the way back.

The effect was similar to the way I imagined weight training
being (I didn't do any "proper" exercise so I wouldn't know), but all
the items were essential — or might be. And I wasn't going to take
the chance.

The tube smelt like anchovy paste and rotting daffodils and
I was glad when it reached Liverpool Street and I was able to
change to a larger, airier train with windows you could open onto
the outside world. I wondered if this was the train *he* had taken,
and shivered.

The new comics, the Manga-Gora series, were better than my old ones, of
which I had a fairly hefty collection by the time I was about twelve. The
Manga-Gora were from Japan, and featured young women with massive

breasts and short skirts, frequently topless; sometimes in more porno-
graphic poses. I suppose that was when my liking for pornography began,
after Jonathan disappeared. I needed something to fill the gap since I
didn't have anyone to swap comics with any more. So I concentrated
harder on building my collection, on my own.

It was a winter day, I remember, when Rick finally let me have the
new comics. I'd gone there on a Monday morning — not having even both-
ered to go in to school, as was becoming my habit by then. My father had
grown more and more distant; my mother even more odd. Dad still brought
me stuff from the plant to test, mainly a new kind of orange drink that
didn't taste of oranges (strangely, I thought) that was going to be marketed
as a kind of "youth" drink. Trendy, or whatever. I later learnt that it was
around this time that my mother had started an affair with some unem-
ployed bloke, Carl, from the estate near where we lived. There were argu-
ments then, constantly. I would sit there sipping my orange death-drink
(it was later banned because of a particular type of additive it contained
and had to go back into research until it was deemed fit for production),
listening to accusations of "bit of rough" and "bigger than mine, is it?"

I had started a new school by then as well, a grammar school in the
centre of town whose principal was a friend of my father. It was pointed
out to me many times that it was on this basis that I had got a place,
which didn't make me feel very enthusiastic about going there. So I
stopped. It must have been around November, my twelfth birthday, the
same time that I got the news comics. Every day I would leave as if for
school, in my uniform, with my bag, and then get changed at the end of
the road behind some bushes on the edge of the park. Then I'd walk
through the park, excited about my comics which I would buy with the
guilt money given to me by both my mother and my father, to make up
for love, I suppose, of which there wasn't very much at that time.

Don't get me wrong. I'm not blaming my parents for this at all, I'm
just accepting that at the time when I went, as my mother later put it, off
the rails, they were very preoccupied: my mother with her lover and my
father with his job. In the evenings, as I said, they were busy arguing.
That suited me. While other children were being told to get on with their
chores (we had a cleaning lady) or do their homework, mine just screamed
at each other, leaving me plenty of time for comic-reading and mastur-
bating, my two favourite activities.

Looking back now, there was something wrong. I mean, all these comics were filled with the big-titted women I have already mentioned, in their spreadeagle poses or whatever, looking alive, red-blooded and, frankly, gagging for it (like that girl Tam, actually). That didn't interest me. To this day, the most exciting experience I ever had was precipitated from the pages of The Atomic Warrior comic, part of the M-G series that I got regularly from under Rick's counter, having assured him I was sixteen. The issue that really did it for me was later banned here and in America, since it featured a particularly violent storyline, in which the evil changeling Goxa (the Atomic Warrior's arch-enemy) masturbated over dead or, more disturbingly, almost dead bodies and on the penultimate page, actually had sex with one; a young boy.

After seeing that image, the boy blond, hairless and with his inanimate head thrown back in accidental ecstasy, while Goxa, having changed (because he was a changeling), fucked him first as a peasant girl, then as an old woman, then as a horse and finally as a snake, I was overcome. If I remember correctly I came all over the bathroom right that minute; looking at the comic while sitting on the toilet with the thin, glossy pages spread out in front of me on the slightly damp bath mat.

Now, before you get the wrong idea, I'm not gay and I'm not perverted. I am actually not interested in sex at all any more, at least, not with real people. What fascinated and excited me about the picture was the lack of animation; the way the young dead boy just lay there, oblivious to what was going on. And it may surprise you to know that I fantasised not about being Goxa, or even the Atomic Warrior. From that moment I wanted to be that boy. It was almost like a premonition: I desired to be a victim. To get screwed.

Rebecca's flat was in a cheap-looking suburb on the edge of East Hertford. I remembered from the magazine story that she had been a photographer working in London, but the flat, when I eventually found it, was on the top floor of a shabby-looking launderette. I wondered what kind of photographer she had been.

In contrast with Tam's house, there was no outward sign that there had been much of a police presence here, probably, I thought, since the murder hadn't taken place on these premises. It had been at the train station, where Rebecca's photograph had been taken.

With a sick chill that penetrated the heat I suddenly realised one of the most obvious things: each of the murder sites was also the site where each woman had been photographed for the magazine. I filed this piece of information away for the moment, with its interesting possibilities, and walked into the launderette.

"We're going to close soon," remarked a thin, slightly shrivelled woman, emerging from a booth marked *Powder and Change*. Her accent was rural and her vowels rounded. She had a kind, overworked face and I smiled warmly at her, noticing that she was breathing heavily, like me, in the heat.

"Long day?" I asked.

She sniffed. "Bloody too long, days, now. Not what they used to be. And they say that they get *shorter* as you get older."

"Yes," I said, intrigued, "I've heard that. It's a proportion of the time you've been alive or something." I trailed off. I wasn't here to talk about this.

The woman took a broom out of the cupboard and started poking some of the dust and soap powder around with it.

"You're not here to do any washing, then?"

"No," I said, "I've come about the murder."

"That poor girl from upstairs?"

"Yes, that's right."

"And are you from the *Metropolitan* Police, like all those others?"

"No."

We stood in silence for a moment, me not wanting to have to explain myself, and the woman clearly not wanting to ask any more questions. However, after a brief pause she started telling the story she must have told a thousand times.

"It was last Thursday," she said. "She went out and never came back. Thursdays she was usually back by mid-afternoon to do her washing. I used to put a load through for her, cheap, like. You know."

"Mid-afternoon?" I said. "I thought she was a photographer working for some company."

"She was freelance, dear. Came and went as she liked. Anyway, I got worried when she didn't come back, but that didn't last long because the police turned up the next minute demanding keys to the flat and all sorts."

"You've got keys to the flat?" I asked excitedly.

"Oh, yes," she continued. "Anyway, I let them in, but they never did tell me what was going on until they'd finished. Effing and blinding about *no forensic here*, just like on TV. Anyway, only as an afterthought, really, one of them comes back in to talk to me. Gives me the keys and says, *Sorry, but there's been an accident. Are you Rebecca Marsh's landlady?* I thought, *landlady?* and laughed at the idea that I owned the place. I said as much and then the young man asked for the owner's name, and the landlord's name, and I kept asking what was going on. Eventually they told me she'd had an accident on the train platform which they were treating as suspicious."

"What that it?" I asked.

"Oh, no. The same evening they were back — different ones, asking about a stalker and a magazine." She looked up at me with frightened eyes. "Did you see it? The magazine, I mean."

I nodded. She continued.

"I couldn't believe all those things had happened to the poor girl, and right under my very nose as well. I must have been dozing or something on that day."

"Oh which day?"

"When that brute came round — from the story in the magazine. Anyone visiting has to come through the shop, you see."

"Isn't there any back entrance?"

"No, I don't think . . . There's the fire escape, I suppose. He must have gone up that."

"So what do you know about Rebecca?" I asked. "Did she have many boyfriends, or visitors?"

"No," said the woman. "No, not at all. Lonely little thing, I think. Moved up from Essex or somewhere, because of some boyfriend, but they split up. At least, he came around a lot for a while and then nothing."

"That's sad."

"Yes. Lovely girl she was as well. Very nicely spoken, like you."

"Oh," I said. "Um, thanks."

"Anyway," said the woman, "I'm about to lock up. Did you want to have a look upstairs?"

"Oh, yes please," I said eagerly, and followed her through a side door and up the stairs.

CHAPTER ELEVEN

REBECCA

THE FLAT SMELT STRONGLY OF VANILLA. It was small, but had obviously been lovingly decorated. The front door opened onto a tiny hallway where an old, sixties-style telephone rested on a small glass table surrounded by art deco prints and black and white photographs.

"What's going to happen to all her stuff?" I asked the lady from the launderette, who had followed me up.

"I don't know," she said. "The landlord will want it out. I know that. Although I'm not sure he'll find another tenant in a hurry. It's such a shame — she's put a lot of work into making the place look nice."

Rebecca's taste seemed very similar to mine, I thought, looking around the flat. Every window was curtained with white muslin which hung ethereally from wooden curtain rails. There were no carpets, just big thick rugs scattered on the pine floorboards: a dark pink and white striped one by the unmade bed; burnt orange and blue in the sitting room. The kitchen floor was tiled in black and white.

The sitting room was the most lived-in room in the flat. An old squashy-looking red sofa dominated the far end of the room. I walked over and saw two books lying on it: one was about a photographer who only took photographs of herself and the other was *Misery* by Stephen King.

A bookshelf next to the sofa contained about two hundred more books — mostly photography and literary fiction titles — and also supported a small portable television. On top of the TV was a small pink badge. *Becky*, it said.

I looked on the bookshelf for more personal items like diaries, notebooks and so on, but found nothing. An old fireplace in one of the side walls had been cleared out and Rebecca had placed an orange vase there in which a bunch of dried flowers was arranged. The mantelpiece above this supported a long line of videos: the whole *Twin Peaks* series, *North by North-West*, *Psycho*, *The Birds*, *Wild at Heart*, *Eraserhead*, *Blue Velvet*, *Cinema Paradise*, *The Unbearable Lightness of Being* and *Misery*. Maybe that's why she was reading the book. Opposite the mantelpiece was a door leading through into the kitchen, and the far wall held a door to the bedroom. I decided to search the kitchen first.

Again I was looking for personal effects, notes, reminders, anything that might tell me who Rebecca knew and what she might have been afraid of, but there wasn't anything here. No calendars on the wall, no notes stuck to the fridge, no Post-It notes or letters.

The fridge contained only three items. Evian, smoked salmon and a pot of Clinique moisturiser. The rest of the kitchen was as you would expect and had been left poignantly untidy. I felt a small lump rise in my throat as I looked in the sink and saw the slightly mouldy remains of a cup of coffee and a small china plate with toast crumbs still stuck to it.

Next, I poked around in the bedroom, wanting to know everything about this girl and desperately trying to find some way in. But it was clear that the police had been here before me, knowing what they were looking for and taking it, leaving almost no trace of the personal Rebecca. Presumably the police would be comparing and contrasting what they'd found with the personal effects of the other two women, looking for whatever it was that linked them.

But I needed something to go on. I searched through all her drawers, in her wardrobe and even in her laundry basket. I was just about to give up when something caught my attention. It was a small evening-size handbag lying discarded under the bed. I looked in it and found a contact book and diary. In the diary these words were written: *Shoot, Mark Moss*, and they appeared in the box labelled Thursday 19 June. *Bingo*, I thought. *So that's where she was going*. If it hadn't been for the comma . . . But she obviously meant photo shoot. I slipped the small books in my bag and continued, feeling lucky.

The search was made rather more difficult by the woman from downstairs following me around tutting every so often, and mumblings things like *What a shame* or *Such a nice girl*. I didn't stay in the hallway long, or the bathroom — a small, dark room (and *darkroom*, I suspected) with only a shower, toilet and a sink.

Once I'd satisfied myself that there really wasn't anything else to see here, I thanked the woman and left. I looked at my watch and saw that it was almost three o'clock. The heat outside had intensifed, and I felt my body grow damp with perspiration as soon as I walked out of the launderette.

We moved back down South not long after that. A combination of events led to this, the first being the appearance of Carl's wife, who discovered that he was knocking my mother off and decided to do something about it.

It was a Monday morning, and I was off school quite legitimately for the first time because of a mysterious infection for which I had to take big, bitter antibiotics. I remember that my mother had just been up to give me my morning dose, along with a glass of milk, which she said was better for me than "all that rubbish" my father brought home. We talked for a while, about nothing in particular. My mother sat on the very edge of my bed and seemed to be trying to get around to mentioning something. I looked at the way she was dressed — probably for the first time — and wondered why she did it. The too-high heels, the thin, thin, thin pencil skirt and the make-up. When I was younger I used to like the smell of it when she pressed her head against mine, or tucked me in and gave me a goodnight kiss. But it seemed like a cracking mask by then, and I wondered if she was going mouldy underneath it.

I remember wriggling around in my sweaty pyjamas as she tried stroking my head. I didn't want her to touch me. She had just started to talk about my comics when the doorbell rang. She looked surprised, but ran down to open it. All was quiet for a few seconds, then I heard the click of the door being unbolted and the rattle of it opening. Then everything became very loud. Women's voices, maybe five of them, rang out in the hallway along with a dull thumping noise and, of course, the screams. My mother's screams. I lay there, prone, not knowing what to do. The voices were saying things like, slag, haven't you got a husband? Whore, and the words my father had often used: bit of rough.

Back on the train I felt frustrated, doing the journey I had done yesterday in reverse. I now had something to go on, but it wasn't much. *Mark Moss.* Who was he? There must have been some other detail, or clue in the flat that I'd missed. Perhaps Mark Moss, if I could locate him, could tell me something about Rebecca.

It had been odd talking to Star last night about Edgar Allan Poe's Dupin, one of my favourite fictional detectives. Here I was in his role, but with the unfortunate problem of lacking the arrogance or the evidence to proclaim the big *Aha!* I still felt moderately confident, though, neither less nor more than in the beginning, and I had a feeling this was going to turn out to be either very much more simple, or very much more complex than everybody thought.

Half an hour later I was in a cab back to Camden, having seen virtually nothing at Sasha's house. The house itself had been easy enough to find, and was so close to London Fields that I could see why she used to cut across the park. I imagined her being followed, running home to the best friend mentioned in the *Smile!* feature (who wasn't in when I knocked) and then convincing herself it was nothing.

And now this.

With grim thoughts in mind I'd approached the big front door. It was white, or had been once, the old heavy gloss paint peeling like a scab. The doorbell hadn't worked so I'd banged loudly. Nothing. I tried shouting through the letter box: still nothing.

Thinking *hard-boiled* for a moment, I had a crazy idea. Two minutes later I'd cut down a side road and round to the back of the house where various gardens backed onto one another. Loud African music was coming from one garden and a big woman swayed on the porch, wearing nothing but a purple and red sarong. She didn't seem to notice me as I made down a short passageway and unbolted the wooden garden gate.

Sasha's garden wasn't as overgrown as I'd imagined it might be. The grass needed cutting, but a variety of flowers grew uniformly in flower beds around the edge of the lawn. This was in sharp contrast with next door's garden, in which two old prams, assorted tyres, a headless doll and half a Ford Capri lay abandoned.

There was a scuffling just beyond the fence and I thought I heard whispering, then nothing. Striding confidently towards the back door, I tried the handle. It didn't budge. Looking around on the ground for something with which to open it, I heard louder whispers. Children's voices.

"Shhh. It's the murderer."

"Let's see!"

"Ouch!"

"Get off me!"

"Shut up."

"Get a description, Peter."

"Fuck off, *I'm* Peter."

Giggling. Then: "You can be Scamper."

"Brown hair. Curly."

"Big bag. D'you think she's got the murder weapon in there?"

More scuffling. By this time I was peering over the fence. There, in the garden, was a group of children in summer clothes. There were about seven or eight of them, the oldest looking about eleven and the youngest about three. The older-looking children were peering at a notebook. The youngest one was holding a pink water pistol with which he was shooting his own foot.

A small red-haired girl looked up at me, her freckled face smeared with the remains of what seemed to be face paints.

"Hello," I said. "Who are you?"

"Shit," said one of the children, an Asian boy of about nine in a bandanna and cut-off jeans. "Call the police, man, before she fucking kills us."

I laughed. "What are you doing?"

"We're calling the police," said a smaller girl loudly. She was wearing a Barbie vest and matching knickers. "We saw you trying to break in."

"But I am the police," I said, narrowing my eyes, trying to scare them.

"No you're not," said a boy with glasses and bruised legs.

"Yeah, show us yer badge," said the red-haired girl.

"I haven't got a badge," I said, adding in a conspiratorial whisper, "I'm undercover."

"Bollocks," said the Asian boy.

"Shut up, *Colin*," said the small girl.

"I'm Jack," he corrected. Some arguing broke out and the smallest child started shooting the others with his water pistol.

"Who are you supposed to be, exactly?" I asked.

"The Secret Seven, stupid," said the red-haired girl, ducking a blast from the water pistol. "We're looking for the murderer."

"Yeah," added the boy. "The one that killed that girl from in there."

"Well, shall I let you into a secret?" I said.

"What secret?"

"Only if you promise you won't tell anyone."

I had their attention now. "We promise," they chorused.

"It's a man."

"What?"

"The murderer. We've found out it's a man."

"Are you really the police?"

"Yes. And it's definitely a man."

"A clue," declared the red-haired girl. "Write it down."

Smiling, I got down from the fence and let myself out the way I'd come in. I'd abandoned the hard-boiled approach. It probably wasn't the best idea in the world trying to break into a murder victim's house with the Secret Seven watching.

Walking out onto the main road, I realised I hadn't had any phone calls all day, and when I pulled my phone out of my bag I could see why: the battery had gone completely flat. Cursing under my breath and lighting a cigarette, I set off in search of a phone box to call Tyler to see if Jess was back yet. No luck — there weren't any phone boxes here. Searching for a cab was fruitless as well. Richmond Road seemed to be the kind of road on which nothing much happened outside the imaginations of children, and eventually I gave up and hailed one down on Mare Street.

CHAPTER TWELVE

NOTHING

THIS TIME HENRI was the first one in when I got home.

"My favourite daughter," he proclaimed as I walked through the door, and then, once he had seen the state of me (mascara running with the heat, hair up in an unglamorous ponytail, my body limp with carrying the bag from hell all day): "Oh, my God."

"Hi Henri," I said, smiling at the look of horror on his face and kissing him on both cheeks. "Did you have a nice day?"

"*Oui*, of course. But what has happened to you?"

"Nothing," I said, wandering into the kitchen to make some coffee. I found some fresh bread and some salami and made a rough sandwich. "I've just been out, um, visiting people."

"*Dead* people, probably," said Henri exasperatedly. "I know what you're up to, I just hope you're careful out there."

"What do you think?" I said, biting into my sandwich and pouring coffee for us both. I laughed. "Anyway, I don't think it would be possible to be further away from the murderer than I am right now. I'm quite safe."

Henri chuckled. "Not having much luck?"

"No, well, maybe. I don't know. It's all so complicated, you know?"

"Don't tell that to Star," he said. "She is very over excited about all this."

"I'd have thought she'd have had enough of murderers and everything with her work."

"Yes, well, I thought so too. There is something about the investigation that she finds fascinating. All these *romans policiers.* What do you call them?"

"Crime novels."

"Yes. She reads so many of them. It is quite incredible."

"Anyway," I said, not wanting to dwell on the murders for too much longer today, "Have there been any calls for me?"

"Yes, your mother rang about half an hour ago."

"Is that all?"

"*Oui.* Whom were you expecting? A young man, perhaps?"

"No, of course not."

"Hmm," said Henri. "What did you think of Cal?"

"*Cal?*" I said, taken aback. "Um, sweet, I suppose. But dull."

"Yes, you would think that. Sometimes I worry that you are too sophisticated for your own good."

"What, you mean I won't fall into bed with the nearest bloke under fifty? I am only *half* French, Papa."

"You may be missing out," he said mysteriously, smiling and taking his coffee cup.

"I don't think so," I said, following Henri as he took his coffee through to the living room. "Anyway, when's Star coming back?"

He looked at his watch. "About seven, I think. Within the next ten minutes or so."

"Has she moved in, I mean, *officially?*"

"Officially, no. We don't want to rush anything."

"No."

"I must say," said Henri, "that you are looking rather healthier than when I saw you when you were living in London, despite your current *désordre.*"

"Must be the country air," I said.

"No, no." He shook his head. "It is more than that. It is like an . . . *inner peace,* I think."

"Well, I'm happy down there, I suppose. I mean, I thought I was just going to go and stay for a while, but to be honest I feel like a tourist already coming back to London. Everything seems so insignificant here all of a sudden, you know, things I used to care about like the price of travelcards and the corruption of the councils. It all just seems so far away."

"Well, it's doing you a lot of good. I, too, would move back to the countryside if it would have me."

"Don't be so silly," I said fondly. "You always hated the countryside. You hated the smallness of it, and the way everyone thought you were a tourist because of your accent."

"*Oui*. I suppose . . . Maybe I will retire to the country, then you can look after your mother and me without having to travel too far."

"You'll be lucky," I said, laughing teasingly. I didn't want to think about Mum and Henri getting old. How old would I be then? At the moment, twenty-five seemed too much — surely it was only five minutes ago that I was twelve.

Without warning, my mind filled with images of Rebecca, Tam and Sasha, my imagination animating the pictures from the magazine and placing the women in their homes. I saw Rebecca on her red sofa, Tam at her yellow table fending off Dean and Sasha in her garden, weeding. Why were they dead? It was all so *wrong*. I must have looked quite vacant, because Henri tapped me on the arm and broke into my thoughts.

"How's your mother?"

"Fine, I think."

"And Sue?" Henri raised his eyebrows when he said the word *Sue*.

"Sue? Oh, yes," I remembered. "You met her at my garden party, didn't you?"

"A very good choice, I think," said Henri, smirking.

"A good choice?"

"Is this the wrong word, I —"

The phone cut through his sentence and it turned out rather surprisingly to be Cal, for me.

"What does he want?" I hissed at Henri as he waved the telephone receiver at me.

"Why don't you speak to him and find out?"

"Because . . . Oh, give me that." Exasperated, hot and confused, I took the receiver from Henri and spoke a terse *hello* into it.

"Lily?" said Cal nervously. "Hi, how are you?"

"Hot," I said. "And tired. And you?"

"Oh, fine. Look, I was wondering . . ."

"Mmm?"

"Well, maybe we could go out sometime."

I shrugged. "Maybe."

"Is that a definite maybe?"

"Sorry?"

"Um," Cal giggled nervously, "I'm not very good at this. Have I caught you at a bad time?"

"Well, kind of. I've just got in and I haven't really got my thoughts together yet. Why don't I call you back?"

"Okay," he said, and gave me his number.

When I put the phone down, Henri, who had been hovering around by his bookshelves, came over.

"Well?" he demanded.

"Well, what?"

"Are you going out with him?"

"I doubt it," I said. "He's not exactly my type."

"Maybe you should give him a chance."

"I would, it's just . . ."

"Just what?"

"I think I'm in love with someone else."

The words had come from nowhere. I was stunned. Was I really in love with Fenn? I felt myself blushing and turned to walk out of the room. Henri seemed nonplussed — he, of course, didn't realise the implications of what I was saying. I wasn't in love with a married man as such, just with one who was about to be married. Oh, God.

I decided to retire to the bath for a long tepid soak, during which I gave myself a severe talking-to about Fenn. He was getting married: there could be nothing between us. It was probably a good thing that I was away from there right now; this talk about love was dangerous.

As I lay in the water I thought through this idea that I *loved* Fenn. He was my best friend, sure. But love? How could I love someone I was so angry with? Okay, so he believed Bronwyn was carrying his baby, but before she told him she was pregnant they'd been strangers (it had been a distant one-night stand) and I had been his friend. And look how he was treating me now.

My mind gradually emptied of Fenn as I repeated the words "infatuation" and "only" to myself over and over again. It soon began to refill: this time with thoughts about the murders. I compiled a list of possible suspects from what I had to go on at the moment. The list comprised: the stalkers from the magazine story, everyone on the magazine staff, Tyler, Jess, Dean and the woman in the launderette (impossible, but I was trying to be scientific). I also added the peculiarly named Mark Moss to the list. He shared the same surname as Tyler. Interesting.

It had to be someone who knew the magazine story was coming out before it did. I knew that. And something else had been bugging me: the murders replicated the magazine feature exactly — but only just. Sasha had been killed walking to work early on Thursday morning, Rebecca *extremely* shortly after that. The delicate timing had, presumably, been the result of some research and preparation; finding out who was going to be where and at what times. The murder sites were the same as the sites for the photo shoot. Whoever had committed these murders had seen the magazine feature a long time before — or *worked* on it. I couldn't wait to get the *Smile!* magazine offices to follow this up.

And then there were all the other connections that I didn't know about. I'd been through Rebecca's contact book and diary. Jess's name wasn't there, and there was no mention of Mark Moss either. Looking under their initials, I found no record of Sasha or Tam. Great. All the people I'd so far connected with Rebecca's murder she hadn't known, at least not well enough to record their numbers.

I dipped my long, curly and already somewhat soggy-from-the-heat hair into the bathwater and wondered again what was going on with Jess. She'd gone away because it was all too much. Fine. Except why had she begged me to come in the first place? She probably knew that everything was not what it seemed, perhaps she even knew why. So why hadn't she spoken to the police? The only explanation was that she had something to hide. But what? And where was the *Stalking* file?

After my bath I went and lay on the bed in my room, enjoying the sound of the cars driving past and occasional voices in the street. This was as silent as London got, in my experience, but at least my thoughts were able to disentangle themselves a bit. I had become rather worked up today, rushing from place to place in the heat, and doing it on public transport hadn't helped. It felt strange having my term-time routine shattered as well, and staying somewhere different. Being a guest made everything an event somehow: meals, chats, outings. Even if you did stuff by yourself, people wanted to know what you had done, what you were going to do next and so on.

Feeling tired, but refusing to succumb to this feeling, I read some of Star's thriller for a while and then wandered downstairs shortly after I heard her key (*her* key!) in the door. So they hadn't moved in together yet? I wondered if Henri had mentioned that to Star.

A pleasant evening followed involving a quiet supper of fresh pasta with Parmesan and garlic and the three of us relaxing in front of the TV. Star didn't ask me many more questions; she seemed to have a lot of paperwork to catch up on. Henri changed channels constantly with the remote control before settling finally on a re-run of *Morse*, which he ruined slightly by trying to remember out loud who the villain was, since he had seen it before. I found it hard to believe this was my father's sort of thing at all, but he assured me that he had always been a fan, proclaiming that it was the only decent thing on TV apart from *Newsnight*. Star laughed at that and added *Masterchef, Home and Away, Top of the Pops* and *Peak Practice* to his list for good measure, bursting Henri's culture bubble and making him almost embarrassed.

Just before I went to sleep I reminded myself of a detail that I really should follow up tomorrow: Tam's odd friends and her art connections. I felt almost content when I went to sleep, except for one thing. Fenn's wedding was in three days' time and I never did come to a conclusion about exactly how that made me feel.

CHAPTER THIRTEEN

TAM

EXCITEMENT GOES TOO FAR

A new exhibit was unveiled at the controversial *Excitement* exhibition at the Heath Gallery in London today which is already causing a stir.

While talk of the unsolved Magazine Murders is still fresh all over the country, ex-art student Dominic Carson has decided to cash in on his six-month relationship with victim Tamara Hunter by staging an installation in which he will talk, live, about their life together, while sitting on a milking stool in a booth in the gallery.

"I do not see myself as an exhibit," said Carson, speaking at a press conference yesterday. "I am merely a vehicle for the installation piece which is itself about life after death. In this way, Tam's memory can live on. It will be an oral history; a living, breathing monument to her and everything she stood for."

Dominic Carson is hardly a household name, yet in the art world he is known for his controversial work in the realm of what is termed "bondage art." A previous installation was branded a health hazard and a fire risk by the Department of Health because it featured a young woman tied to an iron post. Other critics were outraged because the girl, a model hired from an agency, was to be topless, and, during opening times, would not be fed and would only be allowed to drink water from a dog bowl. Feminist and anti-violence groups called this "shocking" and welcomed the Department of Health's ban.

Speaking at the time about his work and the piece, called *Bravado*, Carson said that: "All great artists have been unrecognised at first, and their work dismissed as dangerous. I take this ban as a compliment of the most profound kind."

Carson's five-piece exhibition went ahead, however, but in place of *Bravado* was a piece called *Shame*, simply the Department of Health letter hung on a blood-red canvas.

There are no moves to ban his latest installation, called, simply, *Tam*, which will be only two exhibits away from the publicly slammed *Scene* series, said to contain genuine pictures taken at murder scenes. An insider at the Metropolitan Police said that they were not concerned about Carson's piece, and added that they would probably be sending an officer along to take notes.

I arrived at the Heath Gallery the next day just after lunchtime, having seen the piece in the newspaper. There was an element of fortuity about this: I never usually read the news section of the *Guardian*, simply because it was too big and I resented having to clear the whole table to spread it out on. I only read the tabloid section, which today took me about ten minutes since there was only one interesting piece on the women's page about anorexia. I had always been a big (although firmly *in the closet*) fan of horoscopes, however, particularly the ones in the *Evening Standard*, so taking advantage of being in London I had popped to the local shop at about eleven to buy this, some chocolate and a can of Coke. The piece about the *Excitement* exhibition, and the shockingly *exciting* news about Tam's ex-boyfriend was on page eleven and came as a very welcome surprise, since I had drawn blanks otherwise that morning.

Having started with the mysterious Mark Moss, I'd got precisely nowhere. He wasn't in the phone book, nor was he a member of any of the photography associations I'd called. Thinking I was clever, I'd run all the numbers from Rebecca's contact book as well. No one had heard of Mark Moss, and no one knew anything about Rebecca except that she had been an excellent photographer. She'd been very into her work: that was all I'd established.

It had proved impossible to secure much information about Tam or her friends from Goldsmith's or from Dean, who, when I phoned pretending to be a reporter, simply told me to fuck off. I was on the verge of going to the Goldsmith's student bar to hang around asking questions when the trip to the shop had become appealing. And then there it was: possibly my vital lead.

The Heath Gallery stood grey and shabby at the wrong end of the South Bank, but despite its bad location there was a queue when I arrived. It seemed to be increasing its profile more and more lately. I remembered that last year, when I still lived in London, there had been an exhibition called *Smut*, dealing with issues surrounding pornography and sexuality but which had unfortunately included pieces on themes like paedophilia and bestiality. It was amazing, I thought, that the art world had become such a hotbed — or indeed the safe house — of vulgarity, and it always amused me that only serious art and serious books were allowed to depict scenes which, if portrayed in a general release film, would be almost instantly banned.

The irony for me was that somehow it was films that were deemed to be morally vacant and worthless, while anything in a book or on a canvas was considered culturally important. There was some scheme last summer, I remembered, to encourage more young people and children to read: why had no one simply told them that the dirty or violent bits in books were always much more graphic than in films?

I kept myself occupied in the queue with these thoughts and a cigarette until, finally, I was allowed to enter. I hadn't been to an art gallery for a while, having always been the type of person who *meant* to go; who wrote "visiting galleries" on the hobby section on forms, but who could actually count the number of actual visits on the fingers of one hand.

When my best friend, Eugénie, died, I was nineteen and just about to come to London for the first time to go to university. Of course when I got here, I'd found that none of the people I met could replace her, and had become more and more introverted. I'd indulged in a spate of gallery-visiting then, finding art galleries to be some of the quietest places in the too-loud metropolis, strangely the only places that reminded me of the countryside and enabled me to think in peace.

This was not like any of those experiences, unfortunately. The crowd inside the foyer was loud; a group of twenty-somethings were comparing postcards noisily at the doors of the shop-café on the left, and a group of protesters were being politely but firmly shown out of the main exhibition through the doors off to my right. I stood still for moment, listening to the effect of the for and the against in stereo: *Don't you think the Carson installation was amazing? Should be banned. Look at this one; it's actually got that scene on it from the House of Horror murders, where they found that girl buried in the garden. It's a disgrace. Are they real, do you think? Government money. Art grants. Rubbish. Brilliant!*

Trying to filter out the voices I looked up at the ceiling, which, like the rest of the foyer, was glass. I wondered if these minimalist glass fans could see the irony of it all; how see-through the whole effect was. I found myself being roughly jostled by a group of drunk critics who were coming in behind me, so I moved forwards, through the glass doors, into the glass chamber, to look at the first exhibits.

When my father got home he found us just the way we were: me quivering in bed, not able to get up; and my mother in a bloody heap just by the front door. On her head lay a soggy envelope which had been delivered by second post. It was from my school, saying that there were serious concerns about my attendance.

My father hit the roof. I later discovered that he had been made redundant that same day. The drink still wasn't passing any tests, and management had apparently had enough of his "pissing around." Three things. Always three things. Bad things come in fucking threes.

So he decided we would move. My mother recovered, of course, after a few stitches and a couple of nights in hospital. She started seeing a therapist after that as well, to deal with her desire to shag working-class men, and some other stuff from the past. I stayed with an aunt over this period, and when I came back the house wasn't the same. Everything was in boxes, including the contents of my room. I remember walking through the door and feeling the most horrible, sick, twisted-stomach feeling as I thought of the now hard tissues stuffed down the side of my bed; the illegal comics stacked in my wardrobe.

She looked at me peculiarly when I walked through the front door, my mum. I think she blushed. I knew right then that she'd been through my things, so I calmly asked where the box of stuff from my room was. She pointed her long talon up the stairs and I turned and went; not running, not betraying how important all that stuff was to me, just walking slowly with what I expect other people would call resigned gloom.

They were gone, of course. [Sighs and coughs.] I remember my father following me up the stairs and saying something about organising some kind of "help" for me as well. I remember him putting his head in his hands and saying: "What has happened to my family?"

I think I punched the wall, and I think I walked out, but I can't remember. What I do remember was the van and then the new house back down South. Everything changed then: it was the start of a new era.

The first series of exhibits was called *Still Life in the Nineties*, the title, I assumed, intending to be an art pun with an unspoken *yawn* at the end. *Still* life in the nineties. Ho, hum. The pieces within it reflected this rather obvious and, I thought, pointless excuse to play on words. The first one was a baked-bean tin; a nod, I imagined, to Andy Warhol's tin cans, but since it was a supermarket own brand, it unfortunately lacked the design qualities of the Campbell's Soup version. This, I deduced, must be the point. The next piece was as dull and understated as the first, featuring a muddied, child-size Manchester United football shirt sitting crumpled next to a drink carton. The drink was one of those things full of E-numbers and very popular with kids. I played a game with myself for a while, wondering what the title of the piece was. Once I had settled on *After the Match* I looked at the actual name. It was called *Childhood*. A slightly grandoise but interesting concept, I thought, warming to the collection slightly.

By the time I reached the third artist I was really enjoying myself. I had seen a few pieces which were actually quite absorbing, despite my initial prejudices. My only criticism so far was that the exhibits were on the tame side, although I realised that they would be keeping the really sensational pieces until last. By the time I reached the Carson installation I was so wrapped up in it all that his piece came as quite a surprise: I'd almost forgotten it was there. It was hard to miss, though.

A small crowd had gathered, and as I pushed my way to the front I noted with some surprise that, as anticipated in the newspaper piece, a single plain-clothes policeman was keeping notes.

"I suppose you could say he's part of the installation now," said a man standing next to me, nodding at the policeman.

"Sorry?"

"The copper. He's part of it, I mean, this is *living* art. He's part of the piece, a further comment on who Tam was — on what her life became."

"I suppose so," I said uncertainly, following this idea through in my head to its problematic conclusion: that the murder was then also part of the art.

The man soon drifted off, and when the artist stopped to drink some of a bottle of lager he had under the milking stool, the rest of the crowd drifted away as well. The installation was set in a small alcove between two main rooms, so for a few minutes I was alone with the artist, the policeman and a rather beefy curator-cum-security guard.

"What's he doing here?" I asked the policeman, pointing at the security man.

"They're guarding all the most controversial exhibits," he said, chuckling. "They don't fancy any members of the public *adding* to them, if you know what I mean."

"What, destroying them?"

"Yeah, or in his case, attacking would be more accurate."

"Really?"

"Oh, yes."

We stood there for a couple of minutes silently. Then I turned to Dominic Carson.

"So," I began conversationally, eliciting a glare from the guard and a seen-it-all-before smile from the policeman. "What made you decide to —"

"Please don't speak to the exhibit," interrupted the guard, serious and deadpan.

"What?" I said incredulously.

"You should have said you were a journalist," said the policeman. "He's done the press conference earlier."

"Yes," I said, "I heard. But I'm not a journalist."

"Oh, I see," said the policeman.

"Why can't I talk to him?" I asked the guard.

"Because he's part of an installation," he said exasperatedly. "You just can't *talk* to exhibits, you know."

"Oh, right, so I couldn't *talk* to a painting, then?"

"You could," said the guard. "But you'd soon find yourself escorted out."

The policeman laughed. "Bit of a *police state*, the art world, then, wouldn't you say? What a turn-up, eh?"

"Sorry?" said the guard and I together.

"Well," said the policeman, "I remember a time when art was radical — you know, *for the kids*, smashing the state and so on. The voice of youth, or whatever. Bloody fascists now, these artists."

The security guard sighed loudly and started tapping his foot while I laughed, covering my mouth with my hand in case I got into any more trouble. Meanwhile Dominic Carson sat up on his milking stool, having been straight-faced and unresponsive throughout our exchange.

"He's going to start now," said the guard to me. He gestured at the policeman. "I can't chuck *him* out, more's the pity, but if I hear one more peep out of —"

"Don't worry," I said. "I want to hear what he's saying anyway."

Dominic's talk, or should I say, *rant*, was not what I had expected at all. In fact, I was surprised the press hadn't mentioned that the content of his verbal outpourings was mainly sexual and detailed how, after meeting Tam last Christmas at a Goldsmith's end of term party, she had left college and moved in with him and his flatmate, practising various forms of bondage and asphyxiation which made the policeman grimace and me blush. The talk went on for about five minutes until he reached the recent weeks leading up to Tam's death.

"She was unique," he said. "But no one understood her, what she was all about. She became more demanding, somehow. She wanted more. Stuff I couldn't give her — or I didn't think I could. They were going to throw her out of the house because she owed them money, so she came up with this scam to get money. It was the end of her. The end of us. She did it for money, to so many men. Then she even sold her secrets. We split up. It seemed like the best thing at the time. I still can't believe she let someone else . . . So many others. But that one in particular, the last one . . ."

Something struck me about what he was saying that wasn't quite right. I wasn't sure why, since it seemed to tally precisely with what Dean had said. But then again, Dean had been more than a bit mysterious about all the details as well. I just wish I knew what was going on. After a while Dominic stopped again and I sidled over to the policeman.

"What was that about *letting someone else*, and so many others?" I asked. "Letting them do what?"

"Kill her," said the policeman. "From what I can gather so far, he thinks she hooked up with lots of people after dumping him and did more of that asphyxiation stuff with them. This 'one in particular' we can't get out of him. He can't remember his name, so we're having to do DNA tests on all her clothes now. Anyway, as far as he's concerned she got strangled in a sex game: it was an accident. He obviously hasn't been reading the papers."

"Why?"

"Well, we found the knife from the Sasha Brookes killing in the front room there."

"Oh, yes," I said, remembering the TV report, "of course you did."

"Anyway, what's a nice young girl like you doing hanging around listening to all of this? I'm sure you've got better things to do." He leant his thin face towards me and whispered conspiratorially: "He's not very good."

"Oh, I can see that," I said. "I'm here for the same reasons as you, really. I'm a . . . um, friend of Jess Mallone." Seeing the look that passed over the policeman's face I instantly held my hands up. "But before you ask," I added hurriedly, "I don't know where she is and I didn't see her before she went."

"All right," he said, smiling, "I believe you. So why do you look familiar?"

"I don't know."

"You say you're a friend of Jess Mallone."

"Yes."

"Are you from London?"

"Not any more. I'm living in Devon now."

I started shifting from one foot to the other, embarrassed. *I* knew where he'd seen me before — there had been an item on me in one of those *Police Monthly* magazines, mainly to feature the picture of the Chief Superintendent of our local force giving me my reward. But maybe I was shy, maybe I didn't want to get into trouble — I certainly didn't want to help him figure it out.

He narrowed his eyes and looked at me hard. "You're the one who solved the Stephanie Duncan case."

"Um . . ."

"Yes, it is you. You've got those strange eyes." He smiled. "I always remember eyes. My grandfather was the same, one green and one blue. I remember commenting on it at the time when I saw you in the magazine."

"Okay," I admitted, smiling. "It was me. But I'd been kind of hoping to withhold that information."

"Fancy you turning up here. I suppose you're planning to solve these murders as well, are you, embarrass us again and all that?"

"I'm having a go," I said. "But I haven't really got anywhere yet."

"Look," he said, glancing at his watch, "do you fancy a coffee? I've had enough of standing here."

"Um, okay," I said.

It transpired, over a watery espresso and a stale cake, that Inspector Thompson had volunteered to come down here today because in his words it was "better than knocking on doors." It seemed he had a vested interest in the art world himself anyway, being something of a collector.

"So how far have you got?" I asked eventually.

"What, with the murder investigation? Not far, I'm afraid. The incident room is taking a lot of calls, but most of them don't lead anywhere."

"Is that always the way?"

"Mmm, mostly. But we'd have expected a few firmer leads by now. We're having trouble getting much on the three women, to be honest. I don't know if it's a coincidence or what, but none of them seem to have had close relatives. No *parents* in any case. If I recall, Sasha's body was identified by a girl she worked with, Rebecca's by an uncle who was so drunk he didn't know what day it was and Tam's was identified by some joker from her house."

"Not Dean?"

"Oh," said Inspector Thompson, looking surprised, "you've met Mr. Charisma, then?"

"I've had the pleasure, yes." I laughed and then grew serious again. Some of the things Dominic Carson had said had made me think. "Are you absolutely certain the same bloke did all three?"

"Oh, yes. The knife connects Sasha's killer with Tam's, and of course there's the magazine story. We have to assume that someone was out to get them because of that. There certainly don't seem to be any other connections between the three of them. Also, Forensics have found evidence of the same fibre at each murder scene — probably from a bag or item of clothing belonging to the murderer."

"Do you know what it was?"

"Mmm — denim. Very helpful."

"But what if there is no real connection and the knife was there for another reason? Dominic could be right about Tam dying in a sex game."

"Go on."

"Well, isn't Dean an obvious suspect? What if the knife was in the house because *he'd* used it to kill Sasha?"

"It's an interesting theory," said Inspector Thompson. "But, and I'm telling you this absolutely confidentially, that young man has an alibi as strong as a brick wall."

"What is it?"

"I *definitely* shouldn't tell you that."

"Why not? I could always go and ask him myself. He was very helpful last time I spoke to him," I added, lying.

"Okay. Well, suffice to say that it involves his poor, sick mother, a hospice and about ten witnesses — all nurses — who'll back up where he was that morning."

"Oh, dear. I suppose it would be hard to pin down a motive as well, really."

"Yes."

I sighed. "Never mind, back to the drawing board, I suppose."

"Don't worry, I had the same theory myself for a long time, until we actually brought the bugger in. Disappointing, isn't it?"

"Yes," I said. "But I'll get there."

"Not by doing anything dangerous, I hope?"

"You never know," I said, smiling. "I can't promise anything. Incidentally, what about the other obvious candidates? Who's got an alibi?"

"*Obvious* candidates?" The inspector chuckled. "I don't think anything's obvious about this. But strictly between you and me . . . Let's see. I shouldn't be telling you this at all, but anyway . . . Jess Mallone. She could have had something to do with it. We don't know about her alibi, since we haven't been able to speak to her properly yet. Her boyfriend, what's his name?"

"Tyler."

"Yes, he was at the gym. Goes every morning at the same time. Loads of people vouched for him there."

"What about the artist?"

"What, Carson?"

"Yeah."

"No alibi as such. Although he swears he didn't have anything to do with it. Apparently there was no way he could have afforded the petrol or the train fares to get from London to Hertfordshire and then back again. I must admit, we didn't get much more than that out of him when we interviewed him. That's one of the reason's I'm here now."

"And *Smile!* magazine? Any of them in the frame?"

"All of them, until we rule them out. They've been very unhelpful, to be honest. I just can't wait to start doing some tests, see who this mysterious character is that Tam was knocking off."

"Anything on the stalkers?"

"Nope. This is the most frustrating thing. The phone company don't have any record of Sasha reporting those nuisance calls — they say it was too long ago or something, and since she didn't report it to us at the time we've no way of following that up. We've spoken to all the commuters from Rebecca's train line and none of them can remember seeing a man smiling at her. Mind you, none of them can really remember her, so that's a bit of a non-starter. We've contacted all the counsellors in her area, to see if she may have spoken to one of them. Nothing. Tam Hunter was the strangest one. All that stuff in the magazine story about changing her name and everything? We can't find any evidence of a former name. DVLC don't have any record of her at all, which would indicate that she didn't even have a driving licence, but the magazine article says she'd had two."

"Maybe they were illegal in some way," I suggested.

"That's what we reckon. From the look of her housemates I don't think it would have been too hard for me to get hold of that kind of thing. In any case, we haven't got anything on her stalker, Stuart. This Carson fellow doesn't seem to know anything about him. Neither does Dean."

"Yeah, that's what he told me as well."

The inspector finished his coffee and looked at his watch.

"I'm sure you'll get something soon," I said.

He stood up to leave. "I know it's no good warning you types off, but if you do get anything, please at least give me a call." He gave me his card. "And don't go doing anything dangerous. This really should be police only, you know."

How did your father die?

In an accident, I think.

I wandered around the exhibition for about another hour after that, by this time quite enjoying the atmosphere. I wasn't as shocked as I thought I'd be by the *Scene* series, and found the crime scene pictures interesting, albeit in a macabre sort of way. The framing was what made them so interesting; in each case the photographer had composed the shot around some object other than the body. I thought that the artist who put the series together was receiving rather too much of the credit — surely the unscrupulous but undeniably gifted photographer deserved some acclaim, too?

The moral issue was harder to resolve, though, and I wasn't surprised that from the voices I could hear in the small, appreciative crowd, none seemed to be asking what the relatives of the victims in the pictures would think of their loved ones' last moments displayed like this for all to see.

Beyond the series of photographs was a video playing on a loop, of the "artist" talking about precisely these issues. He was young, and very good-looking. I stood there for a while watching, until I was startled by a tap on my shoulder.

"Hello, Lily," said Cal, as I turned to face him. I must have looked freaked out. The man standing next to him was the man from the video, looking more dishevelled but with a large grin on his face.

"Before you ask," he said, "I'm only in it for the money."

"I take it you're the artist," I said. "Hi, Cal."

"Hi," he said. "This is Jon, my partner."

"He always makes it sound so gay," said Jon. "I think he means *creative* partner. I'm his artist, or he's my writer, depending on which way you look at it."

"And you're hanging around here to see the reaction to your collection?"

"I don't give a shit about anyone's reaction," said John pleasantly. "I'm only here to pull girls."

Jon was taller than Cal and much more interesting-looking. His black hair stood in slightly matted clumps on his head and his almost turquoise-blue eyes shone out of his suntanned face, which by the look of things he had forgotten to shave for a couple of days. He wore a faded T-shirt which exposed his brown arms, one of which sported a snake tattoo, the other a long scar.

I stood there looking at him for a few moments, trying to place him, as if I'd seen him somewhere before. There was something about him; more than a bit of rough. He seemed dangerous. I sighed and looked at the floor.

"Are you all right?" asked Cal.

"What? Oh, yes, I'm fine," I said, looking up and snapping out of my reverie. I pointed at Jon. "What's he doing?"

Jon had walked over to the series of photographs and struck up a conversation with a middle-aged woman who seemed to be getting rather agitated about something. Cal chuckled.

"He's so wild," he said, causing me to cringe slightly. "He's a bad influence on *me*, anyway."

"Yeah, but what's he doing?"

"Right," said Cal slightly dramatically. "You're the great detective. If I give you a clue, you can work it out."

"Okay."

Cal stood there looking up at the ceiling for at least a minute before I became frustrated.

"What's the clue, then?" I asked impatiently.

"What? Oh, um, the clue is, *look up.*"

I looked up, but couldn't see very much. There was the wall, a small alcove and then the ceiling. As I cast my eyes up and then down for a third time, I noticed it: not just the small red light, but the reflection of light on glass. A camera lens. And if there was a camera with a red light — a video camera — up there, then it didn't take a genius to work out who was behind it.

"Presumably Jon's recording people's reactions," I said. "For some dodgy art video no doubt."

"Christ, you are good at this," said Cal, looking impressed. "Hey, Jon!"

"What?" asked Jon, sidling over.

"She's got you sussed."

"I've been sprung? Oh, well, never mind."

"I suppose you're going to tell me the reaction is the real art," I said.

"Got it in one, babe," said Jon, then, turning to Cal: "Where did you find her?"

"She's Henri Pascale's daughter," he explained.

"Cool," said Jon, looking me up and down.

"Anyway," I said. "I really must be —"

"Oh. Well, it was nice to meet you," said Jon, elbowing Cal in the ribs.

"Ow," said Cal. "*What?*"

"Get her to come out with us tomorrow night," hissed Jon.

"I've already tried asking her to come out and she's said —"

"I'd love to," I interrupted. "You did say *us*, didn't you?"

"That's right," said Jon. "Me, Cal and a few mates."

"Great," I said.

"Well, Cal'll pick you up around seven, then. We usually just have a drink and then go on to someone's flat or a club or whatever."

"That sounds fine," I said.

I spent the rest of the afternoon sitting in the garden, drinking Pimm's and lemonade, listening to *Kaleidoscope* on Radio Four. A lovely cool breeze teased its way through my hair and I felt the most calm and relaxed I'd been all week. I read some of Star's book before dropping off eventually, listening to a bird singing in the tree.

CHAPTER FOURTEEN

THE WHOLE TRUTH

THE *Smile!* MAGAZINE OFFICES were situated not far from Henri's house on the unglamorous side of Islington, near where my old flat used to be. I had expected something more *vainglorious*, somehow, but my first impression of the exterior of the building in which the offices were — dirty, grey and uncared-for — was not far off what I found when I went inside.

Two receptionists sat at a semicircular desk, which was neither grey nor beige but somewhere in between. They clashed with each other. Both were bottle-blonde: one dark, one light and silvery. The younger of the two, the dark-blonde one, was wearing cerise and black; the older one wore lime green and purple. They both had on too much make-up, and their long, brightly painted nails were in need of a double manicure.

After telling the older one my name and appointment details, I was invited to sit down on a "comfortable" chair, which was made from some kind of artificial bus-seat fabric and was the same indeterminate shade of dull as the counter. All at once I could see why Kathi hadn't been keen for me to come, and I wondered how many visitors they actually had here.

After about five minutes, Kathi, a slightly overweight but friendly-looking woman, came bustling into reception and shook my hand. We said our hellos and set off down the corridor.

"It's such a terrible shame," she said.

"I know."

"And poor Jess, running away like that. It must be awful."

"What was Jess like?" I asked. "I mean to work with."

"Jess? Oh, she was lovely. Friendly, efficient. I wish all our free-lances were like that."

"I knew her at university," I said, conversationally. "Very pretty, isn't she?"

"Pretty? Um . . ." Kathi seemed a bit thrown by this. We had reached the offices of *Smile!*, denoted by a small plaque next to the door saying *Smile! Magazine*. She opened the door and I walked through first. The layout of the room was as expected: an open-plan office with tables and computers in what I imagined would be called clusters, with groups working together. At the back of the room was a larger, tidier desk which was definitely not part of a cluster, but part of a square. A tall, dark-haired woman dressed all in black sat behind it. We walked to the next desk over from that, positioned to its left.

"This is me," said Kathi, gesturing at her desk. "Take a seat."

"Thanks," I said, smiling at the dark-haired woman who smiled back falsely and got up to go over to the coffee machine. Looking down at Kathi's hands, which were now fiddling ner-vously with a paper clip, I could see that her nail varnish was al-most exactly the colour of *blood*: not "blood red," as such (which wasn't like blood at all); rather, it was only a couple of shades lighter than black, seeming brown now, and then as she turned the small piece of metal slowly in her fingers, dark red, and then, in the shade again, *black*.

"To be honest!" said Kathi, making me jump, "I know you'll think this is a bit weird, and the police had trouble getting their heads around it too, but I never met Jess."

"You never met her?"

"No. I rarely meet freelances. Well, sometimes if they're reg-ular contributors, but not really. We do everything by phone and fax."

"So how did Jess get involved with *Smile!* magazine?"

"She was friends with one of the photographers, Mark, although that didn't really matter. It was her ideas I liked. We've been a bit thin, lately. I mean, the market's flooded with imitators at the moment and we're all competing for the same stories. There are only so many people prepared to have their picture taken and their name revealed in a magazine like this."

"Yes, I noticed that real names were used," I said, not mentioning that I had in fact seen the actual brief for the *Stalking* piece. "Why's that?"

"It's what the readers want," said Kathi, taking a piece of chewing gum out of a packet and popping it in her mouth. "Real names, real photos. So that's what we have to provide."

"But why?" I asked. "Why is it so important?"

"Look," said Kathi, leaning over the desk towards me. "Say I've got a woman out there claiming she's had fifteen babies in ten years. If you were a reader, what would you want to see?"

"I don't know. The stretch marks?"

"You'd want to see the babies, wouldn't you, to prove she wasn't lying. I mean, anyone can say they've had fifteen babies. I could sit here and tell you that, but you'd want to see."

"Mmm," I said, "I can understand that."

"Our readers place great value on truth. Truth and intimacy. So we tell the stories, show the pictures and hey presto. It's kind of institutionalised gossip."

"I see. Do you mind me asking how much the people get paid?"

"What, the writers?"

"No, well, I wouldn't mind knowing that, but I meant the people in the story."

"That depends, really. We've paid two, three grand for a story before. Normally it's anything upwards of two hundred quid per story. If there's more than one case study we divide it."

"And the women in Jess's story, what did they get?"

"I think it was a hundred pounds each," she said, wrinkling her brow with concentration. "Of course, none of them actually received it."

"Why not?"

"We pay out anything up to six weeks after publication. It's how the accounts department works."

"I see."

"Anyway," said Kathi briskly. "I'll show you round and then we'll have some lunch. I started a diet this morning but sod that, I'm starving!"

I lost track of all the people I met. There was Mandy the sub and Rachel, her assistant. Unless Rachel was actually Kathi's assistant — I was already too confused by that point to remember. The editor was called Tordy, her assistant was called Helen and I just gave up after that. There were some features writers and, of course, the Art desk. I asked Kathi to point out Jess's photographer friend, but none of the photographers were in. Apparently they were redoing a shoot that had gone wrong and wouldn't be back now until late afternoon. That was a shame. I'd wanted to talk to the photographer who'd shot the *Stalking* story; I was sure he or she would have some interesting information.

"When will the photographers be back?" I asked.

"Dunno. Hard to say really."

"Do they work with the feature writers, or on their own?"

"Depends, really. For true life stories they usually just go around on their own."

"Really?" This was interesting.

"Oh, yes."

"And who was the photographer for the stalking piece?"

"Mark."

"Mark?"

"Mark Savage. Jess's friend."

"Oh." For a moment I'd held my breath, thinking that maybe Mark would turn out to be Mark Moss and a connection would be there. But, like everything else, there was no way this was going to be that simple.

"Apart from the photographers," I began, speaking slowly, "who would have been able to see the layout of the magazine before it was actually published?"

"What, you mean who would have known what was in the pictures?"

"Yeah."

"God. Um, everyone really. All the staff would have had access to the layouts on the computers. But loads of people could have known where the pictures were taken just by following Mark around. I mean, the whole thing was about stalkers. If someone had stalked the photographer they'd know as much as any of us about the pictures going in the magazine. This is what we've been trying to tell the police. They all seem to think that poor Mark is some kind of major link, but really it could be anyone. They had assumed that only the photographer and Jess could know the identities and the addresses of the three women, but if a stalker had followed either Jess or the photographer, they'd know. If Jess or Mark told anyone, they'd know. If anyone had access to their computers, files or diaries, *they'd* know. For God's sake, I commissioned the feature and I certainly know."

This made sense. I thought through what Kathi had said as we left the building. Of course the photographer was a suspect, and a strong one, but close behind him were a hundred and one others. Not just people at the magazine, but passers-by who'd seen the women pose, friends of the women who may have gone along to give them moral support, and goodness knows who else. One thing suddenly seemed clear to me. If it had been this photographer, Mark, he had set himself up to be caught. Unless he was operating in some kind of bizarre double-bluff world, this indicated to me that he was innocent. And if he was so stupid as to have set himself up so obviously, and he was guilty of murder, why hadn't he been arrested? The police must have ruled him out somehow, and they knew a lot more than I did.

We went to a small restaurant around the corner for lunch. Kathi declared that she was only going to have a starter and loudly ordered a salad, but by the time we'd finished our starters she'd upset the waiter's organisation slightly by ordering a huge main course of tagliatelle. I'd already ordered two courses, and was planning on a third. Small talk soon turned into something like an interview, with Kathi asking a lot of questions about me and my background. Eventually she began quizzing me over the murder I'd solved.

"It would make such a fantastic story," she said once I'd given her the barest bones I could. "You really should think about going public."

"What would you have to do, find two other amateur sleuths to make up the numbers?" I asked, teasingly. Kathi looked at me seriously.

"Oh, goodness me, no. Your story is very, very strong by itself."

"So why do these things always seem to come in threes?" I asked. "I've noticed it in other magazines as well. It's as if two isn't convincing enough or something."

"That's partly it," she said. "But mainly it's to get some variety. For example, the stalking piece wasn't about the women so much as it was about the *phenomenon* of stalking: who's at risk, what to do if it happens to you, and so on."

"So you have one very serious story, one light-hearted one and one somewhere in between?"

"Something like that. It's very important for us to be able to have balance; we don't want to scare our readers, but we don't want to treat a subject lightly either."

"Right." I finished the remains of my pasta and lit a cigarette while Kathi poured more wine. She didn't seem to be in much of a hurry to get back to the office, and I assumed being a media person meant that she could extend lunch as long as she wanted.

"It's like showing all the possibilities of something. Did you see the *Revenge* piece we ran a couple of months ago?"

"No, not really. Didn't Jess do that one as well?"

"That's right. Anyway, it showed what can happen if you push revenge too far. In one of the stories a girl attacked her lover's ex-girlfriend, and in the second someone ruined someone's career. But the third one was quite funny; you know — cress in the carpets and prawns in the curtains. The couple in that story got back together, as well."

"The happy ending," I commented wryly.

"Oh yes, that's so important. At least one story has to have a really happy ending, if there are three. If the story isn't case-study based, you know, if it's just the story of one person or a couple or whatever, then that definitely needs a happy ending."

"Conflict and resolution," I mused.

"Exactly. With emphasis on the resolution, of course."

"Of course," I said. "And there was me thinking that literary theory had no application in real life."

"They're all classic stories," said Kathi, "told in a classic way."

"Because that's what the readers want?"

"Absolutely. They want to be told that you can make something really good from a bad situation, because for many of them their bad situation is never going to get any better. They need to have that hope, that it is possible. A lot of them have been married for ages, to husbands that drink too much, spend all their time working or down the pub and most of the time are selfish, unromantic bastards."

"I can imagine."

"So we get a lot of stories about *awakenings*," she said. "You know: My Husband Lost His Job But Then We Downsized And Lived Happily Every After, or: My Husband's Affair Saved Our Marriage. In all the stories the husband suddenly realises, 'Oh, I've been so insensitive,' rushes out to buy flowers and learns to cook. Or something."

"So it's a fantasy?"

"In a way. It's a fantasy for the women whose husbands are never going to change, but it's reality for the people in the story."

"I can see now why it's so important for them to be real," I said. "I just don't understand where all the stories come from. I mean, where do you find them?"

"Well, we've got loads of freelances that we use regularly who make a living out of it. They spend all their time finding stories and we get faxes from them all the time with ideas we can pick and choose from. Also, if the editor wants a specific piece, we commission it out to someone, you know, give them a brief and let them get on with it."

"I see."

"We also get members of the public phoning in, and wannabe writers with no story ideas or anything cold-calling, because they've got our number from the *Writer's Handbook*."

"That must be annoying."

"Some of them are nice people, but we just have to tell them to get back in touch when they've got some interesting true stories. Then when they do phone back — if they do — they've usually either got really bad stories or ones where the people want their identities kept secret."

"Oh, dear."

"The best thing, really, is when people phone in selling their own stories."

"Yes, I saw in the magazine that you're offering two hundred pounds for them."

"That's right. Of course we still get completely inappropriate ideas that way as well."

"Like what?" I asked, intrigued. "I mean, what are the worst ones you've ever had?"

"Um . . . Oh, there was one where a woman had called from a convent to say that she killed her whole family by accident after leaving a chip pan unattended."

"Not a happy ending, I take it?"

"No. That's why she was in the convent," giggled Kathi. "I shouldn't laugh, really, but I couldn't believe it. We just don't deal in tragedy—not unless it's got a nice resolution."

"Yes," I said, lighting another cigarette.

"Oh, there was another one as well that I remember. Let's see, how did it go exactly? Oh, yes. *My mother's husband was my boyfriend's gay lover.* We do *not* run that kind of story, I can tell you."

"Sounds more Ricki Lake than *Smile!* magazine," I said.

"Exactly."

"So where did Jess get her people from?"

"I don't know, really," said Kathi. "They all have different methods. One of my freelances carries a permanent ad in some local newspapers. Others advertise once they've got the story commissioned. A lot of them, the less regular ones, operate a kind of word-of-mouth thing. Also, I've got one woman who sits around in village pubs listening in on conversations."

"Goodness."

"Yes, she takes it pretty seriously."

"What does she do, just walk up to them and say, 'Hello, I've been eavesdropping . . .'?"

"Oh, no. This is the best bit. Once she knows there's a story there, she just vanishes into the night and then phones the person the next day to say that one of their neighbours is trying to sell the story and advises them to sell it direct themselves."

"That's a bit underhand."

"I know," said Kathi. "Fantastic, isn't it?"

I laughed and finished off my wine while Kathi called for the bill. It was hard to believe the magazine world was really like this: I had always imagined that in reality it would be less desperate than people made out, but instead it was worse. It was easy to see how that was the case, though. A few years ago only *Woman*, *Woman's Own* and a couple of others would have been competing for stories but now . . . After a quick calculation I worked out that since there were at least fifteen women's weeklies, each publishing at least five true stories per issue, that meant there was a market for seventy-five of those things a week: almost four thousand a year. Wow. Maybe I was in the wrong business, I thought. Which reminded me.

"I forgot to ask," I said. "What kind of fee would Jess have received for the story?"

"About six-fifty, I imagine," said Kathi. "Yes, it must have been. We pay six hundred and fifty for a double page and five hundred for a single."

"Goodness," I said. I really was in the wrong business.

"Of course, she'd have made a lot more if she'd stuck around and sold her story to the tabloids while it was still fresh," said Kathi thoughtfully. "Which rather makes me wonder where she's gone, and even if she's got something to hide."

"I expect it was all just too much for her," I said. "And maybe she wouldn't want to go raking over all the details about the poor women with some horrible tabloid newspaper."

"You are joking, aren't you?" said Kathi, once she had stopped laughing. "When did you last see Jess? I may not have met her face to face, but I know for a fact that girl is absolutely ruthless. I'm sure she'll end up working for a tabloid herself one day."

"Oh," I said, surprised. "I didn't realise."

"Seriously," she said, shaking her head and downing the last of her wine. "She's completely loopy. I don't really get friendly with many freelance staff, but one day I was talking to Jess and I'd been crying because I'd just been dumped by a boyfriend I'd been with for a while. She could hear in my voice that I was upset, so she asked what was wrong and I told her. She was working on the *Revenge* piece at the time and I made a joke about how I should do a prawns-in-the-curtains job on the guy."

Kathi paused, looking slightly troubled. "I'd actually forgotten about this, but it's all coming back now. She was just so odd. She went all serious and asked if I really wanted to get revenge on him. Then she started going on about theories of nuclear war, something about launching such a powerful first strike that he wouldn't be able to get me back."

"Bizarre. So what did she suggest?"

"She said I should turn up at the bar where he goes at the weekend and engineer a row with him and get lots of witnesses. Then she said I should go back to his flat, apologise and get him to sleep with me one more time. During sex I was supposed to do something else to make him violent, like call out the name of his best friend or whatever. Then she said I should punch myself in the head, go to the police and say he raped me."

"Bloody hell."

"Yeah, that's what I thought. It was like she just hatched this completely over-the-top plan out of nowhere. All the guy had done was split up with me, for goodness' sake. I tell you what, I pity anyone who gets on the wrong side of her."

"Yeah, right."

Kathi and I parted outside the restaurant, she visibly reeling from all the wine, and me wondering if I actually knew anything about Jess at all. I hailed a cab when one eventually appeared, and disappeared into the charcoal afternoon, seeing lightning begin an onslaught of central London as I went. I'd had a funny feeling all day — like I was being watched — but I put it down to paranoia.

When I returned to Henri's it was still mid-afternoon. The streets of Camden were black and wet since the rainstorm, but the sun was beginning to nudge its way back through the clouds and it was still as hot as ever. I sat in the garden for a while, drinking black coffee and enjoying the combination of smells from the wet lawn: grass, damp earth and flowers.

London smelt fresher than it ever had before and I closed my eyes for a while until I eventually dropped off, dreaming that I was back in the countryside and that Fenn was softly stroking the back of my neck with some freshly cut flowers. The dream soon turned sinister as the flowers became roses and the stalks sprouted thorns. Before long I was covered in blood which ran down my neck and between my breasts. I woke up shaking and almost screaming until I realised that it was okay: I was here, there were no thorns and the blood I had imagined was just perspiration from the intensifying sun.

CHAPTER FIFTEEN

LOOKING FOR THE THRILL

CAL APPEARED AS PROMISED at seven precisely, while I was engaged in an interesting debate with Star about psychopaths. Neither of us heard the car pull up outside; she was too busy talking about the practice of criminal profiling while I was playing with tautologies, like if all sex offenders are first-born sons, then did that mean all first-born sons were potential sex offenders? I was interested in pursuing the act of profiling to its natural conclusion, to argue that if you could establish that a "type" committed a particular kind of crime, then that would surely have implications for the rest of the people in that "type."

"This is exactly the point I've been trying to make with some of my colleagues," said Star. "We have to go *beyond* statistical analysis."

"Statistical analysis?"

"Yes, that's where a lot of the current profiling methods come from. I'll give you an example. Say eighty per cent of serial killers that attack young housewives in supermarket car parks are white males aged twenty to thirty-five who live with their parents and drive Ford Escorts. If you were presented with an offender who has attacked four housewives in four different supermarket car parks, what can you deduce?"

"Er, that he's a nutter?"

"Yes," laughed Star, "apart from that."

"I think I can see where this is going," I said. "Would it mean that he is between twenty and thirty-five, lives with his parents and drives a Ford Escort?"

"Exactly."

"Sounds a bit dodgy to me. I mean, I bet a high proportion of normal blokes of that age live at home and drive Ford Escorts. Or otherwise it could imply that the data was put together from a series of crimes committed by one person. Like, if out of one hundred crimes eighty were committed by one person, it would only be that person's details used to create a *type* using this method."

"That's precisely what I said," said Star. "I'm glad somebody finally agrees with me. This is why I'm trying to get more funding into research on qualitative methods of profiling."

"Aha, quality before quantity and all that."

"Exactly."

"So is this all part of what you're doing now?"

"Yes, but the project will be completed soon, and there is so much more work to be done."

"Isn't the stuff you're doing at the moment about *treating* psychopaths?"

"Yes, supposedly," said Star with a twinkle in her eye. "But it's all to do with the same thing. It's easier to treat them if you can understand them, and any understanding is bound to be useful in profiling. That's what it's all about, really, for me at least. An emphasis on *understanding*."

"So not just what they drive, but why they drive it."

"Exactly. If I knew that eighty per cent of a particular kind of serial killer drove Ford Escorts and I had a similar crime to investigate, I wouldn't be looking at someone else with a Ford Escort, necessarily."

"What would you look for?"

"Well, first I'd look at the remaining twenty per cent, the anomalies that everyone forgets about, and see what the people in that category drove. You can bet that if eighty per cent drive Escorts, then the rest would probably drive similar cars in terms of cost, status and availability — working on the assumption that people from similar backgrounds and in similar circumstances commit similar crimes, which is of course what profiling takes as given. So I'd look at how old the cars in question were, the colours and so on. What I would be asking is not what this person is likely to drive, but why they are likely to drive it. Just like you said."

"It all sounds very interesting."

"Oh, it is. I'll give you an example of where traditional profiling doesn't work. Okay, now say you've got a sexual assault which has occurred in the car park of a busy but remote country pub run by a man and his wife. They've got two grown-up children, one boy and one girl, who both work behind the bar sometimes. The pub was full on the evening in question — there was a pool tournament going on. The landlord and his wife who were working that night say they didn't see anyone leave the pub or come in between about nine thirty and ten fifteen, when the tournament final was going on."

"Right," I said, making mental notes.

"The victim, who survives, tells police that her attacker smelt clean."

"Okay."

"He was wearing button-fly jeans and M&S boxer shorts."

"What make were the jeans?"

"You don't know. The victim didn't see."

"Go on."

"He didn't carry anything, and there was nothing in his pockets."

"Okay. So is this a serial rapist or just a one-off?"

"There have been five other victims in the area who all report the same kind of clothes and the same type of attack."

"Which is?"

"Forced fellatio," said Star, wrinkling her nose.

"Nice."

"Yes. Anyway, the attacker is said to speak with a local accent and knows the area. After the attack is finished he takes a cigarette from the victim and then makes her strip. He dumps all her clothes in a nearby field and disappears."

"Poor girl," I said, feeling sorry for the imaginary victim.

"She's all right," said Star. "Anyway, you are given the following profile. Seventy per cent of serial rapists who attack women under twenty in public places are in their early to mid-thirties and are in a steady relationship. They don't drive, but their wife or girl-friend does; usually a Fiesta or a similar small car. They typically drink heavily and are unfaithful to their partner. This group are unemployed, although their partner usually works."

"What about the remaining thirty per cent?" I asked.

"Very similar, but with one detail different for each one, I think," she said. "They weren't all unemployed. Some worked casually. There were also a couple in their twenties and one in his late thirties."

"Can I ask any questions?"

"Go on."

"What time did the attack take place again?"

"About ten in the evening."

"And this was in a remote area?"

"That's right."

"Did his breath smell of alcohol?"

"No."

"Okay," I said. "I've got all that."

"So what do the statistics tell you?"

"Nothing. It was obviously the pub landlord's son."

"How the hell did you know that?" asked Star, her mouth open with astonishment. "Did you read about it in the newspapers or something?"

"No, I don't think so. Why, was this a real case?"

"Yes." She looked absolutely flabbergasted. "That's amazing."

"Are you serious?" I asked. "Did I really get it?"

"Yes," she said, smiling and shaking her head in disbelief.

"Goodness," I said, feeling a little shocked but very pleased with myself. "That *is* amazing. Maybe I did read it somewhere and forgot."

"Stop selling yourself so short," said Star. "Anyway, tell me, how did you know?"

"To be honest, I ignored the statistics completely and just thought about it. It had to be someone who lived near the pub — or *in* the pub since it was so remote. It wouldn't have been the landlord because someone would have noticed that, but I thought, well, he had this son, and you said only the landlord and his wife were working at the time. He would be likely to be clean and wear nice clothes. He wasn't carrying a wallet or anything, so he'd obviously just come from upstairs, got on with his crime and then gone back up. I would guess his age at about eighteen or nineteen."

"He was eighteen."

"If he was upstairs in the pub trying to keep out of sight I doubt he would have been drinking," I continued. "Which rather made me rule out all the customers."

"Exactly."

"And I would imagine that if he's a serial rapist he might turn into one of those types you mentioned. Drinking heavily and so on, probably getting a girlfriend with a car to drive him around. But that doesn't mean he's like that now. All criminals must have been teenagers once."

"Excellent," said Star. "I said you were a genius."

"I'm not," I said, blushing slightly.

"Well, you can certainly see what I mean about profiling."

"Yes," I said. "I can see how easily it can go wrong. And you're right, you've got to look beyond the statistics. He wasn't any of the things on the list."

"Exactly," said Star. "Therein lies some of the title for my research report: *The Forgotten Twenty Per Cent — Looking Behind the Statistics.*"

"I'd love to have a look at what you've done some time," I said. "I just can't understand why people bother with statistics when all you need is some common sense and a good imagination."

"Oh, I can," said Star. "It's low-cost. The thing is, you can't train a machine to do qualitative analysis. You need a human being for that. But with the statistical methods you could, in theory, create a computer programme that sorts the Ford Escort drivers from the Porsche owners, for example, and then match that up with a central computer record of everyone's names, what they drive, who they live with and so on."

"Police state here we come," I said.

"Well, it's policing by numbers, really," said Star. "They'd need to spend a few years inputting data from current crimes so they'd be able to come up with the profiles, then, when a crime is committed by a particular type of offender, they would just bring up the profile and cross-reference it with all the people who fit the profile who could have been in the area at the time."

"I bet they'd cut down on training," I said.

"Well, eventually the computers could do it all," said Star forebodingly as the doorbell rang. "Imagine that."

I got up from the kitchen table and walked over to the door just in time to see Cal doing his hair in the reflection.

"Hi," I said, opening the door and almost being knocked over by his enthusiastic smile. "Come in."

"I'm on a double-yellow," he said, almost proudly.

"Well, I'm not quite ready yet, so you'll have to wait for a couple of minutes."

"Oh, I think I'll chance it with the traffic warden," he said bravely.

"Hello," said Star as we walked into the kitchen. "I think I'm to blame for Lily being a bit, um, behind schedule."

"Oh?" said Cal.

"Nothing," I said, smiling at Star. "Anyway, it was fascinating."

"My pleasure," she said.

"Maybe some time you could help me do a profile for you-know-who?"

"Yes," said Star. "Or in this case, you-don't-know-who."

We both laughed. "It's only a matter of time, I'm sure," I said ironically.

"What are you talking about?" said Cal.

"Oooh, murder," said Star teasingly.

"And mayhem," I said. We both collapsed into a fit of slightly inappropriate giggles. "Right," I said, composing myself. "Give me two minutes."

I ran up the stairs, full of new-found enthusiasm sparked by my conversation with Star. Despite what I'd said, I really never had read anything about that case, and yet I had solved it on the basis of a few facts. While somewhere deep inside me I was sure it was a fluke, I nevertheless felt very pleased with myself.

The full-length mirror in Henri's bathroom was flattering and showed me that the jeans and T-shirt I was wearing would be fine for tonight. I ran my fingers through my hair, not wanting to chance more frizziness by brushing or combing, and smoothed a blob of serum over it. When it was as sleek and glossy as it was ever going to be, I applied a little black mascara and a coat of red lipstick. As a last thought, I swept my hair up into a high ponytail and secured it with a band. It was a hot evening and I wanted it off my neck, particularly if, as I suspected, we all ended up in some sticky club or pub later on. After a healthy squirt of Givenchy III, the only perfume I'd ever worn, I was ready.

We were all meeting in a trendy (according to Cal) bar in Clapham, which required a fairly long drive. I loved driving through London at night when the streets were less busy, and the Embankment, my favourite road in London, could sometimes be found virtually empty. However, I wasn't driving; Cal was, doing it "defensively," at a snail's pace, swearing and braking whenever someone cut him up or overtook him, and stalling at almost every set of traffic lights.

"I hate driving in London," he admitted eventually.

"Can't keep up with the pace?"

"I don't know." He shook his head. "It's too fast for me. I wish everyone would chill out a bit."

"Do you want me to drive?"

"I didn't know you could drive."

"Oh, yes. I'd have my car here had I not driven it into a tree chasing a murderer."

Cal laughed. "Yeah, right."

"It's true."

"No. You're winding me up."

"If that's what you want to believe," I said. "Anyway, do you want me to drive or not?"

"Er, no, I don't think so," he said, looking nervous as he edged his too-big-for-him Audi around a parked car. "You're not insured."

I wrinkled my forehead slightly as we approached the corner and turned onto Battersea Bridge. "Where did you say we were going?" I asked.

"Clapham."

"Are you sure this is the right way?"

"We'll get there eventually," he said. "I've got my own route."

"I'm sure you have."

"Were you really chasing a murderer?"

"Mmm-hmm," I said distractedly, lighting a cigarette and noticing an attractive Fenn lookalike walking over the bridge.

"You're mad."

We were approaching a roundabout, which seemed to faze Cal slightly, so I shut up while he negotiated it tentatively, missing the turning anyway and having to go round again.

"So tell me again," I said, once we were back on a straight road. "Who are these mysterious people we're going out with?"

"Right," he said. "There's Jon, who you've already met . . ."

"The artist."

"That's right."

"Carry on."

"There's Nick, who's just down from Cambridge, he works in a bookshop there; Sarah, that's Nick's sister, she lives in Brixton; then there's Kirsty and Jules, who went to university with me. They're film-makers now."

"What did you do at university?"

"Film Studies, at Goldsmith's."

"Film Studies," I repeated, thinking, *Goldsmith's*. That was where Tam had gone. "What about Jon?"

"Fine Art." He stopped for a traffic light. "I really want to be a proper writer," he said, looking at me hard. "A novelist. But apparently copywriting is as good a way in as any."

"It worked for Salman Rushdie."

"Exactly. Jon wants to move back into fine art as well, although I think he's mad. He's very talented, just not really very interested in what he does. He wants to be a millionaire, though, and reckons all you have to do is get in with Saatchi or whatever. That's why he did the *Scene* series — for the attention."

The lights changed and we were off again.

"How did you meet Jon?" I asked.

"You're very interested in Jon," he said, slightly jealously.

"I don't *think* so," I said defensively, seeing an image of Fenn in my head appear and then burst, popped by the impending wedding (one day to go if you didn't count today and Saturday).

"Good," he said, possessively. A hideous image passed through my mind at that moment: Cal and Jon, talking about me at the gallery maybe, or afterwards. *Hands off, she's mine*, Cal was saying to Jon in the same tone he'd just used. Hands off, *mate*. I shivered.

". . . and then she organised . . ."

"What?" I said, interrupting Cal who was in full flow, saying something I wasn't listening to.

"The careers woman," repeated Cal. "She was the one who introduced Jon and me. She gave him my phone number, but he never called. We met up eventually on graduation day, blind drunk, and got on like a house on fire."

"Why didn't he ring you in the first place?"

"Well, he never really wanted to work in advertising. I convinced him."

"Was that because he wanted to be an artist?"

"No."

"What did he want to be, then?"

"A postman, he reckons. Like in *Il Postino*."

The bar was certainly trendy; achingly so. Drum and bass seeped out of speakers; background music faster than a human heartbeat, tuneless, hypnotic. Cal and I had to push our way through lots of scantily clad twenty-somethings to the back area, where his friends were gathered around a square table. I looked for Jon; he wasn't there.

"Calvin," drawled a man with a deep voice and shoulder-length mousy hair. "Good to see you."

Cal smiled as the man stood up and slapped him on the back. He looked at me.

"What are you drinking?"

"Beer, please," I said, and watched him walk away.

Left with all these people I didn't know, I sat down, rather self-consciously, next to a woman with short dark hair who was wearing a see-through white top with a bright red bra underneath, and a short red skirt. Next to her sat the mousy man; on his left were two people who were obviously a couple — she was sitting on his lap. I assumed these must be Kirsty and Jules, which meant the mousy man was Nick and the see-through woman Sarah. Not an amazing series of deductions, but it would have been nice for Cal to stick around and introduce us all the same.

Sitting back in my chair, I couldn't help feeling uncomfortable. I affected nonchalance for a while, looking at a distant point across the bar, pretending there was something fascinating over there. None of the others noticed; they were too wrapped up in a conversation about old friends, none of whom there was any chance I would have known. I lit a cigarette and waited for Cal to return.

At last he appeared, carrying two bottles of Budweiser. And there was someone else with him: Jon, looking slightly dazed, with a cigarette hanging out of his mouth.

"Hey, look who it isn't," said Sarah to the others.

They all smiled and the atmosphere changed. There was something about Jon — everyone was pleased to see him.

"Fucking hell," said Jules, tipping Kirsty off his lap and standing up. "Long time no see, man."

"Yeah, right," said Nick. "Where've you been?"

"You know," joked Jon. "Ducking and diving."

"Incidentally," said Cal loudly, "this is Lily, everyone."

"*I* know who you are, babe," whispered Jon in my ear as he slipped past me. When I looked up he was grinning at me, then he was gone.

"Aha," said Sarah, "the identity of the mystery woman is revealed. Hi, Lily, I'm Sarah."

And so the introductions went on. I'd been right about all the names. As the introductions were happening, chairs got shifted and people rearranged themselves to accommodate the new arrivals. I ended up sandwiched between Sarah and Cal, while Jon ended up at the far corner of the table next to Kirsty and Jules, with whom he started an animated discussion.

"So how do you all know each other?" I asked, grabbing a space in the conversation between Cal, Sarah and Nick. "Were you all at college together?"

"Nick was on Jon's degree," said Cal. "We were all at Goldsmith's except Sarah."

"Did any of you know that girl who was murdered?" I asked, pretending to be vague. "She was at Goldsmith's, wasn't she?"

"Yeah," said Cal. "But she was a few years behind us. I think I may have seen her in the bar once."

"What was her name?" asked Nick.

"Tam," said Sarah. "Tam Hunter."

"Did you know her?" I asked.

She shook her head. "No. I covered the original story."

"Really? What do you do?"

"I'm a reporter."

"Yeah, *hack*," called Jon from across the table. "News of the fucking screws."

"Ignore him," said Sarah. "He thinks working for the biggest-selling newspaper in the country is something to be ashamed of."

"They're weird, those murders, don't you think?" said Cal.

"In what way?" asked Nick.

"Well, three women, all unconnected, all in the same magazine. It's odd, that's all." He took a swig from his beer and looked off into the distance thoughtfully for a moment. "I reckon it was all the same stalker."

"Do you?" I said, wrinkling my nose. "Don't you think that would be a bit of a coincidence?"

"Yeah," he said, "but the whole thing's a coincidence, isn't it?"

"Is it?" I said, unconvinced.

"What about old Dominic Carson, getting up there and doing his stuff at the gallery," said Sarah. "Have you seen him?"

"Yeah, he's just along from Jon," said Cal. "He's a fruitcake, isn't he, Jon?"

Jon looked up from across the table. "What?"

"Carson. Nutcase, isn't he?"

"Fucking lost it, mate," he agreed, and went back to talking to Jules.

"Do you think he knows who did it?" I asked.

"What, Carson?" snorted Sarah. "He's just up there trying to earn drug money. If you ask me, the only person who knows who killed those women is the murderer himself."

"Why do you say that?"

"Well, there aren't any decent leads, are there? That feature writer's disappeared with whatever information she's got, and apart from that . . . We've got virtually nothing to write about. If the police know anything they're not telling us. I mean, we'd usually have got some dirt by now. No one seems to know who these stalkers were. No one knows much about the victims, either. And as for the feature writer, well, we could probably do with more on her. I need to find someone who knew her at university or something, ideally."

"I thought you just made it all up," said Cal. I stayed quiet about knowing Jess.

"Yeah, ha ha, very funny," said Sarah. "At least Carson gave us a couple of new ideas but it's hard to see where to go next."

"Don't you think it's voyeuristic?" said Cal seriously.

"What, Dominic Carson?" she said.

"Yeah, it all seems a bit sick to me."

"How can you say that when your creative partner has lined the same walls with pictures of murder?" said Nick. "Surely *that's* voyeurism?"

"I don't think so," said Kirsty, leaning over the table to get an ashtray. "I mean, it's not like people get pleasure from looking at the actual pictures."

"Yeah, they are pretty grim," said Sarah.

"Are you talking about Jon's pictures?" asked Jules. Jon looked up, lighting a cigarette and grinning at me. His teeth were a mess: brown and chipped with the odd gold filling evident at the back when he smiled. For some reason I found this feature very compelling. I couldn't look away.

"But that's not what voyeurism is about, though, is it?" said Kirsty, pressing her point.

"What do you mean?" asked Cal.

"Voyeurism isn't about enjoying what you look at," she said. "It's about enjoying the act of *looking*."

"Yeah, right," mumbled Nick, downing his pint and standing up. "Who wants another?"

By the time we left the bar it had become quite packed, although I doubted that any of the new arrivals were quite as drunk as our group, with the exception of Jon, who was being very reserved and Cal, who, as he kept pointing out himself, was driving. I was getting there, but I wasn't anywhere near as slaughtered (Nick's term, as in: "I'm fucking slaughtered," which he said continually) as the rest, particularly Jules and Kirsty, who was becoming ever more animated the more she drank. The conversation had moved eventually from murder on to sexuality, then back to death (how you created realistic effects in films), then where we were going to eat. Opinion seemed to fall in favour of a small new restaurant down the road, so we all trooped there merrily, Kirsty stumbling in the gutter now and again and Jules steadying her gently each time.

I caught up with Kirsty and Jules.

"So you're film-makers?" I asked.

"For our sins," said Jules. "What about you?"

"Literature lecturer," I said.

"Interesting. You should talk to Nick, he's well into books."

"Yeah, I might do that. Look, this probably makes me seem a bit thick, but have you heard of a film called *Peeping Tom*?"

"Classic," mumbled Kirsty.

"Of course," said Jules. "Like she says, absolute classic. Fantastic film."

"What's it about?"

"It's about all kinds of things. Psychoanalysis, child abuse, murder. There's this psycho going around murdering women and it's all about how he gets caught."

"'S from the murderer's point of view," slurred Kirsty. "*Well* scary film."

"Do you know anyone who has a copy?" I asked, thinking, *I definitely must see this.*

"I don't," said Jules. "Kirsty?"

"Nah," she said. "'S really rare now, apparently. I used to have a copy taped off the telly but then I recorded over it by accident."

We'd reached the restaurant, a glass-fronted single room with tables and chairs scattered haphazardly around. I ended up next to Cal once again, which was a shame because I really wanted to speak to Jon. He was almost opposite me, though, and winked when I sat down. Soon everyone was swept up in a discussion about advertising, dominated by Cal and Jules. Jon didn't say much. He seemed almost sullen except for the odd wink in my direction. Now, what were they for?

Cal left at the end of dinner, making an excuse to do with having to "get the car back." He offered to drive me home and I gratefully accepted, except that just as I was reaching for my jacket Jon leant over and whispered: "Stay."

So I did. We went on to The Grand eventually, an old London cinema that had been converted to a club (as was the vogue) which was running an eighties night featuring back-to-back Soft Cell, Simple Minds, Duran Duran and Human League records. Nick, Sarah, Kirsty and Jules headed straight for the dance floor when we arrived: I headed for the bar, where I settled on a bar stool and waited to be served.

"Get us a Red Stripe, babe," came a voice from behind me. I smiled. Jon sat down next to me; almost too close, his leg nearly touching mine. I tried to stop myself being excited by this. He'd hardly spoken to me all night; he had bad teeth and he was, in some way, dangerous. I repeated these caveats in my mind, but my mind had other ideas. It seemed to focus too long on Jon's body. He was thin, but wirily so, his substantial arm muscles taut under his shirt. His jeans clung in all the right places as well, I noted, feeling my face begin to redden as he caught me looking.

"Are you eyeing me up?" he asked.

"No," I retorted, "of course not."

"I'll tell Cal," he teased.

"Why? What's Cal got to do with anything?"

"I thought you were an item."

"No." I shook my head. "Uh-uh. Definitely not."

"So you're not, you know, *seeing* him or anything?"

"No. He's not my type. Why?"

"Just curious." Jon gulped down a quantity of his Red Stripe and took a cigarette out of my packet. "What about Nick? Is he your type?"

"Nick?"

"Yeah. You seemed to be talking to him for most of the night."

"Did I? I don't remember. Anyway, why are you so interested?"

"Am I? Nah, you're flattering yourself, babe."

"Yeah, right."

He laughed. As he did so his body moved and his leg pressed against mine. I didn't move and neither did he. We drank our beers quickly. After a while Jon ordered two more Red Stripes and opened a fresh packet of Embassy Number Ones. He offered me one and I took it, too drunk by now to care what I was smoking. Without realising what I was doing, I was pressing my leg harder against his.

We didn't speak that much. Jon nodded his head to the loud music; my upper body swayed ever so slightly with every beat. My head had never felt lighter; going to the loo would be a definite no-no until I'd sobered up a bit. There was no way I was going to stagger anywhere, and besides, I felt like I couldn't move even if I wanted to. This wasn't like me. One-night stands just weren't my thing — but with Jon I couldn't even be sure what was on offer. He hadn't exactly propositioned me. *You're flattering yourself, babe*, he'd said. *We'll see*, I thought.

"So," I began conversationally, "what were the responses like, you know, to your *Scene* whatsit?"

"All right. Some old bird got a bit shocked. Most people, they're like, *I've seen it all before.*"

"Where did you get the crime scene photos?" I asked, instantly regretting the question as his face glassed over and his eyes became stormy.

"Um —"

"Don't worry," I cut in. "It was a stupid question. I shouldn't have —"

"No, it's all right. I just promised —"

"It doesn't matter."

"It just, well, it isn't exactly legal, you know."

"I gathered that." I took a swig of my beer.

"So I've been getting some grief about it all. The Old Bill wants to know where I got them, too."

"Really?"

He grinned precociously. "Yeah."

"But that's no problem, I imagine."

"I'm an artist, mate. They can't touch me."

"So it's not really a big deal, then?"

"Nah."

"So what if I wanted some crime scene photos? Would you be able to get them for me?"

Jon laughed. "What the hell would you want with crime scene pictures?"

"Nothing," I said evasively. "It's a hypothetical question."

"People like you don't ask hypothetical questions."

"Whatever," I said. "But could you get them?"

"Some of them aren't very nice."

"Some of the things I've seen aren't very nice either."

"Yeah. Cal told me about you running around after some murderer."

"So?"

"Well, I suppose I could. Do you want a particular set, or will random ones do?"

"The Magazine Murders," I said. "I want those."

"You are a dangerous woman," said Jon, looking at me strangely as if I had done something to surprise or even impress him. "I'll see what I can rustle up for you."

We sat for a while watching the pace of dancing change as *Karma Chameleon* became *Careless Whisper*, and as people, including us, became more drunk.

"School discos," I observed drunkenly. "I remember dancing to this at school discos."

"Oh," he laughed. "This was out when I was at university. Brings back memories all right."

"It certainly does."

"*Fuck a Fresher Week*. Worked every time."

We both laughed.

"You really are morally bankrupt, aren't you," I said as Jon started stroking my leg.

"No," he whispered, "I'm just misunderstood."

"Yeah, well don't expect *me* to understand you," I said, looking into his vacant blue eyes momentarily before he kissed me hard.

The kiss was both softer and harder than I'd expected. It was beery and smoky but sweet; sweet without being sickly, like fine chocolate. He stroked my hair as he kissed me before grabbing a clump of it and pulling me more roughly towards him, making me dizzy with drink and surprise, wobbling slightly on my bar stool. I took this as my cue to pull away and smooth my hair.

"Sorry," he murmured, looking away.

"Don't be," I said. But it was too late. He had already hopped off his stool, downed his can of lager and walked over to the dance floor, from which he shot me only a half-glance before grabbing Sarah and dancing wildly with her. I turned back to look at the bar, not knowing if he was attempting to make me jealous or not. Unsure as to whether I should be following him onto the dance floor (desperate or polite?) or sitting here (cool but stand-offish), I lit a cigarette and listened to my heartbeat in double time to *Save a Prayer* by Duran Duran.

In front of me and on the dance floor, the scene moved to the music in slow motion; it seemed I was watching from a million miles away, the music and the laughter distorted by the distance, with my mind turning one line over and over again: *What the hell am I doing?* As things came back into focus and returned to their normal speed I glanced at Jon. He was standing sullenly on the edge of the dance floor, staring at me and smoking a cigarette. He mouthed something at me when he saw me. I could have sworn it was *I want you.*

Excited and frightened by this I turned away. What about Fenn? He was getting married — I looked at my watch and saw it was gone midnight — *tomorrow.* What was I going to do, be celibate for the rest of my life? *Save a prayer till the morning after,* said the sound system mournfully. The song died out and the lights came on. Ten minutes later I turned to leave, guilty and not alone.

CHAPTER SIXTEEN

THE WALLS ARE CLOSING IN

JON'S FLAT WAS SOMEWHERE IN EAST LONDON. We hailed a cab and drove there almost in silence, me only breaking it once to comment on the hyper-real orangeness of the Rotherhithe Tunnel. It reminded me of somewhere I had been recently, but my mind, sponge-like and soggy from all the drink, wasn't in the mood for remembering. I turned it to other things.

Was Jon regretting this as well? I didn't know. Just as I was wondering whether I should make the cab go on to Camden he took my hand in his and held it gently, the hardness of his skin rubbing comfortingly against the softness of mine. In my mind I kept trying to skip to the waking-up scene, trying to visualize it so that a) it would happen, and b) I could feel comfortable with it. It was always hard for me because I wasn't at all accomplished at one-night stands. With Anthony, my only long-term boyfriend, it had been easy. We both knew what was going to happen and got on with it; unromantic but straight to the point. I used to undress in his tiny bathroom and then emerge into the darkness to find him already in bed waiting for me.

The last one-night stand I'd considered having was, of course, with Fenn. A good deal of preparation had gone into that: perfume, silk underwear and a definite willingness (or was it desperation?) to go through with it. But of course it had never happened, since *that* was the night Bronwyn phoned to tell him she was pregnant. Great timing or what?

So this was very spontaneous by my usual standards. I'd met someone, fancied him and now I was going home to bed with him. I gulped to myself at the thought. Meanwhile, the cab was stopping: pulling up somewhere off the East India Dock Road — surely we weren't there already? Trying to recall all the articles I'd read in women's magazines, I told myself this happened all the time. Women went home with men and slept with them. What was the problem? Jon paid the driver and we emerged, stumbling a bit, into the night.

His flat was large and took up the whole top floor of a pre-war building. Inside, everything was a mess — beer cans, takeaway cartons — the whole set-up clearly said *bachelor pad*.

"Sorry it's a bit of a state," he said. "I wasn't expecting . . . you know."

"That's all right."

"Do you want a coffee?"

"Yes, that would be great," I said, cringing. *That would be great.* I sounded like I should be in an advertisement. That would be great. I'd *like* that. I hoped I didn't sound too drunk.

Jon scooped up most of the mess and took it through to the kitchen with him. The room was clean, at least, if not tidy, and contained items that in my experience only a single man would ever own: black leather sofas (two), a glass coffee table and a PlayStation. I sighed and sat down on the edge of one of the sofas, feeling uncomfortable and wanting something to look at. Getting up again almost immediately, I crossed the room to look at Jon's bookshelves. I scanned the three thin shelves, noting several modern, trendy novels. The rest were art books except for the biggest title on the shelf: a filmography of Pedro Almodovar, which I looked at without much interest for what seemed like hours, all the images blurry in front of my inebriated eyes.

"Coffee," said Jon, re-entering the room and making me jump.

"Cheers," I said, walking over and sitting back down on the shiny black sofa.

"I'll just sort the lights out," he said, fiddling with the dimmer switch, alleviating a lot of the glare and only some of my nerves.

148

"So," I said, watching him come back across the room. I wondered if he was going to sit next to me but he didn't, choosing the other sofa instead. "How . . . how long have you worked with Cal?"

"About six years now," said Jon. "Yeah, six years."

"Right."

"And you're a . . . ?"

"Lecturer. Well, I am now. I used to be an actress."

"Whew. Busy woman. You're young as well, aren't you?"

"Not that young," I said defensively, feeling school-play-groundish. I picked up my coffee from the table and took a sip from it. "I'm twenty-five."

Jon stood up again nervously and I wondered whether he was going to make his move now, but he didn't. Instead he wandered over to the stereo and chose a CD, which he put on at medium volume.

"And you're some kind of Sherlock Holmes as well?" he said.

"Yeah, apparently."

"Seriously, what did you do? You solved a big crime, I heard."

I told him and although he looked bored at first he soon became more impressed, particularly when I got to the end of the story.

"Fucking hell. You're something, aren't you?"

"I'm not sure about that."

"Out of my league," he murmured, running his hand through his thick black hair, which was still standing in clumps on his head.

"Sorry?"

"Nothing."

My mouth was dry and my head began to pound. All the passionate desire I'd felt seeing Jon mouth those words to me in the club was evaporating now and being replaced with another sort of desire: to be at home in bed. This was another reason I didn't get very far with one-night stands: usually at this point I *did* go home to bed, unable to keep up with the pace, not knowing the rules of the game. But this time, feeling I had some sort of point to prove, I gathered up all the courage I had and walked shakily over to the other sofa in the middle of which Jon was sitting, eyeing me suspiciously.

"Do you mind if I join you on there?" I asked, hearing my voice crack slightly. "I'm a bit cold."

"Of course . . . Be my guest." He moved over a bit and I sat down, close to him now but even more nervous than before. He didn't do much to help. No hand on the leg this time; no hard kisses.

The space between us fizzed and hissed like a B-movie force field. He wasn't going to cross it and neither was I. *Sod you, then,* I thought, *I've made my move.* But I found his non-reaction oddly compelling. He was playing hard to get, and it was working. How difficult would it be to reach out and touch his face? Too difficult. My body turned cold at the thought. What if he rejected me? Then, as I imagined him touching me, my body became warm again — accusingly so, every small hair on my arms and every skin cell on me reaching out towards him like a flower turning to the sun; too minute and too subtle to be detected by the human eye but yet . . . He must have seen something, because at that moment he looked up and said: "Shall we go to bed, then?"

What?

"Er, okay," I said, feeling tingly and fearful at the same time. No snog on the sofa first? Surely we were doing this wrong, some-how? Still drunk enough to be up for it, though, I followed Jon in a zigzag line to the bedroom which was right at the end of the hall. I sat on the unmade bed, expecting some fully-clothed foreplay but when I turned around to take his hand (or whatever), Jon had dis-appeared.

I sat there for a while, not knowing whether he would consider me forward if I took my clothes off and got into bed. What if he wasn't really expecting me to sleep here, and I'd made a dreadful mistake? I took my shoes off as a compromise and lit one of his cig-arettes which I found in a box on a window sill by the bed. There were condoms there too — a three-pack with only one left. Was this a good or a bad thing? I wasn't sure. My thoughts made me smile drunkenly, this smile freezing on my face when Jon entered the room, dressed only in his boxer shorts, and hopped straight into bed.

"Aren't you going to get in?" he asked.

"Yes. I was just . . ." Just what? "Having a cigarette," I said, noticing the Embassy Number One smouldering in my hand.

"Well get a move on, babe," he said confidently.

Still sitting on the edge of the bed I undressed quickly not wanting to seem unromantic by asking him to switch off the lights but nevertheless feeling a bit uncomfortable doing it like this. Shouldn't he have peeled my clothes off on the way to the bedroom, leaving them in a tell-tale line up the corridor like a pornographic Hansel to my Gretel (so I could find my way out in the morning)? I hoped all this was going to be worth it. This was the only real one-night stand I'd ever had, and it would be just typical for it to turn out to be a waste of time.

But once I was in bed all these feelings evaporated along with my thoughts. His smell was musty and clean, his skin soft and his limbs strong. Pinning me down, he kissed me even harder than before and I found myself kissing him back; wanting him. Playing teenagers, we wrestled together in our underwear for what seemed like hours. He clearly liked being in control. Whenever I rolled on top of him he pushed me down onto my back; not gently, *hard*, holding my wrists or my hair. When I couldn't stand it any more I took the initiative and pulled off the last of our clothes, watching Jon grin as I did so. The sex was rougher than I was used to but I found this, and him, very exciting.

When I woke up the next morning he was still asleep. Feeling both guilty and curiously proud of myself I dressed quickly and left, hailing a cab and ending up back at Henri's in what seemed like record time.

Let's get back to the events following the murders. You say there was a woman investigating?

Yeah. Lily fucking Pascale.
I thought it would be a laugh at first, you know, someone to play around with. She didn't notice me following her: down the stairs of the Deptford tower block (yes — I was there!), and behind her cab all the way home — seeing where she lived. She didn't see me watch her undress; didn't notice me in the bushes watching her sit in the garden in the hot sun. She had a nightmare while I was there. I loved looking at the sweat building up on her brow and the look of horror on her sleeping face. She gasped before she woke up.
She wasn't getting very far, I noticed. She'd believed all my bullshit

anyway. No one was going to suspect me. Not even her, fucking super-sleuth. Super-slag.

"You're back, then," observed Henri as soon as I walked in.

"Yes," I said, feeling instantly self-conscious about my dishevelled state. "Aren't you supposed to be at work?"

"Yes. I cancelled all my appointments."

"Why?"

"*Why?*"

"Yes. Has something happened?" As I kicked off my shoes and approached the sofa I had the sensation of walking through thick syrup. This was the atmosphere that I had only partially sensed from the hallway.

"Well, *no*, obviously not now. But this isn't what we all thought this morning. We thought you were dead."

"Who thought I was dead? Why?"

"Me, Star, your mother. You didn't come back! Was a phone call too much trouble?"

"Um . . ." I was stumped. That wasn't the reaction I'd expected at all. In fact I hadn't expected any kind of reaction; as I had told myself endlessly last night, women did what I had done all the time.

"You have a mobile phone," continued Henri. "Oh yes, we all know you have the bloody phone — it was ringing half the night. I suppose it's too much to expect you to take it out with you?"

"It is actually," I said, "when it's the middle of summer and I'm not wearing a jacket or carrying a bag. You knew where I was, anyway, since you set the whole thing up."

"Me? What did I set up?"

"*Cal.* And anyway, you must have known I was with him because Star saw us go."

"Yes, and when I spoke to him this morning he said the last time he saw you was about eleven last night."

"He went home early; I stayed on." I shrugged, walked into the kitchen and poured a glass of Evian which I drank quickly. I could still see Henri's red face and relieved expression, which was tinged only very slightly with anger. "I am twenty-five now," I added. "I honestly didn't think you'd be so worried."

"Well, we were," he said more softly.

"Sorry," I said.

The thought that my own father knew what I had done last night made me cringe with embarrassment. Because he and Mum had split up before I hit my later teenage years, we'd never had the chance to develop an easy father-daughter relationship where he accepted that it was likely I would go out, stay out and occasionally sleep with someone. In evolutionary terms I may as well have been about fourteen as far as he was concerned, and I knew that nothing I could say would stop him feeling that way. He would just have to get over it in his own time.

I gave him a kiss on the cheek and persuaded him to go back into work immediately, which he did, leaving me alone to recuperate in the house. I had planned to relax, to watch some daytime TV for an hour or so and then get on with thinking about the murders, but this was marred slightly by my father's parting comment.

"I answered the damn thing in the end," he'd commented from the doorway.

"What damn thing?"

"Your underused mobile phone."

"Oh?" I had thought that it would be Fenn again, and that I would eventually have to talk to him. In the space between my question and Henri's reply I'd decided that today would be a good time to call, with me feeling confident and desirable from last night and Fenn having been made to wait long enough even by my standards.

"It was a woman," said Henri. "Or a girl. Screaming all kinds of things. She said her name was Bronwyn and that you'd stolen her boyfriend."

"Oh," was all I could manage to say before Henri slammed the door behind him.

So my life was a soap opera? Great. And there was me thinking that now I supposedly had this super-deductive brain there wouldn't be any need for me to get embroiled in that stuff any more. Anyway, what was Bronwyn talking about? I found the whole concept of me stealing her boyfriend (or should that be fiancé,) laughable at best. Surely that should be the other way around anyway, since it was obvious that Fenn and I were on the verge of something just before she appeared — or reappeared — on the scene. Unable to deal with any more drama this morning, I gave up thinking about it and made some coffee.

Flicking through the TV channels I soon discovered there was nothing on. This didn't usually stop me watching, but I ended up just sitting on the sofa dreamily, thinking about Jon: his strength, his charisma and his compelling devil-may-care attitude. He hadn't said thank you or goodbye and that, I decided, was the way I liked it. I could still smell him on me; that warm, salty, musky smell of fresh male sweat and excitement. Despite all my other problems — the wedding and the unsolved mystery in particular — I felt as though a spell had been broken. I couldn't believe I had liberated myself with a one-night stand. *Smile!* magazine would be proud of me.

I finished my coffee and went upstairs for a shower, feeling great except for three things: I was too hot; the Bronwyn problem probably wasn't going to go away until I dealt with it; and I still had the uncomfortable feeling of being watched. I tried to shrug my worries off, but my shower was spoilt by the shadows I kept thinking I was seeing behind the curtain and the constant twitching I had to do just to make sure they were in my imagination. In the end I got out before I'd even rinsed my hair properly and wandered through to my room dressed only in a towel which dropped off when my mobile phone, still lying on the bed charging where I'd left it, started to ring.

"Shit," I said, gathering up the towel and picking up the phone. "Hello?"

"You have sixteen new messages," said the robot voice mail woman who always decided to *callback* (their term) at inconvenient moments.

"Goodness," I said to myself. Henri hadn't been exaggerating.

Beep: "Hi, Lily, it's Mum. Just calling to see how you are and . . . There have been some developments here you might want to know about."

Beep: "Lily, it's Fenn. How long are you going to keep this up?"

Beep: (Bronwyn's voice) "Bitch."

Beep: (Fenn's voice) "Lily?"

Beep: "Why is it that every time I press redial the phone calls your number? Are you having an affair with my boyfriend? This is Bronwyn and I think we need to talk."

Beep: "Lily, this is Beth. We're all really worried about you. Bronwyn says you keep phoning Fenn. It's not really fair, is it?"

Beep: "It's Nat. What's going on?"

Beep: "Lily, it's Fenn. I absolutely have to speak to you. Ignore me after that if you want, but I'm afraid something rather unfortunate has happened."

Beep: "This is Bronwyn. Why the hell won't you answer your phone you cowardly . . . cow!"

And so the messages continued. I was shocked: maybe that was what made me laugh. When the laughter wouldn't come any more I just sat there, drained, wondering what the hell had happened to get them all so dreadfully worked up. They were in such a lather, I dreaded to think what must have been happening while I was out having my comparatively innocent one-night stand with the delightfully uncomplicated Jon. Who had said what to whom? I certainly hadn't said or done anything. I listened to the messages again. It was clear that Bronwyn had been making a fuss, telling people that I'd been harassing Fenn. How stupid.

Bronwyn could wait, I decided, getting dressed and going downstairs for a coffee. But as soon as I'd begun to fill the kettle, my mobile began ringing upstairs. I walked slowly up to answer it, arriving just as it started to ring for the second time. An unknown Torbay number was showing on the caller display. It had to be her.

"What do you want?" I asked wearily after Bronwyn had barked *hello* at me.

"I was trying to ring you all last night," she said.

"Well I'm very sorry I wasn't in. What can I do for you?"

I could hear her breathing heavily into the phone, angry and unable to contain herself. In order to win this I was going to have to stay calm.

"There's no need to sound so smug," she whined.

"Yes, and there's no need for you to be so rude. May I remind you that I am still your lecturer." I felt my blood start to heat up as I thought about how outrageous this whole situation was, but kept a lid on it, speaking slowly and deliberately and trying not to lose my temper. "I've no idea why you're phoning me, and even less idea about why you kept half my family awake last night. Is it something to do with your studies?" I added, adopting the blasé tone known for infuriating anyone it was used on.

"Of course it's not to do with my fucking studies," she cried. "You know damn well what this is about."

"Really?"

"Yes, well . . ." Bronwyn faltered and I pounced.

"But I don't, though, do I? I don't know what all this is about since *you* are the one who has manufactured whatever it is. Beth has heard that I keep phoning Fenn. But we both know that's not true, don't we?"

"That doesn't mean you haven't been trying to steal him!"

"Who?" I said innocently.

"Fenn of course. Why . . . why are you being so difficult?"

"Bronwyn," I said slowly, "do you think you might be a bit paranoid?"

"Paranoid?"

"Yes. Apart from the fact that I'm just not interested in whatever problems you and Fenn are having, I've been in London virtually all week and haven't laid eyes on him since we had coffee on Saturday."

"Ha! I knew it! I knew you'd been seeing him behind my back."

"Oh, for God's sake. You really are immature, aren't you?"

"Shut up!"

"Are you really going to keep him locked up for the rest of his life?" I asked. "Is that the only way you think you're going to keep hold of him?"

Silence.

"Because you're probably right. We both know the baby isn't his — although I'm certainly not going to be the one to tell him — and we both know he doesn't love you. If you want to get married under those circumstances then good luck to you. I have to say I told Fenn I thought it was a mistake, but that's because I'm his friend."

Bronwyn didn't correct me about the baby. She didn't say anything.

"So, if that's all you wanted to talk about . . . ?" I said.

"We don't want you at the wedding," she said quietly. "That's what I phoned to tell you."

"What?"

"Throw your invitation away. We don't want you there."

"And is this what all the dramatic phone calls have been about?"

"Partly."

"Well you could have saved yourself a lot of trouble just by looking at your RSVPs. I'm in London, Bronwyn. Do you really think I'd bother coming back just for your wedding?"

"I don't know. I thought —"

"And if you think I can't see what you've been doing then you're even more dim than Fenn thinks you are," I said, instantly regretting my bitchy tone but not being able to help it. "Obviously you've set up this pernicious rumour that I'm still going after Fenn, or whatever, as an excuse to keep me away from the wedding. What a stupid waste of time."

"So you're definitely not coming, then?"

"I told you, I've got better things to do. So you needn't worry that he's going to take one look at me and jilt you." I stopped myself. This was going too far. I softened my voice a little, feeling slightly sorry for her. "Look, I'm not going to tell you there was never anything between Fenn and me. Obviously there was. And look, maybe he *does* love you. In any case, you have to understand that I don't want someone who belongs to someone else." I hesitated. "Now, I think we should pretend this conversation never happened, okay? We don't want problems when the new term starts."

"What, because to you I'm just a student?"

"You are a student, yes."

"Well in that case you'll be pleased to hear that I'm not going back to university anyway."

"What?" I asked, shocked and genuinely concerned.

"You heard. I'm not going back."

"Have you discussed this with your tutor?" I asked, forgetting momentarily that I was her tutor.

She laughed bitterly. "I don't think my *tutor* cares either way."

"That's not true," I said. "I care about you as a student."

"You've got a funny way of showing it," she mumbled. "Anyway, I've discussed it with my husband-to-be. He thinks it's for the best, and so do I. I'm only taking a year off."

"And I assume you've cleared this with someone?"

"Not yet. I didn't know I had to."

"Well I'm sure your *husband-to-be* can tell you what forms you need to fill in. Bring them to me and I'll make a decision as quickly as I can."

"Make a *decision?*"

"Yes. I have to decide whether or not to support your taking a year off. You can't just leave university for a year whenever you feel like it."

"Oh. I didn't know."

"Well you do now. Don't worry," I added. "You are having a baby and that's a very good reason. I can't see that there'll be any problems."

She said a quick goodbye and hung up. I sat there feeling drained. Had I meant all that stuff about not going to the wedding, anyway? If I was honest with myself, the RSVP hadn't been returned because I'd forgotten, and also because I didn't want to make the whole thing seem real. But not to go? I'd kind of assumed I would, eventually. But then again, it was already Friday afternoon and I wasn't in Devon, no clothes were washed and no plans had been made. It was hard to see how it could have happened; all along it was clear that I wouldn't — or rather *couldn't* go. I hoped Fenn would forgive me, and then, remembering Jon's hard, rough arms around me last night, decided I didn't care. It was time to be single again.

I went downstairs to make a coffee, feeling the silence in the house press against me uncomfortably as I went. For some reason this feeling — the one of being watched — had become almost impossible to shake off. Despite my certainty that it was just some sort of paranoia, the feeling stayed with me as I boiled the kettle, poured the water in the cafetière and took a mug from the cupboard. My imaginary audience made me aware of my every move, the way I stretched my arm to open the cupboard; the line of my body as I swilled the coffee in the bottom of the jug.

The tension was broken only when I switched the television on again. Sitting in front of it with my coffee and my notepad, I decided it was time to make a list of suspects. If only I knew how to start. At that moment everyone in London seemed to have as much motive, means and opportunity as anyone else. Nevertheless, once

I started writing down names I felt better as I saw three clear categories emerge. Tearing the sheet of paper from the pad, I organised my suspects into their categories on a new sheet.

People connected to women	Smile! *People*	*Jess People*
Dominic Carson	Kathi	Jess herself
Goldsmith's students	Other staff	Tyler (why?) — alibi
Tam's new boyfriend (who?)	Mark Savage	
Mark Moss		
Stalkers		

Desperately, I stared at the names, but none jumped out at me. I had a feeling it might be someone I hadn't included, but who on earth could that be? The phone rang, making me jump, but when I answered it there was no one there. How appropriate.

I must have dropped off on the sofa because the next thing I heard was the sound of a key in the lock and then Star's voice saying, *Hello, is anybody in?* Groggily, I sat up, my legs feeling spongy and my brain like mashed potato. Sleeping in the day always had that effect on me — which was why I never usually did it. But then last night hadn't left many opportunities for sleep.

"Lily!" said Star gratefully. "Thank God you're back."

"Sorry I worried you all," I said. "I didn't think to let anyone know my plans."

"Well, why should you?" she said, putting her bag down on the table and walking into the kitchen. "You're a grown woman now."

"I see my father's hysteria wasn't catching then," I said.

Star laughed. "He does fuss. I said you'd probably met someone and spent the night with them. That seemed to shock him somewhat."

"I can imagine."

"So, where *did* you go?" she said, coming through with a bottle of white wine and two glasses which she filled before I had time to protest.

"Oh, just back to someone's flat," I said vaguely. "You know how it is."

"And I take it this was a *man's* flat?" she said, raising an eyebrow and smiling.

"Oh, yes," I said, taking a sip of my wine and smiling slowly. "But of course."

Star giggled naughtily and asked questions for a while then went to get changed, after I refused to give her any more details. Henri arrived shortly afterwards, his mood of this morning dispelled, it seemed, by a productive day at work in which he had taken on two new celebrity clients: a writer with panic attacks and the writer's cat.

"How can you psychoanalyse a cat?" asked Star, over dinner.

"You can't surely?" I put in.

"For the prices this woman's paying I would psychoanalyse her front door, her garden furniture and anything else she's got lying around," said Henri affably, reaching for the salad.

"Who is this *writer*, then?" asked Star. "Is she very famous?"

"Oh yes," he said. "Very. How did you know it was a 'she'?"

"I just did." Star smiled her ever-so-slightly smug smile.

"Surely this *writer* would know that cats don't have an unconscious," I said. "I mean, they don't, do they?"

"I read somewhere that they dream," said Star, "which shows something."

"Oh, yes," I said, thinking of my own cat and the strange movements and noises she often made in her sleep. "I suppose they do."

"Stop it," said Henri. "You'll have me convinced, soon."

"Mind you, I find it hard to imagine what cats would repress," said Star.

"Maybe guilt about all the rabbits and voles they eat," I said, dissolving into the giggles that had been coming thick and fast since the first glass of wine.

"Anyway, how are your psychopaths?" asked Henri, looking at Star fondly. "Not giving you too much trouble, I hope?"

"None of them like fish."

"What?" he asked, confused.

"Oh, they have to eat fish — you know the *fish on Friday* thing they have in institutions. They were all complaining about it this afternoon. I'm still wondering whether or not to add it to their profiles."

"What," I said, *"likely to be an eldest son who drives a Ford Escort, lives with his mother and doesn't like fish?"*

"The world has indeed gone mad," said Henri.

"Quite," said Star. "Anyway, Lily, how's the investigation?"

"Slow. Frustrating."

"Maybe you will give up?" said Henri, hopefully.

I shot him a withering look as he got up and started clearing the table. "I don't think so. It just seems like I need one big thing — a breakthrough of some sort. I've got one firm lead, of sorts, but it's proving impossible to follow."

"What's that?" Star asked excitedly.

"I don't know if it means anything, but . . . I'm not sure how to explain it. Jess, you know, the girl who's disappeared . . . ?"

"The journalist?"

"Yes, that's right. Well, her boyfriend — the one I went to see — says that *she* said Peeping Tom did it."

"What, as in *Peeping Tom*, the film?"

"I thought so, but I can't find it anywhere."

"Have you tried all the video shops?"

"Oh yes, I even rang the BFI. They say they've only got it on sixteen millimetre, whatever that is."

"So you say this girl knows who did it?" asked Star suspiciously.

"Well, I don't know," I said. "It doesn't make any sense if she does."

"Mmm."

"I mean, why would she have called *me* but not told the police anything? That's what I don't get."

"Yes, that makes no sense at all," said Star thoughtfully.

"Anyway, I still think it would be worth looking at the film — if I could find it."

"Maybe you could try some Film Studies departments at some of the universities, or the BBC archive or something."

"That's a good idea," I said. "I can see why you do research and I don't. You're brilliant at all this."

Star laughed. "Hey, Henri," she called. "Tell your daughter she can stay for ever. I love these compliments."

Henri looked up from the dishes. "What are you two yakking about?"

"*Peeping Tom*," said Star. "I remember seeing it when it came out. Such a classic film."

"I feel like I'm the only person who hasn't seen the bloody thing," I said.

"*The* classic psychoanalysis film," mused Henri. "My favourite film. So what about it?"

"Lily needs to see it," explained Star.

"And?"

"Well, she can't find it on video anywhere."

"Have you tried the bookshelf in the living room?" he asked, smiling smugly. "I believe that's where I keep my copy."

"You mean it's been here all along?" I asked, incredulous.

"Yes." Henri laughed like he'd just heard the best joke ever.

"Thank you," I breathed gratefully, to no one in particular. "Thank you."

The phone started to ring while I was on my way to the book-shelves to find the film.

"Can you get it, please?" called Star from the kitchen.

"Me?"

"Yes, and tell whoever it is that your father is otherwise occu-pied."

I picked up the phone to hear a familiar voice say: "Is Lily there?"

"Yes," I said, "speaking. Who's this?"

"Jon."

"Oh, hi," I said, surprised.

"Am I disturbing anything?"

"What? Oh, no. We were just having dinner."

Silence.

"So what did you . . . I mean . . ."

"I need to see you. Can you meet me?"

"Yes, I suppose so," I said, hoping this wasn't what I thought.

"Don't worry," he said, as if reading my thoughts. "It isn't what you think. I've got something for you."

"Something? For me?"

"Don't get excited. It's just that stuff you asked me about last night. I can't talk on the phone. Look, you're in north London somewhere, aren't you?"

"Yeah, Camden."

"Okay, I'll meet you at Café Toto."

"Café Toto?"

"It's right near MTV."

"I'll find it."

"Half an hour?"

"Fine."

It was almost ten when I left the house, closing the door on Henri's protestations (*Where are you going at this time of night? Don't you know there's a murderer out there . . . ? At least one murderer. Shall I drive you?* and so on), and stepping out gratefully into the now cool summer evening.

I'd calculated that Café Toto was only a five-minute walk from Henri's house so there was, unfortunately, no need to call a cab. I enjoyed walks on this type of evening, but some of Henri's warnings had stayed in my head. There was definitely a murderer about, and I still felt like I was being watched. I'd tried to dress casual but sexy for my meeting with Jon — there was no chance of me sleeping with him again. Despite his being very good in bed he wasn't someone to get *involved* with — but I still wanted to keep up appearances. I'd opted for a low-cut grey T-shirt and a short denim skirt. I just hoped I wouldn't get any trouble on the way there.

Super-slag came out dressed like a soap star, all done-up hair and make-up. Her skirt was short, showing her legs. But that wasn't what I was enjoying: I was just enjoying playing with her, like a puppet but with longer legs on the end of the strings.

I took up a slow pace, keeping about fifty feet behind her on the other side of the road. If she saw me there would be trouble — I mean, I couldn't exactly pretend to be anyone else. I'd been enjoying stalking her, though, over the past day or so. She was interesting; the way she moved about and the choices she made fascinated me. Like now, would she turn this way or that? She took the first turning onto the main road and, I

163

may have been mistaken, but I thought then that she was a bit frightened.
She wanted to be with people.

I was relieved to be on the main road, surrounded by people out
enjoying the mild evening. Pubs and cafés spilled onto pavements
as they always did at this time of year, and the atmosphere was
calmer than usual: after a long day in the sun, most people seemed
to want to relax quietly.

Glancing at the big silvery MTV building I saw that not much
had changed since the last time I was here. Some teenagers were
gathered, as always, outside; hoping to see a celebrity on the loose,
going in or coming out of the doors. Without stopping to look for
long (lest I get mistaken for a teenager or a celebrity), I walked a
bit further down the road to Café Toto, went inside and looked
around for Jon.

CHAPTER SEVENTEEN

A FOOL'S ERRAND

HE WAS SITTING ALMOST OUT OF SIGHT in the back area of the bar, which wouldn't have been my first choice of position had I been waiting for someone. He looked a bit out of it too, but sexy in tight blue jeans and a check shirt.

"All right?" he enquired as I walked towards him. A cigarette was smouldering in the ashtray and a brown manila envelope lay flap down on the small table.

"Yes, thanks," I said, eyeing Jon and the envelope with equal suspicion.

"I trust you got home safely this morning?"

"Yes. Um, thanks for . . ."

"A great shag?"

"You could put it like that." I smiled, embarrassed. It took a lot to make me blush, but I did now.

"Sorry," he said. "But it was."

"Was what?"

"A great shag."

"Um, yes, I suppose so," I said, blushing even more. "I'm going to get a drink. Do you want one?"

"No. I'm meeting someone else in a bit. I just wanted to give this to you." He nodded towards the envelope. Not wanting to be pushed around or hurried by him, I turned and walked towards the bar anyway, ordering a vodka, lime and soda before taking the cool glass and walking slowly back to the small table.

"Why didn't you call me?" he asked as I sat down.

"When?"

"Today."

"Today?"

"Yeah. Why didn't you warn me?"

"What about?"

"Your old man ringing Cal last night. He knows about what happened with us, you know."

"Who does?"

"Cal."

"So?"

"So, he told me to lay off you the other day at the gallery."

"Why didn't you, then?"

"It takes two to tango, Lily," he said, letting a small half-smile play across his lips.

"I didn't notice doing the *tango*," I said, with mock innocence.

Jon laughed. "You're pretty cool, babe, you know that?"

"So?"

"So maybe I want to see you again."

Jon let his fingers dance over the brown envelope as he spoke, looking down at it the whole time. Surely he wasn't embarrassed about asking me out again.

"Maybe I'll call you," I said.

He laughed like he didn't care either way. "Yeah, right. Of course you will."

"You never know," I said teasingly, pleased that I was in control again.

"Whatever."

"Are you sure you don't want a drink?"

"Nah," he said, sounding quite drunk anyway. "Like I said — things to do."

"Okay. Sorry I can't tempt you."

"Oh, you tempt me, babe." He laughed and then let his voice drop to a whisper. "You fucking *tempt* me all right."

I looked around the bar, slightly fazed by this sudden show of emotion (or was it raw lust? I wasn't sure). I could hear French voices in the other corner — a lesbian couple, judging by what they were saying, thinking they were being discreet because they were speaking a foreign language. On the next table was a man sitting by himself, reading an autobiography of some man I'd never heard of, Michael Powell. He looked familiar beneath his glasses and stubble, but I couldn't work out where I might have seen him before.

Jon touched my arm. "Do you want to tag along?"

"Sorry?"

"This bloke I've got to see — *man about a dog*, you could say — do you want to come? We could go on somewhere afterwards, if you like. Then, you know . . . *whatever.*"

"I don't think so," I said, wincing. "I think I'm a bit old for *tagging along.*"

"Suit yourself." He stretched out both arms and I watched his muscles become taut under his skin. His tattoo warped and became a fairground reflection of itself: a serpent in a house of mirrors. He pushed himself up from the table, which wobbled precariously under both the pressure and the lack of balance, proving that he really was drunk. As he leant over me I smelt a warm cloud of alcohol: Scotchy and lagery all at once. *Chaser* breath.

"Be good," he whispered as he rubbed his right hand lightly over my neck, as if he wasn't sure whether to strangle me or pin me down and make love to me. Both ideas made me shudder, particularly considered together.

Even though I didn't want him to touch me, the sensation made me feel curiously warm and tingly. Unfortunately a small moan left my throat, uninvited, and I bit my lip in case more memories of last night slipped out. It was too late, though. Jon moved his hand and laughed.

"You want me bad, don't you, babe?"

I shut my eyes for a second, not knowing how to react. When I opened them he was gone. The envelope was still there, containing, no doubt, the last pictures taken of Sasha, Rebecca and Tam. I opened it slightly to confirm this and was almost sick when I saw a train line covered in blood. Pushing the photo back into the envelope I swiftly looked around to check that no one had seen. I was safe: the lesbians were too wrapped up in each other and the man was buried in his book. Gulping down my drink and picking up the envelope, I left, breaking into a run as soon as I left the café, and not stopping till I got home.

The house was in darkness when I arrived and I turned my key in the door with a shaking hand, frightened by the dark and the loneliness. Once inside I felt better, although my body was still pumping with adrenaline; from the run and from Jon. What was it about him that made me so uncomfortable? And where had he got the idea that he could treat me like that? I certainly wouldn't be calling him, since he'd already provided the only two things he had to offer me (one being the photos and the other better left unremembered) but for some reason I couldn't get him out of my head.

Tossing the envelope on the sitting-room table, I walked through to the kitchen to pour a glass of wine. A note was there, in Star's handwriting, which said: *Hope your mysterious meeting went well. Fenn called, sounded upset. Said you could call him if you're in before half past eleven.* I looked at my watch. It said eleven forty-five. Oh well, Fenn would have to wait.

The wine slipped down nicely, its crisp, comforting coldness making up for the mushy, dirty heat outside. Settling down on the sofa, I lit a cigarette and looked at the envelope for a while, scared to open it, knowing what would be inside. Instead I reached over to the bookshelves and located the hitherto unobtainable video: *Peeping Tom.* I set it next to the envelope as if both items were exhibits in a trial and looked from one to the other, drawing on my cigarette thoughtfully as I did so. Something told me that each item would lead me in a different direction, like the doors in that riddle about the brother who told the truth and the one who always lied. As with the brothers, I had a feeling that one of these would lead to truth, the other to confusion. Which was it to be?

Finishing my wine I yawned ungracefully. *Neither,* said my tired brain as it began to fall asleep. I rubbed my eyes, feeling them wet, achy and heavy in my face. Tomorrow, then, I thought, and took both the envelope and the tape upstairs with me for safe keeping. Part of me was desperate to open the envelope now. But I wasn't just too tired, I was too scared. This was a task better done in daylight, I decided.

While I was asleep I dreamt. In my dreams Fenn was chasing me, calling me constantly and watching me through the windows and from a discreet distance every time I went out somewhere. Whenever I turned to look for him, though, I saw an old hag in his place: an older version of Bronwyn, I decided, taunting me with his image and the fact that I couldn't have him.

Thinking I was hearing my phone ringing, I woke up at half past ten to find silence: no ringing. It had just been part of my dream in which rings, knocks and raised voices had figured large. My first thought of the day was, is Bronwyn already in her dress? For those few moments after waking I imagined it all: the dress, the car, the ceremony (with tears, perhaps), the car again, the reception and the cake. There. Now the wedding was over, I was able to get on with my day.

Henri and Star were already bustling around downstairs, being early risers and presumably wanting to make the most of their weekend — not having the luxury of academic holidays like I did. In the kitchen was a jug of freshly brewed coffee. Star was sitting at the table with her hair in an elegant French pleat. I touched my tangled nest self-consciously as she looked up and smiled.

"We thought we'd let you sleep in," she said. "You must have needed the rest."

"Thanks," I said, taking a mug out of the cupboard.

"How was your rendezvous?"

"Brief," I yawned, and sat down at the table. "Useful, potentially."

"Oh?"

"I'll tell you if anything comes of it."

Having poured my coffee I picked up the *Guardian Weekend* from the pile on the table and flicked through it. It was hard to concentrate, though. The photographs beckoned, and I knew it would be impossible to do anything else until I'd looked at them. They excited me in a way — think of the answers they might hold! But they also terrified me: their obscenity and their graphic content not a problem for my stomach as much as my mind, which struggled to accept the idea that these scenes could be photographed at all — that they could even *exist*.

Back upstairs I sat on the bed looking for the envelope for

longer than necessary, the coffee I'd just drunk swilling uncomfortably as my stomach twisted around itself. There were so many reasons not to open it — so many ways in which this shouldn't be any of my business. I drew my legs up onto the bed and crossed them, setting the envelope in front of me. I reached over to the bedside table for a cigarette and found one, lighting it with a shaking hand and inhaling deeply.

After a few more moments, I picked up the envelope slowly and pulled the flap open, drawing out the glossy sheets and laying them in front of me on the bed. I didn't look properly as I was laying them out; their images appeared blurred and unrecognisable. But once I'd stopped sorting it was time to look. There, juxtaposed to me as to the murderer, were these three — as far as I knew — unconnected women.

And they were all dead.

Shaking slightly, I looked at the door, afraid that someone might come in and see, more embarrassed than I would be about pornography or drugs; ashamed that I was looking at *this*. Death — more real than I'd ever seen it before.

I hadn't intended to lay the pictures out in any order, but there they were: Sasha, covered in blood in the park; then Rebecca's remains on the train track, recognisable, but only just; then to the right of that, Tam, strangely serene in her sitting room which now looked just like her *room* — her bedroom.

Feeling sick, I stared at the images, waiting for something to happen. How long did I sit there? Fifteen minutes, maybe less, hypnotised by the horror, trying to pretend the pictures weren't real.

It took me a while before I noticed the detail that was to confirm something I had already unconsciously worked out. Needing to compare and contrast, I leant down and pulled *Smile!* magazine out of my bag. Opening it at the double-page spread I was struck by the poignancy and terrible sadness of these murders: bodies laid out in front of me in the same places that they had been photographed for the magazine. The train station, Hertford East, looked the same in both pictures. The park, London Fields, looked brighter in *Smile!* and fresher, confirming that the picture had been taken in the crisp spring and not the stultifying summer. The police picture looked humid, sweaty and nasty; and the girl who had stood there in her shift dress was now lying face down on the path in a blood-covered business suit.

At first glance the same was true of Tam's pictures. The *Smile!* version had been taken in a tidier room — but then, of course, poor Tam never knew she was going to be posing for crime scene photographs. In the police pictures the room seemed darker: a large African-style drape was drawn over the patio doors at the far end and a dim light bulb cast a dull glow over the room. In the far right-hand corner was a large table, seeming to function as a laundry, wardrobe and art table, with clothes and paints jumbled together on its surface.

In the *Smile!* photo the table had been cleared and a painting had been propped up on it. The Rizla packets and ashtrays had been cleared away too, these being scattered liberally around the room in the police photo, all the butts appearing to have come from joints rather than from brown-tipped cigarettes. As my gaze lingered on the photo I noted other differences, but they all seemed insignificant in view of the small limp, body lying on the sofa.

Except for one thing.

In both photos, Tam didn't have many posters up. I'd noticed a pale rectangle on the wall in the *Smile!* picture when I'd originally seen the story. An empty patch; from something that had been removed, I'd thought. And now, in the crime scene photo, there was the missing poster — not a poster as such, rather, it seemed to be a framed magazine. To be specific, it was a copy of *Stella* magazine, glossy and bright, and looking almost exactly the same as any edition of *Smile!*, *Woman* or *Take a Break*. So why had Tam hung it on her wall?

I thought I'd drawn a blank but my mind was quicker than I gave it credit for. *Why indeed*, I muttered to myself as I leant over the bed again and pulled my notebook out of my bag. There inside was all I needed to know, in my descriptions of locations I'd visited and my thoughts on Monday, when I had travelled the sticky triangle between these poor women's homes. I knew why Tam hadn't wanted the framed magazine to be seen, and it was nothing to do with inter-magazine rivalry. I knew that, because it was now clear why it was there in the first place.

Slipping the picture back in its envelope I located Inspector Thompson's card and ran downstairs with it, taking the envelope as well. I was going to talk to Star first, though, now I had something exciting to tell her.

She was still reading the papers.

"Jess made it all up," I declared, slightly breathlessly, sitting down opposite her.

"Made what up?" She looked up and took off her reading glasses.

"The *stories*. The magazine stories. They're not true!"

"Not true?" Star laughed. "Well, that's not a very big surprise, surely. Don't they invent most of that stuff anyway?"

"No," I said. "I used to think so as well, until I had lunch with Kathi."

"Kathi?"

"Trimbull. The features editor at *Smile!* magazine. She was explaining that the stories have to be completely true — with real names and photos to prove it. They make sure, as well, by paying the money to the subjects in the form of a cheque made out to the full name they're given."

"So . . . ?"

"So the *women* were real, obviously, but I think that's where it ended. I'm sure now that they were never stalked."

"God." Star rubbed her eyes and picked up a pen from the table, turning it over in her fingers thoughtfully.

"I'm just about to phone the police and tell them," I said, my voice quickening with excitement. "The thing is, the only people who knew that the stories were false would have been Jess, and the women — who obviously aren't in any position to tell anyone now. The police must be barking up the wrong tree entirely. No wonder they still haven't got any leads on the stalkers."

"What about relatives? Parents? Wouldn't they have put the police straight?"

"No. Well, that's one of the strange things. None of them really had parents. Inspector Thompson told me — Rebecca only had an alcoholic uncle of some sort, Sasha's body was identified by a work colleague and Tam's by one of her housemates."

"Strange."

"Mmm. I thought so, but I couldn't see what it pointed at."

"What does it point at?"

"Nothing in itself, except that none of them would have much to lose, presumably, selling their names and photos to be attached to a bogus story. I imagine it would be hard for Jess to find people willing to pose like that. I mean, what if their parents saw the pictures or something, and thought the story was true?"

"Yes, I can see that." Star narrowed her eyes into slits as she rolled the pen up and down between both hands. "So, are you sure? I mean, how could you tell?"

"There were loads of things. Here," I said, opening the magazine on the relevant pages. "You see in the section about Sasha, where it says that the stalker was calling . . ."

". . . *from the phone box facing her house. He really could see her,*" read Star. "Spooky."

"Except there *is* no phone box facing Sasha's house," I said. "I needed to use one when I was there on Monday — my mobile battery had gone flat — but I couldn't find one anywhere. I didn't make the connection at the time, but now . . ."

Star thought for a moment. "Aha!"

"Precisely."

"What about this one," asked Star, pointing to the picture of Rebecca. "What's wrong with her story?"

"Nothing, as such," I said. "Except the detail about the stalker going into her house."

"Go on."

"Well, she didn't live in a house. She lived in this poky flat above a launderette — I visited it the other day. It says here that when the man came round she was just getting out of the bath, but she didn't have a bath, just a shower. Anyway, the woman working in the launderette said she couldn't believe she hadn't known about the stalking incident. Apparently Rebecca told her all sorts of details about her life, but didn't say anything about that."

"The plot thickens."

"Mmm. Also, the lady said the stalker would have had to pass her to get into Rebecca's flat if he came in the day."

"Which rather makes you wonder why Jess made it occur in the day," said Star, scanning the story.

"Exactly. I wondered that as well. So I think Jess never went to the women's houses, not even Tam's — and she lived just across the road from her. If she had, she wouldn't have got those details wrong."

"I see."

"There's more," I said. "I only linked it all up about five minutes ago." I toyed with the flap of the envelope, trying to decide whether or not to show Star.

"What's that?" she asked, nodding at it.

"It's, um . . ." I looked at her uncertainly. "Would it be right to assume you've seen hideous pictures before?"

"Oh yes," she said, sounding intrigued. "The worst. So what's in there?"

"Crime scene photos," I said, watching her instantly raise her eyebrows. "And before you ask, no, I'm not going to tell you where I got them."

"I wouldn't dream of it. So come on, let's have a look."

"Well, there's only one relevant one really," I said, drawing out the picture of Tam. Laying it on the table next to the magazine, I lined up both items so the pictures were easy to compare. I looked for a reaction on Star's face but there was none, just a kind of wrinkled-brow concentration.

"Different, aren't they?" she commented, studying them carefully. "But what's the key difference, I wonder? *You've* obviously seen it."

"Yep," I said. "But it took me a bit longer than this. Look closer."

She sat in silence for about five minutes staring at the pictures, while I made some coffee and lit a well-earned cigarette. I was concerned that Henri might walk in, but then Star probably knew him as well as I did now, and could easily just close the magazine on the picture if he did. I set her coffee down next to her and she thanked me vaguely, concentrating desperately on the photos. She was one of those people, like me, who had to solve something if it was there in front of them and who just would not give up.

There was this game I'd bought a couple of years before which I'd seen advertised on the tube. All it involved was solving riddles, and it was the best game I'd ever had. When people asked what it was about, I always quoted the ad (not exactly as it had been worded of course) from the train: it was a riddle and went as follows.

Question: A man leaves a country pub and walks to the car park around the corner. There are no street lights, he has no torch and his car is black. However, he spots it immediately. How is this possible?

Answer: Because it's daytime.

Star was looking at the pictures closely now, picking up first the magazine and then the police picture, looking from one to the other and shaking her head.

"It's hard to see," I said nicely.

"It can't be that hard," she said, clearly frustrated. "I'll give up in a minute."

"I'll tell you if you want," I said, hinting: "It's connected with all the other stuff I've been telling you."

"Hmm," she said, still staring at the pictures. She raised her head abruptly and took off her glasses. "Okay, I give up."

"Are you sure?"

"Yes, just tell me."

"Okay. The first thing I thought was weird was this pale bit here," I said, pointing at the *Smile!* photo of Tam in her room.

"Yes, I saw that too."

"And here," I pointed at the framed picture on the wall in the crime scene photograph. "This must be what had been hanging there originally."

"I can see that," she said. "But what is it?"

"It's another magazine."

Star picked up the picture and stared at it closely. "*Stella.*"

"Yes. And if you look closer still?"

"Um . . ."

"There," I pointed. "I know it's tiny, but doesn't that look like Tam to you?"

"Where?"

"In that little picture by that headline or whatever you call it."

"*My Adoption Hell,*" read Star. "Hmm. And you think that's Tam?"

"Yes. But then I cheated. I already knew that Jess had written a story for *Stella* on adoption. I've got the notes for it upstairs."

"So . . . ?"

"So they've pulled the same scam together before. I'm sure that's what it is. Why else would Tam have a magazine like *Stella* framed and stuck on her wall? She probably thought it was cool or something and showed it off to her friends."

"And you don't think the police have seen this?"

"Well, they must have *seen* it —"

"No, I mean noticed the connection."

"There's only one way to find out," I said, spinning Inspector Thompson's card around on the table.

CHAPTER EIGHTEEN

A MAGIC CAMERA AND
WHAT IT PHOTOGRAPHS

"WHAT, YOU'RE GOING TO PHONE THE POLICE?" said Star, sounding appalled.

"Yeah. It's a pretty important discovery, don't you think?"

"Oh yes, there's no doubt about that. I just . . ."

"What?"

"Well, I think you'd win in a game of Scruples."

"I don't follow you," I said.

"Scruples, you know, that eighties party game all about what you'd do if your kid . . ."

"Yes, I know what Scruples is," I said. "I just don't see how it's relevant to this."

"Okay," she said. "Here's the question. You're a sleuth who's solved one crime and become quite well-known for it locally, but people soon forget a celebrity and before you know it you could soon be just a literature lecturer again . . ."

"Very cheerful," I commented.

Star ignored me. "Anyway, you're working on a new investigation and you've made an amazing breakthrough. Do you a) investigate further, b) hand the whole thing over to the police, knowing they'll take all the credit for it?"

"Um, I suppose I'm proposing the second option," I said. "I mean, the police have got so many more people who can investigate this and it's not about taking the credit, it's about justice being done."

"And you, a crime fiction specialist," she said, shaking her head and tutting.

"I don't understand."

"I can't see Dupin or Sherlock Holmes handing *their* evidence over to the police."

"Yes, but that's fiction," I said. "This is real life. Anyway, what if this person kills again? I'd have it on my conscience for ever."

"He won't," said Star.

"What do you mean, *he won't?*" I said. "How do you know?"

"He's made his point," she said simply.

"What point?"

"That's what you've got to work out."

"Or the police. Maybe I should leave it to them."

"Come on, Lily, we both know you love doing this!"

I paused and thought for a moment. "Well, love's a strong word," I said eventually. "But I suppose I do get an unhealthy kick out of it."

"And I bet you haven't even watched *Peeping Tom* yet."

"No."

"Look," she said in an eminently sensible voice. "Why don't you just keep going for a while? Imagine trying to explain all this to the police. You'd certainly have to tell them where you got the photos and drop whoever you got them from right in it. And even if the police understood what you were trying to tell them, what do you think would happen next? They'd go public with it. They'd have to, since they haven't got much else at the moment and then, of course, the murderer would know — about you and about the magazine stories."

"Unless he already knows."

"Well, that's what you've got to work out."

"I suppose so."

What Star said did make sense. Maybe this information was best kept to myself for the time being. Maybe. Still uncertain, I walked upstairs and into my room, eventually deciding to leave the police out of it until I had something else — but only until then.

* * *

Sitting on the bed, I opened my notebook at a fresh page. *Jess*, I wrote. Then: *False stories*. What did it all mean? The events of the past week began to replay in my mind. At least Dean's strange words now made sense. *Yeah, right*, he'd said. *She would have loved that.* He'd been suspicious about the existence of a stalker and now I understood why. Jess had made it all up: the stalkers, their actions, their reasons and probably lots of details about the women as well. I wondered whether the killer had in fact been aware of this. Either way, it put a new gloss on the whole thing.

Before long my thoughts were flowing too fast for my pen to keep up. If there had been no stalkers, and if the women were otherwise unconnected, the only thing they would have had in common was the *Smile!* magazine feature. That meant that the only people they had in common were Jess and the *Smile!* employees, particularly Mark Savage and anyone he knew. I remembered what Kathi had said: even if the connection was the magazine feature, there were a hell of a lot of suspects. But one thing was for sure. The connection *was* the feature.

I was still interested to know how Jess had chosen the women. She must have known them, or at least known someone who knew them. That made me wonder whether there was another link in that direction — a mutual friend or something, perhaps. My head started to fizz and pop with all the information, preparing for shutdown like an overheating computer. I sighed and lay back on the bed.

The house was full of tangled webs and anaemic, see-through spiders; one such spider was clinging to the wall above my head preparing, no doubt, to fall onto my face or into my hair. Shuddering slightly, I sat up again. What was I going to do next? Having all this information made me want to offload it on someone, and telling Star wasn't enough. But we'd agreed: no police for the time being.

A voice from downstairs startled me out of my thoughts.

"*Lily*," came Henri's voice again. "Lunch!"

And I hadn't even had any breakfast yet. My stomach rumbled as I walked back downstairs, reminding me that I had to feed it properly in order for everything to work. The smell of roast lamb greeted me as I entered the kitchen, along with hints of rosemary, garlic and steamed vegetables.

"Can I help with anything?" I asked lamely, seeing the table set and the wine and glasses already out.

"No, no," said Henri, moving the lamb from its roasting tin onto a plate. "*Merde!*" he added as it almost slipped off onto the floor.

"Are you okay?" asked Star, stroking his back soothingly as she moved past him across the kitchen.

"Yes," he said, placing the roast on the table between a bowl of spinach and one of new potatoes. "I think that's everything. Lily, help yourself to vegetables. Star, sit down and stop fussing."

"I'm looking for something to make gravy in," she said, slamming one cupboard door and opening another.

"*Gravy?*" said Henri, sounding disgusted, saying the word *gravy* the way children on their first fishing trip said *maggots*.

"Yes," said Star, ignoring his tone. "You like gravy, don't you, Lily?"

"Oh yes," I said. "With lots of red wine in it usually."

"See," said Star, looking at Henri triumphantly. "It's only you who doesn't like it."

"Humph," said Henri. "All mad." He looked at me curiously. "Obviously no daughter of mine."

"Ignore him," I said to Star. "I'm sure you've encountered Henri's views on *sauces* before. I wouldn't mention mint sauce if I were you."

"Urrgh," said Henri. "The worst. I don't know why you English want to smother the flavour of meat with the flavour of *toothpaste*."

Both Star and I raised our eyebrows. Neither of us was entirely English. But Henri was in full flow now, so while he ranted about English cuisine Star knocked up a sauce and I carved the lamb. No one mentioned murder.

Discovering I was ravenous I ate quickly, not joining in the conversation they started having about some new wonder drug being tested to treat depression. After lunch I took a coffee and a cigarette upstairs and went back to my notebook, jotting down every idea I had; every lead that would need following up. *Jess*, I kept writing. Why had she disappeared? I could see now what she'd meant when she'd said she knew something. She knew the magazine stories were false. And when she'd said how "fucked up" everything was, she hadn't been joking. Her career would have been on the line if she'd told the truth.

As I wrote, smoked and drank a question came into my head. Had Jess even met the women? I'd already worked out that she hadn't been to their houses because of the details she'd got wrong. Of course, if she'd made up the stories herself, there would have been no need to interview them. I was fairly sure they weren't actually friends of hers. The words I'd overheard from Dean's telephone conversation now made sense as well. *No, mate, I don't know her . . . Yeah, well weird. I know that Tyler vaguely. You could try him I suppose . . . Wouldn't bother if I was you. Don't know really, too stuck-up . . . I think it was all through him . . .* Now I realised he must have been talking about Jess, telling someone that "it" (presumably the magazine story) had all been organised through Tyler. Jess hadn't appeared in Rebecca's contact book. So her connection with Jess must have been vague as well. I wasn't sure about Sasha, but again, because of the inaccurate detail, Jess couldn't have been to her house. And if she hadn't been to her house, she probably didn't know her that well.

If this was true then there were other implications, like, how would the murderer have known where the women lived if he hadn't followed Jess? There must have been some other way; for example, that he worked at the magazine — or he had followed Mark Savage, the photographer. So I was now looking at two possibilities. Either the murderer was a *Smile!* employee, or he had obtained the information about the addresses of the women from someone connected with the magazine. And he would have to have known either Jess or someone from the magazine in order to be aware that the story existed at all.

But there still didn't seem to be any motive.

My notes seemed circular and snakelike, eaten up by their own spiralling logic. So many of my conclusions appeared to be based on guesses, and that wasn't going to be very helpful. Maybe I was wrong about everything. My watch said ten past three. I wondered how the wedding reception was going.

Getting off the bed and stretching, my head thick and heavy with facts and humidity, I took some money out of my jacket pocket and walked to the local paper shop for some more cigarettes. I needed to watch *Peeping Tom* and I needed to smoke. A lot.

You know how she looks, don't you? Tall, thin, but with well-rounded, medium-sized tits that looked prominent in her white T-shirt. That curly brown hair: so much of it, and those eyes. One green, one blue. If she'd looked more closely out of the blue one she may have seen me sitting on the wall watching. No skirt today, I noticed. Back to the usual Levi's and trainers. No date, then. [Laughs]

She must have walked only about fifty yards when her yuppie mobile phone rang. I listened eagerly: to whom was she going to speak? Would she tell them anything of what she knew about me? Feeling excited that I was going to hear her on the phone, I leant up against a wall while she stopped, turned and then turned again, sticking one finger in her ear to drown out the sound of a large removal van going past. See how much detail I remember? You must be very excited about this.

Anyway, I listened.

"What?" I heard her say angrily into the phone. Someone was obviously bothering her. "What?" she repeated, incredulous.

Silence, while I lit a cigarette, mirroring her doing the same.

Whoever she was speaking to could certainly talk. Five minutes elapsed before the poor slag got a word in.

"So you're phoning from the reception? That's really low," she said. "Where's Bronwyn?"

Silence. The third party saying something on the other end of the line.

"And what happens when she finds out you've phoned me? What does that mean — yet another round of hysterical phone calls from family and friends telling me to leave you alone? Maybe you could find the time to point out to them that I haven't called you since last week."

Poor super-sleuth. Obviously having romantic difficulties.

"So you're married now, then?"

Curiouser and curiouser. Her illicit love had just got married. I thought this was bizarre: very tabloid.

"Are you happy?" she asked. I assumed the answer was "no" because she continued: "Well, what the hell do you expect? And if you thought I was going to ring you back last night to help talk you out of it, you were wrong. It's just not my responsibility, Fenn. You know that."

Fenn? What kind of a stupid name is that?

"I'm sorry," she continued, sniffling a little now, looking around to check no one was watching her cry. "I'm so sorry it's come to this. But Fenn, everything will be all right. Um, God . . . I suppose at a time like this I think God moves in mysterious ways. Sorry? Well, Catholic, actually. Yeah. No reason why you should know. Anyway, look, what are you going to do? You're going to have to try to make a go of it now, I suppose. What? Why? Well, your wife phoned and asked me very politely not to come. I think she thought we'd run off together or something . . . Don't say that." She wiped a tear from her cheek. *"Don't say that, Fenn. Why couldn't you have seen all this before saying 'I do'? I'll always be here for you, you know that . . . What? I'll move on, I suppose. You know, there are plenty more fish to fry . . . In the sea? Oh, yeah, I suppose that's what I meant."*

She was pulling out a cigarette again, fumbling for her lighter and then dropping it.

"You can't be jealous, Fenn. Yes, I know, but she's your wife now. I mean, you've got to try and love her. Isn't that what you were telling me? Well, of course it makes a fucking difference."

The tears had stopped now and she was getting angry. I'd never heard her swear before. The way she said the word, though. Fucking. Now that was dirty.

"Anyway," she was saying, "I'm seeing someone else now."

Naughty girl. I knew that was a lie and so did she. Her voice betrayed it, too, if Sven or whatever his name was had been listening. She was silent for a couple of minutes while he said his piece at the other end. The last word she said before ending the call was "Jon." I laughed so much I had to retreat back around the corner.

Returning, I found the house empty. Henri and Star had gone out, it seemed: a note on the table confirmed this, adding that they had gone to a friend's and would not be back until late.

Desperate now to see the film, I went to take my place in the sitting room; ashtray, cigarettes and chocolate all collected and assembled next to me on the sofa. Fenn had phoned me on the way to the shops, telling me what a huge mistake he'd made and asking why I hadn't stopped him. I had told him it was his life and, basically, his mistake. Thus the chocolate. But there was no way

I was going to let the whole thing get to me. And I certainly didn't have the time to think about it now, I decided.

Instead, I pulled the video from its sleeve and inserted it into the VCR, which automatically began playing it. I quickly flicked onto channel nine and settled back on the sofa, tucking my legs underneath me and lighting a cigarette.

Opening my notebook I wrote the word *Dartboard* and then the word *Eye*, since these were the first two images in the film. Almost instantaneously, though, I gave up taking notes, transfixed and at the same time puzzled by the film. It was old — older than me — I knew that, but all its conventions seemed peculiar: the music, the lighting and the framing were like nothing I had seen before.

Nevertheless I was instantly gripped. On the screen a hidden camera was picking out a woman. It had cross-hairs, like a gun, which sent a prickle up my neck.

"It'll be two quid," says the woman.

Then the footsteps, while I was thinking: two quid for what? Not sex, surely? Footsteps still, clicking ones, like those made by those metal things people used to wear on the heels of their shoes. As she goes up the stairs the seams of her stockings both date her and whore-ify her. Definitely sex.

"Shut the door," she says. She had blonde curly hair. She starts to take off her skirt.

She is distracted (as are we) by something clicking into place. It's on the camera — the secret wind-up camera which has been filming this entire sequence. Slowly, terrifyingly, her expression changes and she shrinks back screaming, *No*.

Turning my head away for a second, I caught my breath. Had I realised this was going to be a horror film? *Was* it a horror film? I wasn't sure. It was horrible, though. I gulped. Had *that* been the look on Tam's face as she recoiled from the strangler on her sofa just over a week ago? I gulped again and lit another cigarette.

Meanwhile on screen a camera rolls (a projector, in fact). A man watches. Who is he? He watches the murder — the murder he has just filmed. The music — a piano — tinkles and flirts with a melody before crashing into a tuneless crescendo as the voyeur (the Peeping Tom) reaches some sort of climax.

Then, back on the street, he films the aftermath of the murder. He tells someone he is a reporter from the *Observer* (*ha ha*, I thought, without laughing). Then he is in a newsagent's, setting up a photo shoot: some kind of early sixties porn, it seemed.

Then I had to rewind.

"Hold on, Mark, I've got a question for you," says the shopkeeper.

And rewind again.

"Hold on, Mark, I've got a question for you." *Mark*. Oh, no. I hoped this didn't mean what it seemed to mean. Feeling dizzy now, and very ill at ease, I let the tape play on. On-screen, the shopkeeper and Mark, the murderer-photographer, begin to talk about girls and magazines.

Suddenly this seemed very important. The film was good, and I could see why it was a classic. It was frightening, too, although I wasn't sure whether this was partly because of the reason I was watching it. The film seemed more real because to me, murder was no longer confined to fiction.

The murderer's name was definitely Mark, with a K, spelt out on the director's chair next to the projector on which he played back his murder sequences. *Mark Lewis*, it said. As the story developed it became clear that he was a sympathetic character with whom the audience was intended to identify. He killed, it seemed, because of his childhood, a gruesome affair in which his father subjected him to months of scrutiny-by-camera.

On-screen: "Why?" asks Helen, the love interest.

"He was interested in the effects on the nervous system of fear," replies Mark.

This became Mark's fetish, then: *fear*. He was a product of what had been deemed interesting about him. Seeing a woman frightened turned him on. Being turned on made him want to kill.

Maintaining a critical distance from the film for a while succeeded in keeping my fear at bay, until I became wrapped up in the mystery. I was intrigued when the police established that the look of fear frozen on the dead face of the prostitute victim was something unique.

"What was it she saw?" asks one of them, the inspector.

"A man coming towards her with a sharp weapon?" suggests the other, stating the obvious.

"I'm familiar with that kind of fear," says the inspector. "This is something new to me."

When the secret was revealed at the end I almost threw up. It was one of the most terrifying things I'd ever seen, but I watched, absolutely gripped, until the end. When the credits rolled I felt drained, like a voyeur who had just *looked*, for too long at too much stuff. I stood up from the sofa and walked through to the kitchen to make a coffee, wanting to do something normal to try to dilute my queasy feeling. But as I walked past the phone it rang, and when I picked it up nobody was there. Again.

The sun may have been shining brightly outside, and I could even hear children playing in the next-door garden, but to me the moment was as chilling as the darkest, remotest night.

For what seemed like hours *Peeping Tom* still played on some internal projector in my mind, as flickery and scary as Mark's images had been in the film. I tried to do normal things: drinking coffee, smoking cigarettes and even, later, watching *Match of the Day* to confirm that the world was not just real but also innocent. I wanted it to appear full of un-sinister things. But still, when I wanted to go to the loo, I found I couldn't. The thought of going upstairs in the dark, away from the front door (in my irrational mind the first door I would open if anything dangerous happened) and into the shadows was too much. So I just sat on the sofa, forcing myself not to think about murder, not to imagine it might be me next and desperately trying to find a film or a TV programme I could watch which would not make me feel worse.

The cable channels got my vote in the end, since terrestrial TV seemed to offer only murder-mysteries or horror films (*Taggart*, *Vampire's Kiss*, *The Hitcher*) or snooker, from which I could just as easily die of boredom. In the end I settled for an old rerun of *Beverly Hills 90210*, finding it both comforting and disquieting all at once: a good-looking bloke called Dylan was having to choose between two women, a dark and a blonde one. He chose the blonde.

Henri and Star came back eventually. I felt better once they were in the house and soon started thinking properly again. The film had spooked me, but what did it all mean? Did it mean Jess thought Mark Savage had done it? All of a sudden there seemed to be too many Marks. Mark Moss, Mark Savage and Mark Lewis from the film. All connected somehow with the murders. All connected with Jess.

It was just gone ten. I walked through to the hall and picked up the phone. A couple of minutes later, when I had the number I wanted, I dialled again. I wanted to speak to Sarah, to make absolutely sure that what Jess had done was actually possible, and find out how she would have gone about it. Sarah was a tabloid journalist. She had to know.

"Hello," said a loud, male voice on the end of the phone. In the background I could hear music and voices.

"Hi. Is Sarah there?" I asked.

"Hang on." I heard the mouthpiece being covered and then a muffled *Is there anyone called Sarah here?* A few minutes later there was some scuffling and Sarah's faint voice. *It's my fucking house, moron.*

"Sarah Edwards," she said.

"Sarah," I said, "it's Lily. I met you the other night."

"Oh, yes," she said. "You're the one who had it off with Jon."

"How do you know . . ."

"I didn't until you said that." She laughed. "Sorry if it's a bit loud here. My boyfriend decided to throw a party."

"Look, Sarah, I wanted to ask you a few things."

"What about?"

"Um, I can't really tell you. But I can probably get you a major exclusive if you help me."

"Really?" I heard the sound of a door being slammed and the music became more muffled and quiet. "I'm listening."

"Okay, Sarah, look. This is hypothetical, all right?"

"Whatever you say."

"What would happen if you made up a story and published it in your paper?"

"I'd get fired."

"How would they know?"

"What do you mean?"

"Well, say you made up a true life story, like, I don't know, a bloke who's slept with ten thousand women or something."

She laughed. "Sounds like our kind of thing."

"Well, say you got a bloke to pose as him, got pictures of him and everything. Who would know?"

"My editor would know for a start. We have to check people out, you know, properly. The other week I covered a story about this fifteen-year-old kid who'd fathered two children. I got pictures of the boy, his girlfriend and the kids, consent from the parents and everything, but my editor still wanted photocopies of the babies' birth certificates just to make sure. Also, we had to contact the registry offices where the teenagers were born to check they were the ages they said they were and cross-reference that with their birth certificates. Otherwise these kids could have just borrowed the babies from somewhere and made up their ages and made us look really stupid."

"You really do it thoroughly, then?"

"Yeah. All the tabloids are the same. People take the piss and say we make stuff up, but we just don't do it. Even celebrity stories usually have a grain of truth somewhere, despite what the actual celebrities say."

"What about magazines?"

"What do you mean?"

"These women's weeklies. What if you wanted to make up a story and get it in one of those?"

"Piece of piss. People do it all the time."

"Do they?"

"Oh, yeah. We pick up the odd story from them sometimes, but with loads of them, when you follow them up, you find out they're just bollocks."

"Really?"

"Yeah."

"I was talking to a features editor about this the other day. She swears they're all true."

"Yeah, well, she would, wouldn't she? They've got advertisers to keep happy and everything."

"So why is it so different? Why can you get away with it in a magazine but not in a paper?"

"They're more emotional, I suppose. You know, we deal in facts, they deal in feelings. They are quite careful in the sense that they watch out for libellous stuff and other legal complications, but to be honest, they're so desperate for material they can't afford to be too picky. I mean, they have to fill a whole magazine with that *I slept with my best friend's husband* kind of shit. We wouldn't touch most of the stuff they run because it's just not sensational enough for us. And, you know, most of what they do isn't that remarkable anyway. Like these case study things about jealousy or whatever. Everyone's felt jealous at some point, and who's going to be able to prove that you didn't feel something?"

"But what if it led someone to do something? They do have some outrageous examples in these things, like someone who's attacked their boyfriend's ex-girlfriend or slashed her car tyres or something."

"If it hasn't gone to court, the magazine wouldn't be expected to publish third-party names and details, not if they didn't have a contract with them. And again, if it hasn't gone to court it would be difficult to prove one way or the other. That's another difference between them and us, really. We won't touch anything where there isn't any paper trail; court appearances, birth certificates and so on. With these magazines it seems as if real names and photos are enough. The people who are in them can say what they want."

"That's the impression I got as well." I paused. Sarah was being more helpful than I'd anticipated. "How do you know all this?"

"We've all done feature-writing, babe."

"Certainly seems that way," I said, letting a smile creep into my voice.

"So. Are you going to give me anything on this big scoop? Any background information I can work on or anything?"

"I can't tell you yet. But I promise you, there is something at the end of all this."

"I'll be waiting for your call."

"Incidentally," I said, suddenly thinking of something. "What's the secret in making up a feature and getting away with it?"

"Um, make sure no one finds out, basically."

"So you'd get the people who were posing for you not to tell anyone about it?"

"Absolutely. Especially in London. Otherwise, before you know it, so-and-so's told their mother, who's told her friend who's told her son who happens to be the MD of the publishing company or something. Yeah, keep it quiet is generally the fail-safe rule, Does that help?"

"Yeah. Cheers, Sarah."

"No problem."

Sarah gave me her mobile, pager and office numbers for me to get back to her. And I would, once it was safe to go public. But now I was able to be certain. Of course Jess made up the stories: it happened all the time.

Chapter Nineteen

In Your Face

SUNDAY MORNING FOUND ME BREAKFASTING quickly and pacing endlessly around the kitchen. I wanted action. I wanted to get back in touch with Kathi and try to delve deeper into the world of *Smile!* magazine. But it was Sunday. What could I do?

"What's the matter with you?" asked Henri, eventually, looking up from the *Observer*.

"Sunday," I said, letting out a sigh and rolling my eyes. "What a pointless day."

"I think maybe *God* would not agree with you there," he said.

"No. Well, I've just got so much I need to do next and . . ." There was no way I could explain all this to Henri. How could I tell him that the reason I hadn't contacted the police with my new information was because Star had made me promise not to? I couldn't explain the Peeping Tom conclusion either — that tomorrow I was going to the *Smile!* offices to confront Mark Savage myself. No, Henri wouldn't like that at all.

"Relax," he said. "Why don't you read a book or something?"

"Um, yes," I said, getting an idea. "Actually, I think I'm going to go for a walk. See you later."

"Oh, right, goodbye," he said, confused.

I grabbed my jacket and a notebook and left the house before I changed my mind. Once up on the main road I hailed a cab and told the driver to go to Deptford. It was time I had another look in Jess's flat, and that at least could be done on any day of the week.

I saw her from the window. She was coming in the door, then, I assumed, up the stairs. The "security" in the flats was still down, so she was able to come straight in. I thought then: how fucking impolite can you get? To be fair, she did knock first, but no one answered. "No one" was waiting to see what she'd do next.

The thing is, there was already an intruder in the house. He was sniffing around, doing what she'd done so recently: looking at the computer files, making little notes and then hiding when he heard her knock. So you see, when she came in she was not alone.

There was no one in when I knocked. Jess was obviously intent on staying away, and Tyler must have been out. The door was slightly ajar, though, so in the end I just walked in, glad that I didn't have to break in, which had been plan B.

It was too hot in the flat. None of the windows was open and a viscous, dirty, clinging heat with a rotten aroma had clearly been creeping up the block of flats for some time, like a fog, rising in the heat. I hadn't worked out what to say to Tyler if he came back; my strategy was more to do with speed than anything else, my rationale being that if I hurried then I'd be unlikely to run into anyone. Or so I hoped.

I'll set the scene for you.

Girl walks slowly into flat, looking around, checking no one is there.

Man is hiding in the kitchen, thinking she won't go in there.

(The atmosphere is heavy with stealth and deceit.)

Girl heads straight for the study. She seems to know what she wants.

Man decides to venture out of the kitchen, looking to see what she is doing.

Girl spills something in the study. "Shit," she says.

Man hears her and freezes, looking for somewhere new to hide.

Girl leaves the study again, coming out with wet hands, looking for a towel.

Man hides behind the sitting-room door, pressed up against the wall.

Girl walks past the door, pressing it against him as she goes.

Man peers out. It's safe, she's in the kitchen.
Girl finds a tea towel and dries her hands.
Man approaches kitchen.
Girl approaches kitchen door to go and clear up the mess in the study.
Man approaches kitchen.
Girl approaches kitchen door.
She screams.
I laugh.
Man jumps back.
They look at each other.

Everything would have been a bit quicker had I not spilled the by then very mouldy tea on Jess's desk. Having cursed myself I walked out of the study and through to the kitchen to get a tea towel to dry my hands, and something to clear up the mess of the tea which was now all over the desk, the files and everything.

As I walked through to the kitchen two things were bothering me: first, the *tea* bothered me. I hadn't noticed it before, but now I got to thinking about just *why* someone would make a cup of tea and not drink one drop of it. Had Jess been called out in a hurry? The second thing was the banging and the footsteps coming from the upstairs flat as someone walked up and down and up again. Wherever I was, the footsteps seemed to be above me.

Not thinking about that more than was necessary (now I just wanted to get out of there), I found the tea towel and walked back out of the kitchen.

There in front of me was a man I'd never seen before, dark-haired and wearing glasses. It wasn't Tyler, it was an intruder. *The murderer?* I screamed and felt my heart try to escape from my chest even faster than I wanted to escape from the flat.

I backed into the kitchen slowly, knowing I was cornering myself but needing to get away from this man who was now raising his hands and saying, "Whoever you are, please, I'm not going to hurt you . . . I'm . . ."

"Get away from me," I hissed as he followed me into the kitchen.

"Okay, look . . . Are you Lily by any chance?"

"How do you know my name?"

"Are you?"

"Yes."

"It's okay, Kathi told me all about you."

"Kathi?"

"From the magazine."

With every sentence I edged about a foot back and the intruder followed, moving about half as far each time.

Question: A murderer is following you. If every step he takes is half as long as the last, and the first step was half a metre and you are standing ten metres away, how long will it take him to reach you?

Answer: He never will.

"So you work for *Smile!*, then?" I asked, now edging along a unit towards the sink, in which I'd noticed a big knife.

"Yes," he said. "I mean, I've got my NUJ card if you want to see some ID. Look, I'm really *not* going to hurt you."

I may have wanted to believe him, indeed, his tone seemed pleasant and convincing enough. But I couldn't help visualizing the moment when I would drop my guard and he would lunge at me . . . How would he kill me? Would he stab me like Sasha, or strangle me like Tam? Never having felt fear like this, I became virtually paralysed, moving more and more slowly, becoming a parody of my own puzzle. (Answer: *She* never gets there.)

"Oh fuck," I found myself whispering. "What the . . ."

"Please don't be frightened," he continued, moving closer.

"Who *are* you?" I asked, the words turning to acid in my throat and leaving as a whisper.

"I'm Mark," he said. "I'm just a photo —"

"No," I whispered. "No!" I screamed.

Filled with an energy from nowhere I kicked him, hard, in the stomach, needing to get him out of the way so I could leave the room and run for my life. He fell back into a vegetable rack and lost his balance. Before he had the chance to scramble up, I ran out of the kitchen and out of the flat, moving down the corridor as fast as I could go.

I sprinted like crazy out of the building and crossed the main road, turning right and heading for Surrey Quays tube station. Looking behind me, it was clear I hadn't been followed but this didn't make me stop. I hailed the first cab I saw and told the driver to take me back to Camden. Fast. By the time it rolled up outside Henri's door my heart still hadn't stopped beating and my muscles were tense and painful. All the sweat that had poured out of me in Jess's kitchen had cooled, though, and I felt damp, cold and still very scared. Paying the driver with shaking hands I stepped out of the cab, feeling my legs almost give way beneath me as I did so. Walking unsteadily to the door I banged on it hard, not thinking to get my key out, just wanting to be inside as quickly as possible.

Star answered the door.

"My God," she said when she saw me. "Lily, what on earth —"

"Star," I said in a strangled voice. "Just let me in and shut the door."

"Of course, come on, I'll make you a drink."

She ushered me into the kitchen and listened while I told her what had happened.

"A *photographer* called *Mark*," she mused when I'd finished.

"Yes, cornering me in the bloody kitchen," I said, my voice still trembling. "Oh, Star, I'm not sure whether I'm cut out for this after all."

"It must have been terrifying."

"It was. I've never been so scared in my entire li —"

The doorbell rang, cutting through my words.

"I'll get it," said Star. "You stay there."

She was gone for several minutes, leaving me reflecting on whether I should continue with this. I knew I had to, really, but the whole thing had turned a bit too *chilly* for me.

Star came back into the kitchen, but there was someone else with her. My whole body tensed when I realised it was him — *Mark the photographer* — and that Star had invited him in.

"What's he doing here?" I demanded.

"It's all right," said Star, smiling. "He's explained."

"Explained what? That he was trying to murder me?"

Mark stayed on the other side of the room, looking slightly frightened.

"I just came to return this," he said, holding out my mobile phone. "You left it behind."

"Oh," was all I could think of to say. Then: "How did you know where I was?"

"You've got your home number programmed in," he explained. "I just dialled it and, um . . . Your mother was very helpful."

"It's a good job he's not the murderer," commented Star.

"How do *you* know that?" I asked her, hissing through my teeth.

"He's . . ."

"I've got an alibi," said Mark.

"Yeah, right," I said.

"No, seriously, I was, um . . . this is a bit embarrassing." Mark looked at Star for help, but she just smiled smugly. I wished someone would tell me what was going on.

"What?"

"I was in therapy," he said. "With, um . . ."

"Your father," finished Star, looking at me and smiling.

"My father?" I said. "Oh." I thought for a minute, still unconvinced. "So you were in therapy *all morning?*"

"Well, no," he said. "But on my way there, at eight-thirty, I bought some petrol." He fumbled in his pocket. "Here's a copy of the receipt — I showed the police as well. I used my credit card, so it has to have been me. That was when the first girl was being murdered. Then I was actually in therapy between nine and nine-fifty, making it impossible for me to have committed the next one."

"Oh," I said.

"Sorry about the confusion," he said, turning to go.

"Where are you going?" I asked.

He looked at me curiously. "Well, I suppose I'd better get back."

"Maybe, but I think we've got some stuff to talk about."

"Like what?"

"Like, if you're not the murderer, what you *were* doing creeping around Jess's flat."

"I'll make some coffee, shall I?" said Star, and walked over to the kettle while Mark, still eyeing me suspiciously, sat down at the table.

Now I had my chance to look at him properly while he sat, eyes down on the table, and started playing with a table mat. His fingernails were unremarkable, neither foppishly manicured nor slobbishly bitten. But his hands themselves were strange, somehow: bigger than ordinary hands; suntanned, lined. His eyes were wild behind his round glasses. Wild, blue and furtive, glancing this way and that at his hands and the table mat, not looking up at me. His light brown hair was a mess and I couldn't work out if it was curly or just very tangled. His clothes, although casual, were expensive. His cashmere sweater hung just as it should over his designer jeans, and his brown leather jacket looked soft, well-worn but of high quality. Briefly, I wondered how he would afford all that (and the therapy) on a photographer's salary, then met his eyes as he looked up.

"I'm really sorry I scared you," he said, "I can see how it must have looked."

"So what were you doing in there? You're a friend of Jess, aren't you?"

"Yes. Well, I'm more Tyler's friend, really. Those two, they've been on and off since we were at school."

"You were at school together?"

"Tyler and me were, yes."

"So you were at the flat quite legitimately, then?"

"Not exactly, no. Although, I suspect, rather more so than you. You know I could be asking exactly what *you* were doing there."

"I was, and still am, trying to find out who murdered those women," I said simply. "Jess asked for my help before she went away."

"You?"

"Yes," I looked him up and down. "I was trying to contact you earlier in the week. I came to the magazine offices but Kathi said you were out on a shoot."

"Yeah, that's right. She told me about you. Said you were barking up the wrong tree."

"How?"

"By focusing on the *Smile!* connection."

"She would think that, I suppose."

"Yeah."

"So you were just visiting Tyler, then? In the flat, I mean."

"Not exactly." He looked uncomfortable. "As I'm sure you know, Tyler's gone away."

"Has he? Since when?"

"Same time as Jess, I thought."

"Where?"

"He wouldn't tell me."

"Hang on, did you say he went at the same time as Jess?"

"Yeah."

"He can't have done. I saw him at the flat on Monday."

"But he phoned me and told me he was going away. He said he was going to be away for at least two weeks, staying with an ex-girlfriend. I wasn't supposed to tell anyone that," he added.

"Well, I definitely saw him there."

"Strange." Mark shrugged his shoulders. "What did he say to you?"

"Not much. He was a bit odd. Sullen, I suppose."

"He didn't say anything about his suspicions?"

"No. Mind you, he had plenty to say about Jess's suspicions. Apparently she thought Peeping Tom did it."

"She . . . *Peeping Tom*. Mark the photographer. Me. I see."

"That's why I . . ."

"Got freaked out. Of course. I'm Mark the fucking photographer." He breathed out heavily, anger dragging over his features. "Fucking bitch."

"What do you mean?"

"Well, Jess, implying I had something to do with it. I can't believe Tyler passed that information on, though. He knows me. And . . ."

"And what?"

"And he thinks she did it. So do I."

"You think Jess murdered those women?"

"Absolutely. Either that or she set it up somehow."

Star walked over with the coffee and placed mugs in front of Mark and me. She sat down on the other side of the table and looked at me, raising her eyebrows.

"You don't think much of Jess, then," she said to Mark, in a tone I hadn't heard her use before. It was probably the one she used with her psychopaths, although I was beginning to realise that Mark didn't fit into this category at all. He had the air of one wrongly accused; bitter, angry and seething inside. These emotions were now directed towards Jess as he began to speak again.

"You know the funny thing? I'm not in the least bit surprised. I'm not surprised that she managed to have those women killed — or murder them herself. I'm not surprised she set me up either; getting you down here, telling you a crock of shit about (here he managed a very good imitation of Jess, high-pitched and whiny) *Peeping Tom did it* and then fucking off. Tyler knows she did it as well. He found evidence and everything. Why do you think he's gone too? He can't face the idea of her being a murderer."

"What was this evidence?" I asked.

"A blood-soaked T-shirt," he said. "Now, what would Jess have been doing with that in the house?"

"When did he find this?" asked Star. "And why didn't he tell the police?"

"He found it on Thursday night, after the murders. I don't know why he didn't tell anyone. He told me, of course. That's when he decided to go away."

"Why haven't you told the police?" I asked.

"I don't want to drop Tyler in it for withholding evidence or aiding and abetting, or whatever you'd call it."

"So you were in Jess's flat . . ."

"Looking for alternative evidence. They burnt the T-shirt, I know that. Then the way I heard it, Tyler went away. Said he couldn't handle it. I don't know what he came back for, though. He hasn't been in touch with me and I haven't been around there, until today, of course."

"I suppose," I said, wondering why all of this didn't sound right.

"I've just got to find something. I'm not cut out for being prime suspect in a murder investigation."

"But why would you be prime suspect?" said Star, sounding confused. "You've already explained where you were that morning."

"I slept with one of the victims," said Mark, looking embarrassed.

"You *slept* with one of them?" I repeated. "Which on?"

"Tam," he said. "It started after the photo shoot. That's why I've got my alibi off pat. I've lost track of the amount of times I've been over it with the police."

"But you didn't mention an alibi for the time that Tam was killed," I said, suddenly remembering. "What was it?"

The phone started to ring.

"Excuse me," said Star, and got up from the table.

"I'm not here," I said. Then, turning my gaze back to Mark, "Well?"

"I don't have one. That's the problem. I mean, I hadn't said anything to the police about being involved with her. Then that wanker Carson started going on about her seeing someone else and they did some tests. When they cross-referenced them with the *Smile!* employees they struck gold — or so they thought. They wanted to charge me but they couldn't, because, luckily, the killer left that knife there, and there was no way I could have had the knife because I had alibis for the other murders. But I'm not quite off the hook yet. I'm not allowed to leave the country or anything until I'm ruled out."

"Goodness."

"Now you can see why I'm so desperate to get some evidence on Jess."

"Do you really think it was her?"

"Uh-huh. The bloodstained T-shirt is proof enough of that, don't you think?"

"Well, I'm not sure. What motive could she possibly have had?"

"Furthering her own career for one thing. If she didn't get caught she would have been hot property for the newspapers, if not as a journalist then as some kind of celebrity. She's so in your face that I wouldn't put it past her at all. It's all I can think of. I honestly don't know why. It just seems like Jess, that's all."

"Someone said she was ruthless," I mused.

"She is."

"But murder?" I shook my head. "It doesn't seem right somehow."

"I don't know. She's fucked me over a few times."

"How?"

"She's a user. She used me to get in with Kathi at the magazine, and then dropped me. It's always the same. Tyler's her great dreamboat and I'm just his ugly, easily manipulated friend."

"Sounds a bit unpleasant," I said, remembering the way Jess had dropped me as a friend once I'd introduced her to John. "But a track record in not being a good friend doesn't add up to someone becoming a murderer."

Mark looked me straight in the eye. "You don't know Jess all that well, do you?"

"What do you mean?"

"You'll work it out," he murmured, "I'm sure."

As I showed him out, Mark made me promise to let him know if I discovered anything. It seemed that he was as desperate to clear his name as I was to solve this whole thing.

As I watched him leave I pursued some themes from the conversation in my head. It was clear who Mark's prime suspect was: *Jess*, and I couldn't work out why. What could she have done that would lead him to such a dreadful conclusion? How could he think she was capable of *that?* I thought back to my conversation with Kathi about revenge. Maybe Jess just had an overactive imagination, I thought. After all, she had made up all those stories. But lots of people seemed to think she was more sinister than that, and to some extent there was evidence there. Even so, I didn't think she was a murderer.

Shutting the door after him, I found myself feeling even more confused. Could it still have been Mark? There was something not right about him, and Jess herself had implicated him with that *Peeping Tom* stuff. Or had that just been what *Tyler* had wanted me to believe? And, I suddenly thought, what on earth was he up to? Here one minute and "away" the next. No wonder he hadn't answered any of my calls. But why had he just upped and left? What was the significance of the bloodstained T-shirt? And even more peculiar: if Tyler knew Jess did it, why had he asked me to stay and poke around? And if Jess knew Mark did it, why hadn't she just told the police?

As I went over Mark's words and my own experiences of the past week, one thing was clear: this was a lot more complicated than I'd thought. Someone had wanted to implicate Jess with the T-shirt (assuming Mark was telling the truth) and then Tyler had helped her cover it up. That implied to me that he didn't really think she was guilty. But Mark said he did — so much so that he'd gone away himself. Then again, it had been Tyler who'd passed on Jess's hunch about "Peeping Tom" being the murderer. Had he known that was a code for Mark? He can't have done, otherwise why would he have given me the clue? And as for Mark's ideas about Jess's possible motive for killing the women, they simply didn't ring true. What did he know that he hadn't told me?

"So, who done it?" said Star, coming into the kitchen and taking me by surprise.

"I have no idea," I said. "I'm even more confused than before. Who was on the phone, by the way?"

"Oh, no one," she said. "Wrong number, I think."

There was no way I could explain to Star the strange hunch (as they always called it on TV) that I was suddenly beginning to have. A couple of things Mark had said had really made me think. All at once I found myself rewinding desperately over every short conversation I'd ever had with Jess, every movement and flick of her hair that I remembered from university. There had been something odd about her even then; something partly hidden, partly exposed, like her scar. I walked upstairs thoughtfully and reached for my address book.

In here were all the phone numbers I had ever collected, religiously filed under the first letter of the first name. It was pink, or had been once, battered by overuse and neglect, sometimes lying dormant in old bags full of dust and sweet wrappers for weeks before I remembered where I'd left it. But I'd never lost it. As I flicked through the pages I quickly became nostalgic. Eugénie's name and number were here — inserted in the green pen I'd thought was so cool when I was about ten. The other pages were filled with our old friends from school, boyfriends from college and, here and there, in the blue Bic biro I'd favoured since university, names that were simply mine. One of these was John Poole, my friend from university and Jess's ex-boyfriend, and I needed to speak to him next, to find out everything I could about Jess.

There were four numbers under his name and all but one was crossed out; student residences, if I remembered correctly, each superseding one another until the moment when there were none, when he left university and went . . . where? We had promised to keep in touch but of course we never had. The only number left was for John's mother, his only point of contact after university. Holding the book open I hurried downstairs and dialled the number. I didn't recognise the 0702 code (now 01702, I assumed) but I remembered that she lived somewhere in Essex.

"Hello?" I said, when a woman's voice answered the phone. "Is that Mrs Poole?"

"Yes, dear. Is it double glazing?" she asked, her voice weary and resigned to the fact that strangers phoned even when you didn't want them to.

"No, I wanted to see if I could get a new number for John," I said. "I knew him at university and I was trying to track him down." My words came out jumbled, a side effect of trying to make them so friendly and nonchalant.

"You're from the university?"

"No. Well, yes, I *was*." I took a deep breath. "I'm trying to get hold of John. Does he have a new number?"

"What, dear, on his mobile?"

"Yes, or a home number would be equally good."

"Home number?"

"If you have one for him."

The woman clucked on the end of the line. "I'm having trouble understanding what you want, love. Are you selling something?"

"I just want to speak to John," I said.

"Oh," she said. "Why didn't you say? *John!* Hang on a minute, love, and I'll call him again. *John!*"

So he was living with his mother?

"Hello?"

My thoughts ended abruptly. John was on the line, sounding strange and distant, his voice a pastiche of its own familiarity; well known and forgotten at the same time.

"Hi, John. How's it going?"

Silence.

"It's Lily. From university."

"Oh, my God," he said. "*Lily*. How long has it been?"

"Don't," I said, "you'll make me feel old. I'm sure we've got a few years before we start saying that."

John breathed out deeply. "I can't believe how many people I've lost touch with."

"Yeah, me too."

"I suppose you heard I split up with Jess?"

"Yes," I said. "I'm sorry."

"And I suppose you know she's disappeared?"

"Yeah. I'm trying to find her."

"So are the police," he said. "They've been round three times now." He paused for a moment. "Why are you looking for her? I didn't think you got on all that well."

"We didn't. But she rang me out of the blue and said she needed my help. I soon found out why when I saw the news and I came straight down. The problem was, she'd gone by then."

"Is she in trouble?" he asked.

"I don't know."

"What's going on, Lily? I haven't told the police anything at all because I'm too scared I'll drop her in it; but it's all getting a bit much. I just don't understand anything about this. She left me, fucked off to London and I haven't seen or heard from her since. Then I hear there's been a load of women murdered and . . . Christ. I just don't get it."

"Well, to be honest, neither do I." I said. "Look, maybe we could help each other out. Are you free this afternoon?"

Chapter Twenty

Poison

JOHN'S DIRECTIONS MADE THE JOURNEY to Southend sound more convoluted than I suspected it was. If I went by train I would need to get to Fenchurch Street. If I hired a car, or borrowed Henri's, all I would need to do would be to whizz down the A13. Tough choice. Of course, the other factor was my own personal stalker, whose presence had been becoming more intense. The feeling that I *might* be being watched was no longer with me. Now I was almost certain.

Thoughts of my stalker occupied me while I gathered together the things I would need for the journey and put them in a bag. Henri was playing golf, apparently, so it seemed there would be no chance of me taking his car, and the hire companies said they needed to see my driving license, which was sitting uselessly in Devon in my chest of drawers. So it would have to be public transport again.

Having noticed that my stalker only followed me on foot and on public transport, I decided to call a cab to take me to Fenchurch Street. As I dialled the number, and while I was booking it, an inner voice told me I was just imagining it all. It was possible; I was still shaken up by the Mark incident. However, I didn't want to take any chances.

* * *

She came out of the door and onto the pavement, walking to the end of the road before turning a corner. Back in her usual jeans and T-shirt today she looked sexy — but not as sexy as when she had retreated into the kitchen. Of course, I couldn't actually see her then, but I could hear. And imagine.

But I didn't reach the house in time to hear what they were saying. What did he tell her? Fuck. [Shakes his head.] That wasn't part of the plan at all. At first I thought it was amusing that they'd bumped into each other. She had been scared off — or so I thought — and neither of them got what they came for.

Anyway, at that point I still thought there was no way she could know anything. I mean, who the hell would be able to make the right links? It had been thought through so carefully: it was just too bizarre for anyone to be able to work out. Maybe if I hadn't stayed around watching like that . . . But you wouldn't want me to skip to the end, would you? You like it chronological. You like me taking my time.

So maybe I should fill you in on the girl, then, Jess: the one they all thought had disappeared of her own accord. This would make such a good film, you know? The girl sitting there, naked in a small room. The room boarded up. A derelict building all dark and full of rats. I hope she is still there, I mean, I never did go back to check on her. She had a notebook, a pencil, a box of Special K and a bottle of mineral water. That would keep her alive long enough to write the story, I thought. That would be the end: the written apology.

Super-slag got in a cab, then, around the corner. Bitch. She thought she was clever. She didn't even get it to pull up outside the house. So it was too late for me to follow her. That was bad, because at this stage I needed to see where she was going.

Liverpool Street was busier than I'd thought it would be. Back-packers milled aimlessly from croissant shop to underwear shop and back again, never going in a straight line. Trying not to swear at people, I dashed through the crowd towards platform thirteen. There it was, the Harwich train, with only one minute to go before its departure at three thirty-five. Shenfield was the first stop, so it looked as if my journey wasn't going to be too long after all. It hadn't looked good at first: I had been to Fenchurch Street, since the direct train went from there, but when I'd got there the line (usually referred to on the news, according to another passenger, as the "misery line") was closed for repairs.

When I boarded the train I found I was on my own. No one followed me in, so I sat down and tried to relax, thinking about the questions I would ask John, hoping I was on the right track (as it were).

The train took almost an hour to reach Shenfield, which it did tortuously, squealing and grinding over decrepit-sounding points and stopping at almost every available opportunity at horrible-looking places like Romford and Harold Wood. Outside, the day seemed to grow more muggy and this, combined with the heat coming from a strange "ventilation" strip by my feet, conspired to give me a pounding head and sheen of grimy perspiration.

Shenfield station was deserted except for about two people waiting on the opposite platform, onto which I also had to change, according to the guard I asked. My watch said ten past four. I took a seat on a bench and lit a cigarette. Picking up my mobile phone I dialled Tyler's number, interested to see whether he was there and to ask him some probing questions if he was. Maybe Mark had been wrong about him going away. He had to have been: I'd seen him for myself on Monday.

Uncomfortable thoughts came back to me, thoughts of this morning, of Mark and my aborted mission at the flats. What had I thought I was going to find there? That file: the missing *Stalking* file, which now seemed more important than before. I'd wanted to check whether it was in the flat or if it had definitely, as I'd suspected, gone. If it was missing there was a fair chance the murderer had it; how else would he have got the details of the women?

Unless he worked at *Smile!* magazine.

But this had become my B theory. My new A theory, and the one that my hunch had come from, was that this murderer was much more connected with Jess than with the magazine. And one easy way this person could have known about the women — their addresses, phone numbers and details — would have been from her file. As I'd worked out only yesterday, this person could not have *followed* Jess, since she'd never visited the women. I'd considered for a while that the murderer had followed Mark instead, as

Kathi had suggested, but now I wasn't sure about that either. The man I'd met when I first went to the flats had mentioned break-ins. Surely that wasn't a coincidence. The murderer must have been in to get information from Jess's flat. The file was missing. It must have gone with him.

Which meant the murderer was unlikely to be a *Smile!* employee, since they would have had access to the information at work. But who would have known there was a story with a file to find? I'd considered this, but the list was potentially endless. Any of the women could have confided in a friend; Jess may have told a whole number of people. But what was baffling me the most was the apparent lack of motive. Lots of people *could* have killed those women, but nobody seemed to have a very good reason for doing so.

Someone had gone to an incredible amount of trouble to kill three women, on the morning of the publication of a magazine they were appearing in. I was sure that meant the magazine connection was important. Could it be someone with a grudge against the magazine, someone whose sordid life story came out as a result of an overheard conversation in the pub; or a pissed-off employee? All these things seemed almost possible, but there was just not enough substance there. Those women hadn't been killed in anger, or even hate: they had been carefully *executed*. The thought made me shiver, but I knew I was right. There had been something calculated about those killings. But what?

As my thoughts finished ringing in my head, so did Tyler's phone. The answerphone cut in, offering to take a message for me. I wondered then whether he'd been screening the calls, remembering the way he had picked up while I was leaving a message last time. He'd convinced Mark that he was away, but had seemed eager to speak to me. Why?

"Hello," I said to the answerphone. "This is Lily Pascale. I'm afraid I've nothing to report as yet. I'll call again if anything develops."

He didn't cut in this time. Maybe he really was away.

The rest of the journey was uneventful. The train, when it eventually came, took me to Southend Victoria, a grim, colourless station with grey concrete steps leading to a deserted sixties shopping centre. Flies buzzed torpidly around as I made my way out into the close, dirty air. Inside, the station had smelt like any other suburban Sunday, with discarded bits of Friday and Saturday night still rotting in the corners.

Outside it wasn't much better. Traffic fumes from the nearby dual carriageway made the air seem cheap and second-hand. I jumped straight in a taxi and gave the driver John's address. Five minutes into the journey, after an incomprehensible series of left then right then right and left again turnings, the air changed slightly and I saw the sea; clear, blue and comforting.

"The sea!" I said, squealing like a small child. "I'd forgotten this was Southend-on-*Sea*."

"Westcliff," commented the taxi driver. "This is *Westcliff-on-Sea*, really, now. And that," he said, gesturing at the mass of blue in front of us, "is actually an estuary."

"Oh," I said, noticing that we were pulling up.

"Manor Road," he announced, pointing at a small road off to the left bracketed by two No Entry signs and leading to the beach. "One-way system. Can't go in unless you want to spend even longer going around the back. But the one you want is the guest house down there."

"Cheers," I said, giving him a fiver and telling him to keep the change.

I hung around all day in the heat, not having anywhere to go, planning what I was going to do next. I decided then, sitting on the kerb around the corner from her house, that when she came back I was going to kill her. She'd pissed me off, tricking me like that. And I didn't know where she'd gone.

John was pleased to see me.

"Lily!" he enthused the moment he opened the door. "It's . . . um, you look wonderful. Really well."

"Thanks," I said, wishing I could say the same about him. He had been growing bald when we were at university; now he *was* bald. He'd lost weight, too, something that he couldn't afford to do, and his clothes hung on him as if he were a wire coat-hanger.

"Come in," he said, moving out of the way for me. "I've been to the bagel shop and bought cakes. We can sit out on the porch."

"Great," I said, and followed him through the house.

Inside it was dark; the darkness made more thick by the layers of dust coating all the windows and the numerous surfaces in the expansive hallway. Underneath the dust sat hundreds of icons; some obviously Catholic and others less easily distinguishable. There were various sailing motifs set against the chipped Virgin Marys, which gave the house a strange, transient feel, as if its past tenants were either on their way to sea, heaven or both.

The porch was pleasantly secluded and overhung by trees between which it was possible to catch glimpses of the sea. Here and there a sailing boat bobbed past, or a reckless swimmer, far out beyond the buoys. Watching while I waited for John, I felt more relaxed than I had done for days. The water calmed me and I remained hypnotised by it until he returned.

"Here we go," he said, placing a tray on the wooden picnic table.

"Thanks," I said, taking out my cigarettes and sighing. "That was quite a journey."

"You got here in the end."

"Well," I said after we sat in silence for several seconds. "You're looking . . ."

"Shit?"

"No, I . . ."

"It's okay. I know I look rough. I've had trouble getting work around here."

"So you're living here permanently? When did you leave London?"

"A couple of years ago, I suppose. It was when Jess's old man went bankrupt. We both lost our jobs working for him and came here."

"Jess's dad went *bankrupt?*"

"Yeah."

"And you both lived here?"

"Yep. Me and Jess and me mum. *Very* cosy."

"God."

"So. Anyway. Have you seen her? How is she?"

"I don't know. I spoke to her on the phone just before she did a disappearing act and she seemed . . . well, she was upset, naturally."

"Don't count on it," he said wryly, through his teeth. He shook his head. "Done a runner. That's our Jessica."

"What do you mean?"

"First hint of trouble, she's off. Don't feel sorry for her, Lily. I made that mistake for too long."

"I thought you were really happy together."

"No. Not really. I protected her, looked after her and let her play victim for years before I realised she was just selfish."

"Really?"

"Yeah. Oh, it's all complicated. Someone cut her with a knife when she was younger, before we met. I don't know if you ever saw her scar. Anyway, she just, I don't know . . . It sounded pretty horrible, I mean, the bloke, whoever did it, was definitely out to get her. But I just thought, Christ, how many years is she going to keep playing on this?"

"What do you mean, playing on it?"

"She just came over as the big victim all the time. If she wanted something from the shop but couldn't be bothered to go out, she'd get me to go, saying that she kept remembering this bloke *getting* her and she couldn't eat or sleep or go out of the house. She made me look after her, and then, once she felt better, she managed to get out of the house, all the way back to London, to live with her fucking childhood sweetheart."

John laughed bitterly. "I just wasn't any competition. *Tyler Moss.* Educated at Ivy Lane and due to be left five million by his father. Can you believe it? I don't blame Jess, really. I mean, she'd been used to the good things in life. It wasn't any surprise to me that she went chasing after money; I was just surprised she didn't do it sooner."

"What do you mean?"

"After the bankruptcy and everything. She just didn't have anything any more."

John took a sip of his tea and looked out thoughtfully over the water. "So I suppose everyone thinks she murdered those women?"

"Well, some people seem to, but I don't know why. It's such a male crime, don't you think?"

"I suppose so."

"Why do you think people think she could have done it?"

"She's just a bit brutal. She hurts people, uses them, tramples on them. She sucks people in, takes what she needs from them — being all sweet and little-girlish — then fucks them over."

"I've heard that."

"Do you know how many times she's been in touch with her old man since he lost the business?"

"How many?"

"None. She blamed him — can you believe that? She blamed him for losing her the BMW and her allowance."

"I can see why someone like that would have run off with someone like Tyler."

"Yeah. Mind you, he hasn't got his money yet. But she'll probably engineer his father's death to make sure they get it soon."

"Does he really not have anything? I noticed he was living in a council flat."

"By our standards, he's loaded. He gets an allowance, but he spends it all making films about poverty and dabbling in what he calls art. But I think she's happy to wait. And she's so blow away with the whole London scene. Wanting to be a journalist and everything. It was when she got her first commission from *Smile!* magazine that she fucked off. Went to live some kind of media high life or something."

"I see. But *Smile!* magazine isn't real journalism, though, surely?"

"Oh, she knew that. But she thought if she could get in somewhere and make the connections, gather together some cuttings and so on, she'd have a chance with the big newspapers."

"And she hasn't been in touch since?"

"No."

John seemed to have worked himself up into a temper. He lit a cigarette and sat shaking his head for a while. He'd cleared up some things for me already, like why Jess was poor, in London, in that flat and writing for *Smile!* magazine. The trouble was, despite what everyone was saying, this all seemed quite innocent to me and made loads of sense. There was no other reason for her to make up those stories than to further her career. Ruthless and imaginative: yes. Murderous? No.

"And she's always in trouble," continued John. "She attracts trouble. Weirdos, nutters. The stabbing wasn't the only time she's been threatened."

"Oh?"

"Do you want to see something?"

"Sure."

John stood up and went into the house, excusing himself as he went and saying he'd only be a moment. I nibbled at the edge of a cake and sipped my tea. For a moment everything was still except for a solitary bird flapping in one of the trees as a small white cat attempted to pursue it. The sunshine still flared from the sky, intensifying into a hot, early-evening haze.

"Here you go," he said when he returned, startling me. "Have a look at those."

He placed a large brown cardboard box on the table. Inside there seemed to be hundreds of white envelopes, exactly the same size and texture. After picking up a couple of them I established that they all seemed to have been sent by the same person: the handwriting was the same on each one, thin, small and spare, the letters barely formed. The name and address were the same on each one. Miss J. Mallone, Manor Hotel, Southend, Essex.

"What are these?" I asked.

"Hate mail, for Jess. A lot of hate, don't you reckon?"

"Mmm." I sifted the envelopes through my fingers. They felt almost weightless. "Why are some of them unopened?"

"I couldn't be bothered to open them after a while. They all say more or less the same thing, anyway."

"You? But they're addressed to Jess."

"Yeah, but I couldn't let her see these." He sighed. "Look for yourself. You'll see what I mean."

Taking one of the open envelopes carefully between my fingers I eased the single white sheet out from inside it. It was a small, thin piece of paper, the same size as those letter-writing pads you get, folded carefully in half. There was no return address at the top, just the following message.

Dear Miss Mallone,

Do you ever think about going back and changing the past? Do you look at your photo album and wish there were different pictures there?

I have visions, sometimes. I see you being carried on a stretcher out of a building. There is a blanket covering your face.

Regards,
An ill-wisher.

I pushed the paper back into the envelope, frightened by the words written on it. John saw the expression on my face.

"Not nice, are they?"

"No." I gulped. "Poor Jess. She must have been frightened half to death."

"She would have been if she'd ever seen them."

"Did you keep all of them from her?"

"Yep."

"So she didn't know someone was sending her hate mail?"

John shook his head.

"But how did you know what was inside them?" I asked. "She must have opened the first one?"

"No." He looked sheepish. "When I saw it in the post I suspected it might have been from a lover or something. I don't know. It was an odd thing for her to get a personal letter. I suppose I just wanted to know who it was from. I steamed it open and when I saw what it said I couldn't believe it. There was no way I could let her see it. She'd been going on all the time about being depressed and suicidal and everything. I don't know if she was just saying all that stuff to manipulate me, but at the time I believed it. Anyway, the next day another letter came, exactly the same. I opened that, too. It said the same kind of thing so I put it away with the first one. The next day, another one, and so on for about a year."

"Goodness."

"I'm quite glad I've told someone, actually. No one's ever seen these."

"What about the police?"

"Nope."

"Why didn't you show them the letters?"

"Well, they're not relevant, are they? I mean, they're just trying to find her. They don't need to know about this kind of thing."

"What *did* you tell the police?"

"Not much really. Just that I hadn't seen her for months and didn't have any idea where she would be. They seem to think she was hiding out here, but she definitely wasn't. I don't want anything else to do with her, and if she had come here I'd have told her to fuck off."

"Did they ask you anything about her background?"

"A few questions. I expect they would have got most of that stuff from her parents."

"Mmm. I suppose."

"So what do you make of the letters?"

"I'm not sure," I said. "Can I take them away with me?"

"Gladly. They spook me out sitting around here."

"Thanks." I got up and started folding in the flaps on the box. "Incidentally, you said they came for about a year. Roughly from when until when?"

"Um, I think they would have started about the summer before last and finished last summer," he said. "Give or take a few weeks. Why? Do you think they might be important?"

"I'm not sure."

The box was heavy in my arms as I left the hotel and walked back up the road where I had a cab waiting. The familiar feeling of being watched resurfaced when eventually I came out of Camden tube station.

It scared me, the thought that this person was trying to be with me everywhere I went. Who was he, and what did he want? Confronting him was probably not the best option so I walked home defiantly, pretending the heavy box was light and that I had nothing to be afraid of.

It was only when I was safely inside the house that I was able to relax a little. I put the box down in the hall and breathed out deeply. A lot of hate, like John had said. And all for Jess. What could she possibly have done that would have had that kind of effect on someone?

In the kitchen Henri was fussing over some kind of pasta sauce and Star was nowhere to be seen. I walked up and put my arms around my father, giving him a little kiss on the back of his head.

"My unpredictable daughter," he exclaimed. "How are you this evening?"

"Frustrated, confused," I said, taking a piece of bread and dipping it in the sauce before sitting down at the table.

"You're not still chasing this murderer, are you?"

"Of course."

Henri tutted. "I shouldn't be allowing this."

"I'm twenty-five," I said good-naturedly, pouring a glass of red wine and turning to leave. "Anyway," I lied, "I'm still not getting anywhere near him, so there's nothing for you to worry about." I picked up the box and the files and walked upstairs.

Sipping my wine on my bed, I thought through what John had told me, the contents of the box now scattered around me. There were clues in the letters, I was sure of that. If Jess was somehow the centre of this whole thing then there could be vital information about her here. I'd heard somewhere that you learnt more about people from their enemies than from their friends, so maybe . . . Unless of course the box of letters, like the magazine article and indeed the victims themselves, was just another red herring.

So, getting back to the actual murders. Why did you do it?

Finally, I thought you were never going to ask. Why? Such a little question but yet such an important one. Well, there were two reasons: one, I could get away with it (or so I thought), and two; revenge.

The thing is, before the murders I thought I'd finished with all the revenge stuff. I'd thought cutting her would banish the demons. I thought the letters would get them out of my system. But they just didn't go away. In fact, she continued to exacerbate them.

By four o'clock in the morning I had read all the letters. They made me feel sick. Each one contained not a threat, specifically, but a desire to see Jess dead. They were all quite short, like the first one I'd seen, each no more than three or four lines. Some were straightforward: *I can't wait to watch you die,* for example. Others were more enigmatic, like: *If U set your mind free baby, maybe you'll understand.* The line was familiar, but I couldn't work out either where I'd heard it before or what it meant.

It didn't take me long to put together a list of common themes and motifs that ran through the letters. First, of course, there was the menace. Whoever had sent the letters wanted Jess dead. Or so he said. I got the impression that he actually enjoyed the idea of her suffering. Otherwise why send the letters, why not just go and kill her?

Each of the letters had the same tone; oblique, almost coded. They bore the hallmarks of a secret language that only two people would understand; lovers, maybe, or old acquaintances. There was a lot of use of words like *remember* and *the past*. They were referring to an old wound, I thought, like Jess's scar.

Then there were the words and phrases that kept cropping up. *Building* was there in most of the letters. This was the building out of which the sender wanted to see Jess carried, on a stretcher. The line I had seen in the first letter, *with a blanket covering your face*, was used a number of times as well. What did it all mean?

Eventually, my eyes feeling painful and my body ready to give up, I put the letters back in their box and fell asleep. My dreams were as you would expect: Jess being carried out of various buildings, on a stretcher, with a blanket covering her face.

CHAPTER TWENTY-ONE

THREE IN A BED

"I'M BEING WATCHED," I said to Star the next morning, over breakfast. Henri had left for work, but Star apparently didn't have any interviews today, so she was going to be working from home.

"How do you know?" she asked.

"It's a feeling, mainly," I said. "But it's definitely happening. I haven't seen him, but I know he's there, if you know what I mean."

"And you think it's the . . ."

"Murderer? Yes."

"*Lily,*" she said sternly. "Why haven't you called the police?"

"You told me not to!"

"Yes, but this is different. You weren't in danger when I told you not to get the police involved."

"I know. But even if I did call them, what would I tell them? *I've got a feeling I'm being watched?* This is London, and I can't see them chasing around because of some *feeling.* Also, I haven't been threatened, I haven't had a look at the guy and, basically, I don't have any evidence."

"Yes, I suppose so." She frowned. "So what are you going to do?"

"I don't know," I said. "Something, I just don't know what, yet."

After breakfast Star retired to the garden to read through some documents while I headed straight for the phone. I took out the numbers Sarah had given me and dialed thoughtfully.

"Newsdesk," said the man on the other end.

"Sarah Edwards, please," I said.

She was breathless when she answered. "Lily, hi. How's it going?"

"Okay, I think," I said. "You?"

"Yeah. Great. So, is this about my exclusive?"

"Possible. No, definitely. Look, Sarah, you know you said you'd worked on the initial reports about the magazine murders?"

"Yeah."

"What background did you get on Jess Mallone?"

"Um, nouveau riche family, very well off till father went bank-rupt, she went to boarding school, sh—"

"Where did she go to boarding school?"

"Cambridge, I think."

"Go on."

"That was all really. We were focusing more on the victims. Why do you want to know?"

"I need you to get me some background information on Jess and also on Tyler Moss and Mark Savage."

"Oh? What do you need to know?"

"Schools, family histories, scandals . . . I don't really know, anything that seems out of the ordinary."

"Okay." She sounded uncertain. "And how is all this going to help me?"

"It's all going towards your exclusive."

"Are you absolutely certain about all this? Are you sure you're not wasting my time?"

"Positive. Just trust me, Sarah. I can't tell you any more than that for the moment."

"Okay, but you'd better be right. I'll make some calls and then give you an update later."

I replaced the telephone. While Sarah was working on Jess, Tyler and Mark, I wanted to go through all Jess's documents again. All the way upstairs, and all the way down, carrying the box and all the files, I only had one thought: there had to be something here I hadn't yet seen.

After making some coffee and settling down on the sofa, I read the *Stalking* article again, double-checking every word. Then

I read the *Revenge* file. Nothing. The adoption piece had initially struck me as potentially the most important of the two older articles; after all, it was the one in which I was certain Tam had posed. But after reading it three or more times I couldn't see anything of use in it. The whole piece, obviously Jess's first, was clumsily put together and read like any other article on adoption. I'd seen it all before.

Lighting a cigarette, I tipped my head back and closed my eyes. I wondered how Sarah was getting on. I wasn't sure what good the background was going to be, but all the recent pieces of information I'd had seemed to point towards Jess, Tyler and Mark. John had said that Jess and Tyler had been childhood sweethearts. Mark and Tyler had been at school together. They were the three people, apart from the murdered women, who had definitely known about the *Stalking* piece. I couldn't be sure who had known it was false apart from Jess, but that didn't matter. They had all known about it, and they'd all had access to information about the women. If the murders had anything to do with any of them — or someone they knew — then maybe there would be some small fact from their past which would make sense of it.

I rubbed my eyes and leant forward. Why wasn't anything making sense? In a last-ditch attempt to find something I tipped the contents of Jess's files onto the floor and went through them again; every piece of paper checked, every article scoured again.

Most of the bits of paper were A4 size, and until now I hadn't noticed the smaller piece of paper, the Post-It note Tyler had given me and that I'd casually slipped in between the sheets I'd printed out. And I hadn't felt any need to look at it again. All it said were those few words: *Goodbye. Back sometime.*

Except that this time I recognised the handwriting. The "G" had been casually formed; it was big, faint and lazily executed. The "o"s were too small; almost dots, set apart from one another. There were no serifs on the next three letters. The "e" could have been an "o"; it was also too small.

My heart was thumping uncomfortably in my chest. The box of letters sat on the sitting-room table, caught in a white splinter of sunlight coming in the window like a knife-edge.

Getting to my feet, I opened the box and, with a shaky hand, removed one of the letters. Even on the front, there was the same "e" in "Mallone," the same "o" in "Southend." Cross-referencing with the rest of the goodbye note, one thing became absolutely, heart-stoppingly clear. The man who had written these letters had also written Jess's goodbye note, which meant only one thing. This wasn't a goodbye note at all. She hadn't run away or disappeared: she'd been kidnapped. By him.

Getting up and pacing the room, the letters left strewn on the table, I could have kicked myself. I should have known. She'd asked me to come, after all, and then she'd just disappeared. It had never seemed right. Except that Tyler had confirmed it. The *note* had confirmed it.

But how it all fitted into place, now! The murderer had known how to get into Jess's flat — he must have been the one who had broken in, and on one of these occasions had, presumably, taken Jess's *Stalking* file. But on the last occasion, once the murders had taken place, he had gone into the flat and taken something else. *Jess*. That explained the undrunk tea and the uneaten chocolate biscuit. Had he walked straight out of Tam's house and into the flats on Evelyn Street? That wouldn't make sense, since it wasn't until the next day that Jess phoned me.

Except that it actually made *perfect* sense: the murderer did go straight into Jess's flat — to plant the T-shirt; no doubt stained with blood from the real murder. He then watched and waited. But what had he planned? Tyler walked out, I knew that from what Mark had said. But if the murderer had wanted to frame Jess, why had he not just phoned the police and told them about the T-shirt? Maybe he'd wanted Tyler out of the way so he could abduct Jess. If that was the case, I wasn't entertaining great hopes of finding her alive.

Lighting another cigarette, I forced myself to concentrate. I sat down again and started pulling out all the letters, one by one. Who was this man? What had Jess done to make him so obsessed?

Reading through them again was more unnerving than it had been the first time, now I knew this person actually had Jess. This made me go slower as I loaded every word with more significance, more malevolence than I had the first time round. Did he have her in this *building* he kept mentioning, waiting to see her carried out on a stretcher? Probably. But there were a lot of buildings in the country, and to know that Jess was in one of them didn't help me too much.

The clock on the wall said one o'clock. My stomach felt empty, my head light. I got up and walked through to the kitchen, barely noticing what I was doing as I made a sandwich. All I could think of was poor Jess, holed up God knows where, or even dead. And the man who had her, the letter-writer. He had to be the murderer.

But who was he? I walked through to the sitting room and looked at the letters again. Something about their uniformity bothered me. All the same envelopes; the same paper; the same postmark. They had all been posted from a small town in Sussex. Turning one of the envelopes over and over in my hands, I thought this had to mean something: everything the same, all the time. Possibly this man had just lived in this town and had a predilection for this paper, these envelopes. But something told me it was much more than that.

He was an obsessive, sure. But he was also a man who liked plotting and planning. He liked intricacies and codes. Maybe it was all that talk with Star about psychopaths, but I had a feeling that if the uniformity of the mode of sending had been important to this man, then he would have sent the same message each time. I'd heard that some people did that. It would be like a strange form of torture — the same envelope dropping on the mat each morning containing the same paper and the same message. But these letters were different. They betrayed an unpredictability in the man who'd sent them. Each day he was differently menacing, in a slightly modified tone. I was therefore sure that the consistent nature of the paper and envelopes had been unintentional.

Another thing — what had made him continue sending these, every day, for a year? Did this guy not have a life? And what was so special about that year in particular? I would have understood if he had been obsessed with Jess all the time and sent letters every day for years, but for just one year? Odd. Another strange thing I'd noticed when I'd first seen the letters was the way the address had been written. It was as if the sender knew where Jess lived, but had never seen the actual address written down. There was no postcode, and the sender had made the same mistake as me, calling the area Southend when in fact it was Westcliff.

Scratching my neck thoughtfully I reached for another cigarette. Looking at the postmark on the envelopes I noticed that it was the same collection each day. Four forty-five. So he didn't work nine to five? I shook my head. That wasn't it. It was something else.

Suddenly I developed a theory. What if this man really hadn't had a life, just for one year? Not necessarily as a result of unemployment, but something else. Something institutional, perhaps. That would explain the uniformity of the letter packaging. Institutional notepaper; institutional envelopes. The phone cut into my thoughts. I walked through to the hall to answer it.

"Lily?" It was Sarah. The line crackled, like she was on a mobile.

"Yeah. How's it going?"

"This is fucking bizarre. You're not going to believe the amount of dirt I've got on those three."

"Go on," I said.

"Okay. Well, you were right, they definitely knew each other when they were at school. Jess went to Saint Helena's and the boys went to Ivy Lane — both schools are in Cambridge. She used to sneak out at night to go and see Tyler, apparently. I spoke to her old headmaster. He's retired and bitter and was more than willing to talk. He reckons Jessica's old man used to pay him off whenever she got in trouble, stumping up for new libraries and science blocks and so on to stop her getting expelled."

"God."

"Yeah, that's what I thought. Anyway, the boys did very well at their school. They were in the upper sixth when Jessica was in the fifth form. Tyler was head boy and Mark was a prefect. Their headmaster was very unhelpful when I spoke to him, he said the school had closed down now and refused to comment, but there was something a bit funny in his reaction when I asked about Tyler and Mark, know what I mean?"

She stopped to breathe and then carried on. "So I called Tyler's mum. Again, nothing. She sounded very posh, though. Scottish. Mark's parents were on holiday, but his sister was there. She clammed up when I asked about her brother's schooldays, and I smelt a rat. Anyway, when I offered her cash it was a different story.

I'm just driving back from there now. Apparently, Jessica, Mark and Tyler were caught in a three-in-a-bed romp when Jess was only fifteen!"

"Sounds like one of your headlines," I said.

"Yeah, absolutely," she said, laughing.

"So what happened? Were they expelled?"

"Not exactly. After Mary — that's Mark sister — had coughed up that much information, I got back in touch with the headmaster of Ivy Lane and threatened to go public with the three-in-a-bed scandal if he didn't talk to me. There wasn't any point threatening the school as such, since it's being demolished soon, but he's some hotshot educational adviser and everything now, and certainly didn't want the story to come out. So he talked. It turns out all this happened in July 1987. Apparently it was common knowledge that Jessica used to sneak into Tyler's study at night but the school turned a blind eye, what with him being the head boy and so on, and them being fairly discreet."

"Bet they didn't turn a blind eye when they caught the three of them in bed," I said.

"Well, that was the funny thing. Apparently it was a younger boy who found them. Then there was the scandal that followed, which the headmaster remembered in great detail. Apparently, Jessica decided that she would 'get' this boy to stop him from spreading rumours about what he'd seen. It sounds like she'd been reading too much Sidney Sheldon or something. She hatched this major plot to basically ruin his life so he wouldn't spill the beans — you'd have thought she could have just paid him off or denied the rumours or something — but instead, she pretended to be his girlfriend for ages, got his trust and made him fall in love with her. She took photos of him wanking himself off, probably saying it turned her on or something, and, on the first day of the autumn term, she pinned them up around the school. Of course, the stupid cow hadn't realised that he'd have nothing to lose after that, so he spilled the beans all right — in a suicide note. Trouble was, it was the next academic year at that point, and Tyler and Mark were already at university. But Jessica did get expelled, the headmaster thinks, or at least, her parents withdrew her from her school."

"Goodness," I said. "What about the younger boy? Did he die?"

"Oh, no. He was discovered in one of the bathrooms with blood everywhere, having tried to slash his wrists. There was no press involved at the time, so this is the first anyone's ever heard of all this."

"Did you get his name?"

"Yeah," she said, loudly flipping through her notebook. "But I'm fucked if I can find it in my notes. Shall I give you a call back when I find it?"

"Yeah, could you? Also," I added, "could you see if there's any kind of mental institution around Eastbourne?"

"Sure," she said. "I think there is, actually. Why?"

"Because I think the guy whose name you can't find was there for a while, and if he was, it's almost certain he's the murderer."

"Fucking *hell*," she exclaimed. "Are you serious?"

"Deadly. I've got a pile of hate-mail letters he sent her here, all postmarked from this place near Eastbourne. And they all refer vaguely to 'the past' and to some photographs. The idea that he was in an institution — that's just a guess. But I've known for a while all this led back to Jess somehow. It couldn't have been about Tam, Sasha or Rebecca really, because there wasn't anything that connected the three of them — except Jess. All that stuff I was asking you about making up stories? Well, Jess certainly made up the *Stalking* piece. That's what got me thinking along these lines, like what if someone had actually used the murders as a way to get to *Jess*. In that sense the victims weren't even part of it, except that they were connected to her."

"Fuck," she said again. "Hang on. I'm pulling over. *Shit*. When you said 'exclusive' I thought you meant some kind of three-in-a-bed thing. I never realised we were going to break the solution to the biggest crime in the country."

"But the three-in-a-bed element is there," I said, not meaning to joke, but being intrigued that this was what had started it all. Jess, Mark and Tyler.

"So you want me to find out whether it was the same guy who was in Eastbourne?"

"Yeah. I've a feeling he was in one of these places, but he might just have lived in the area. We need to find out if it is the same guy. I'm pretty sure it's all going to add up, but if it doesn't then we've got problems. I can place this hate-mail guy at the scene of Jess's disappearance, but . . ."

"How?" She sounded on the verge of exploding.

"Jess supposedly left a goodbye note, except it turns out it's in the same handwriting as these letters I've got."

"So if he forged her note, then . . ."

"Yeah. Jess hasn't disappeared, he's abducted her."

CHAPTER TWENTY-TWO

THE KING OF ROCK AND ROLL

"OH, MY GOD," breathed Sarah. She was silent for a moment, like she was adding things up in her head. Her mobile crackled some more and I heard the sound of a large vehicle passing her car.

"Are you still there?"

"Yeah, I just can't believe it all. Are you absolutely sure you're right about this?"

"Yes. Well, as sure as I can be. I suppose I could call the police next."

"No," she said, too quickly. "Don't call the police."

"Sorry?"

"Look, I'm going to assume for the moment that you're not mad and that you're not winding me up. If everything you say is true, then this is going to be the biggest story of my career. I know it's selfish, but I *need* this exclusive."

"But what about Jess?"

"We're going to find her, rescue her — assuming she's still alive — and you're both going to be on the front page, babe. We can sort this out ourselves in far less time than it would take to go through it all with the police anyway. And think how embarrassing it'll be if we're wrong. No: we can call them when we find her."

"But we don't know where she is."

"Yeah, and that's what you're going to work out. I mean, you've got the rest, this can't be too difficult, surely?" Her voice quickened and became more professional and brisk. "I'll see what I can get on this bloke's identity, see if we can match the schoolboy with the hate-mail guy, and you try and work out where he may be hiding Jess."

"Okay," I said, uncertainly, feeling like I was obeying orders but not knowing how on earth I was going to fathom out where Jess was.

I replaced the phone and walked, in a daze, back into the sitting room. Sarah's words played like an old film in my head: Jess, Mark and Tyler in bed together, in a school. A boy walking in on them, taking them by surprise, scaring the shit out of them. I imagined Mark and Tyler freaking out. What if they were caught? What if they were expelled? Then I saw Jess, thin, pale and over-dramatic, assuring them that she would take care of everything.

Sarah had said that this all happened ten years ago (could that be significant?) just before the summer holidays. Jess must have thought that the only way to shut the younger boy up would be by making sure he had something bigger to hide; that *he*, rather than *they*, would be the laughing stock of the school. Stop the problem developing by destroying its root. That was exactly what she would have done.

This all sounded just like the Jess I knew, and the Jess everyone had spoken about. She had attacked, harder than she thought her target could defend. But in her strange nuclear-war world, the small country she hadn't thought would survive a first strike was now bombing her back, even harder, using more sophisticated weaponry.

I still didn't understand why this guy had murdered the three women, though. But there would be time for that later. I had to work out where Jess was. Sitting back on the sofa, lighting a cigarette and taking a sip of cold coffee, I thought I was in for a lot of hard thinking, but it proved a bit easier than that. Blindingly.

In my dreams Jess had been carried out of all kinds of buildings on a stretcher. Now, in reality, as I shut my eyes, I knew that the building had to be the Ivy Lane school.

* * *

When I called Sarah she was still on the motorway.

"Lily," she said when she answered, "you were right. The guy's name is Elvis Wilson. He was in an institution just outside Eastbourne for a year, between 1995 and 1996. His mother checked him in, apparently. I've double-checked and he definitely was the boy Jess distributed the pictures of."

"God," I said. "So . . ."

"So this is definitely our man." She sounded excited. "Any thoughts on where we go next?"

"Oh, yes," I said, and told her what I'd worked out.

Sinking back against the wall in the hallway, my body was gripped with an ominous fear, like I didn't believe what was happening. Gathering my wits together, I realised we would need someone to show us where to go inside the school, so I picked up the phone and called Mark Savage. He was at the office, luckily, but about to go out on an assignment.

"Forget that," I said quickly. "Meet me at the Ivy Lane school as soon as you can."

"The school?" he said, sounding confused. "My old school? I thought they were going to demolish it."

"Yes. That's what I'm afraid of."

"Lily, what's going on?"

"I'll explain when you get there."

"Okay," he said, sounding suspicious. "Incidentally, Tyler's back. The ex-girlfriend threw him out."

"Great, well, bring him too, if you can," I said.

"Sure."

With a shaking hand I replaced the telephone and walked into the sitting room. How was I going to do this? I needed to get out of the house and to Cambridge without being seen. After pacing the floor for a few minutes I had an idea: not a good one, but the only one that might work.

"Star," I said, walking through the kitchen door and into the garden.

"Mmm?"

"Could you come inside for a second, please?"

* * *

The two women emerged from the garden and into the kitchen. The stick-insect one with the skirt and the done-up hair, and super-slag, in her jeans again, curly hair up in a frisky little topknot.

They were talking animatedly, then moving off to the left where I could no longer observe them through the sitting-room window. The sun and the net curtain had an eclipse-like, silhouetting effect but at least I could keep an eye on her. It was going to be today: the day that we would finally meet. She had the letters I'd sent to Jessica; I saw them scattered on the table. Clever girl. If she had an ounce of intelligence she would soon be on to me. But I wasn't worried about that, because I was going to kill her.

She came out of the kitchen and walked quickly through to the hall and, I assumed, up the stairs. Yes, a minute later, there she was in her bedroom, back to the window, reading a book.

Star's white shift dress fitted me perfectly, except for being a bit tight around my chest. It didn't take long for me to clip my hair up and to stick hers in a high, slightly backcombed ponytail as she struggled into my jeans and old T-shirt.

"This isn't going to work," she giggled.

"It has to," I replied seriously. "Just keep your back to him for a while. He'll realise eventually, but it won't matter by then. I'll be long gone."

The gate at the end of the garden led to an alleyway, stretching off in both directions, hitting different roads at either end. Henri's car would be parked off to the right, Star had told me. It was a good thing he'd taken the tube to work this morning.

Out of breath and shaking, I unlocked the car and fell in, immediately locking all the doors behind me and looking around to see if I'd been followed. There was no sign of anyone, so I started the engine and pulled off with a sharp squeal of tyres. I deliberately chose a snaking route of little roads and side streets, cutting through Camden the back way to Finsbury Park and up to Tottenham, constantly checking my rear-view mirror for signs that I was being followed. It didn't take long to reach Seven Sisters, at which point I was able to accelerate out of London, cutting up the odd bus and slow-moving tourist until I reached the motorway, at which point I calmed down.

I'd done it — I'd escaped.

As my heart rate slowed so did the car, until I was within the speed limit — or almost. Cruising along at about eighty I was able finally to think and act without being watched and followed. And so I kept wondering: who was Elvis Wilson?

Hoping Mark, Tyler and Sarah weren't too far behind, I moved into the fast lane to overtake a lorry. I had to get there fast.

I sat in the car across the road. If she came out on foot I would get out and follow her; if she drove (which I didn't think she did) I could be right behind her. No one knew I drove; that was one of the ways in which the murders had been so ingenious. Because I went by train, they would be looking for someone who didn't drive. Very clever.

That was the problem with all this criminal profiling. It never took into account that criminals, killers and psychopaths are often highly intelligent. Look at me: even after changing schools more times than I care to remember, I got four A-grade A levels. That's why I don't see anything wrong with killing. Human life. It's so unimportant in the scheme of things. The army think that. Heads of state think that. But the masses have their morality. Their rules and codes. Right and wrong. You see, my theory is that the brighter you are, the less removed you are from notions of right and wrong. The more able you are to see logic in things rather than emotion. Do you remember the King's Cross fire? I always imagined being in that, wondering what I would have done. Someone once asked me who I'd save in a choice between a baby and a middle-aged man (I think it was in some management conference when I went to work before I went completely mad and my mother had to get me locked up). I'd save the man, of course. Wouldn't you? Babies are nothing. They haven't grown into people yet, they don't have personalities. They don't feel pain as much as adults do.

Do you know why that is, incidentally? It's because they don't imagine. They don't see a knife coming toward them and think, I'm going to be stabbed; it's going to hurt; I might die. They don't know it's a knife or what it does because they haven't been taught that yet.

But the point I'm making is that two groups of people kill: really stupid people and really intelligent people. People who are beyond either end of the law, of morality. Sick people kill. And I'm sick. Shall I tell you what the disease is? It's an allergy. An allergy to humanity.

But that doesn't mean I'm not clever. And I was clever. At that moment, sitting outside Super-slag's house in the black Mondeo, I thought I was really clever. I was going over it in my head.

You see, the plan was that any police investigation working logically would not find any way of connecting me to the crimes. I mean, why would I have killed those three particular women? In the sense that all I knew about them was their names and addresses from Jessica's file, they were random victims. To me.

That's the important part, you see: they were only random to me. There was no motive. Or not one that anyone would be able to understand. People would read so much into the killings, looking for a set of logic to lead to the killer. But I hadn't left any logic behind. No clues; no logic. I'd learnt a lot from Jessica Mallone. Hit hard, imaginatively. And that's what I did. It was appropriate, I thought. After all, she was fucking imaginative about ruining my life.

Choosing women who had been stalked — what could have been better? The police would suspect the stalkers and go looking for them; boyfriends, ex-boyfriends, people at the magazine. Jess. Tyler. Mark. And I tried to help that line of enquiry along. That eternal "love" triangle was well due for a good shattering. I mean, that was why. And since none of them even remembered me, who the hell was going to make the connection?

"Lily Pascale," I said into the mobile phone once I'd fumbled in my bag for it.

"It's Sarah."

"Hi," I replied. "Where are you?"

"I'm just coming off the M25. Where are you?"

"I'm not sure. I'm closer than you, but not much. I've got Mark and Tyler coming as well. I thought they could show us where to go in the school."

"Well done. Now all I've got to do is find a photographer."

"Is that going to be a problem?"

"Dunno. Since I haven't told my editor what I'm working on, it might be."

"Well, as a last resort we've always got Mark."

"Mmm." Sarah sounded distracted. "I think I might take the pictures myself. I get double the exclusive that way."

"Well, don't get too excited, she might not even be there."

But she had to be, and all I cared about was getting her out of there. Something about Sarah's attitude disturbed me, but then her tabloid attitude came with her very useful tabloid skills, so who was I to complain?

Before long road signs appeared telling me I was twenty miles away from Cambridge, then ten, then that my turn-off was the next one. I exited the motorway and drove around a large round-about, selecting the road for the city centre.

The countryside around me was yellow, rape-ish and flat: a complete contrast to Devon in the summer. I wondered where this school was. Accelerating down the narrowing country road, I started to plan in my head: I needed a map and I needed an address.

The black Mondeo became hot: stifling. I got out and walked for a while. The girl was still reading by the window so I went to the shop for a can of Coke. I drink it on the way back, the whole can, and then took up my usual position near the front garden.

After a while she moved from the window. Where was she going? To answer the front door. Why? Because I was ringing the bell.

The Ivy Lane school was just across a park in the middle of the town. The tall, grey brick building had clearly seen better days, and I could see why it was being demolished. Part of the roof had crumbled away and the whole building looked altogether unstable. Boards covered its large windows and skips, scaffolding and other workmen's stuff was stacked outside.

It had been impossible to take the car up the large gravel drive-way to the school, since this too was blocked off by diggers and workmen, so I walked, ducking behind hedges and trees when any-one came near, until I reached the large front doors of the ex-school.

There was no sign of Sarah yet, and Mark wasn't here either.

How was I going to get in? I had to get in. But then where would I look? Wishing the others would hurry up, I walked around the back of the school to an overgrown cricket pitch. And here I sat, smoking a cigarettte, waiting. Wondering how Star was getting on, I pulled out my phone and dialled the number.

* * *

The phone rang inside the house. She answered it. I rang the doorbell again. Faintly, I could hear her say, "There's someone at the door, you'll have to call me back." Then she opened the door.

As planned, I immediately grabbed her by the throat; a professional doorstep, if I say so myself (rule: don't think before you act — take them properly by surprise) and pushed her back inside the house, slamming her up against the wall on the left while kicking the door shut with my left leg.

She wasn't screaming, or shaking. Just looking at me. And as I looked back I finally realised: it was the wrong fucking woman. The Asian one, the stepmother, with her hair all backcombed, wearing Superslag's clothes.

You.

"You're angry, aren't you?" you said calmly, your words choked by the pressure on your neck.

You know, there was something in your voice that got me then. How many people have spoken to me like that before? Asked for my secrets? Talked about my childhood — always choosing the wrong fucking things to talk about. Jonathan's disappearance (and the bit I always forget: the bit when I found the body, putrid and cold, in the park, by the swings). My father's death. The wrong things. Never her. Jessica. The end of my fucking life.

You kept asking me to let you go; not to hurt you so much. I'm sorry about that. But at the time I told you to keep quiet, keep moving.

As I spoke I was pulling you — away from the wall. Then pushing you — in through the facing door. We were in the sitting room. It looked different from the inside. Less hazy. Bigger. I pushed you onto the sofa and took out my big knife. A new one: I'd bought it specially for her. But you'd have to do, I thought.

"If you so much as fucking move . . ." I said. Threatening.

"I understand," you said.

The phone began to ring again.

Still waiting for Mark, I tried Henri's number again. I was a bit worried about Star. Someone had been at the door. What if . . . ? It didn't bear thinking about. I just needed to check she was all right.

I asked you who it was going to be, on the phone. You were straight with me, weren't you, when you said it was going to be Lily? I was really blown away by your honesty, you know? I didn't know why you were doing it. For a while I thought it was a tactic, to wrong-foot me and get me where you wanted me. But I let you answer the phone. You pointed out that if you didn't answer, she'd know something was wrong, since you were supposed to be here posing as her. I told you I'd cut your throat if you told her I was here or said anything that sounded funny. You didn't seem scared at all.

After what seemed like an age, Star answered.

"Star!" I said. "I was worried about you. Is everything all right?"

"Yes," she said, slightly shakily.

"Who was at the door?"

"No one."

"Are they still there?" I asked, suspicious because of something in her voice, wondering whether she couldn't talk for some reason.

"No. Everything's fine."

"Are you sure?"

"Yes." Her voice became artificially bright. "Anyway, I've got some work to be getting on with. I'll see you later. Guess what? We fooled him. He's gone somewhere, but I didn't get a look at him. Will you be back soon?"

"No. I'm waiting for Sarah and Mark. Then we're going in. Are you sure you're okay?"

"Yes. Stop fussing."

"Take care."

When I looked up there were two figures walking towards me. One was Mark, the other I'd never seen before. Still slightly confused by something in Star's tone, I watched them approach until they were standing right in front of me.

"So," said Mark. "What's going on?"

I didn't understand why you didn't alert her to the fact I was here. Then you told me: you told me you wanted to interview me for some project, that you work with — what did you call them — sadistic murderers all the time.

You still weren't scared. That's what really freaked me out. I think you actually scared me a bit. You told me all those stories about people who kill babies and rape children for fun. That did my head in. Do you really know people like that?

Those men sounded pathetic though. They have no reason for what they do. I have reasons. And I know my case is fascinating. So that's when I agreed. Yes, you could interview me on two conditions: 1) that I get to kill you afterwards, 2) that you don't play for time unnecessarily.

I tied you to that chair at the kitchen table — I hope you're not too uncomfortable — and went to get your tape recorder from the garden. On the way back in I played some of the tape, it was some bloke talking about how he'd killed his own daughter. He sounded completely mental. And that's why I decided to speak to you, to prove I was cleverer than all your crap child-killers; all your mundane multiple murderers. The ones who'd been caught.

The tape began recording.

"I'm Star," you said.

"And I," I declared, speaking in my Scottish voice, "for these purposes at least, am Tyler."

"This is Tyler," said Mark. "Although you've already met, I think."

"No," said the man, looking confused and shaking his head.

"This isn't Tyler," I said slowly, feeling my thoughts expand uncomfortably.

"I think you'll find it is," said Mark, looking at me curiously.

"Oh, shit!" I said. "So the bloke in the flat was . . ."

"Not me," said Tyler.

"Elvis Wilson!" I said, feeling all the hairs on my body prick up when I realised that it had to have been him, that I'd been alone in that flat with the murderer. I looked at Tyler and Mark, at their blank faces, and realised they didn't know who I was talking about. "Don't you remember him?"

"No," said Tyler. "Should we?"

"The king of rock and roll?" said Mark, joking.

"The bloke who found you both in bed with Jess," I prompted, "ten years ago."

"Oh, fuck," said Mark, looking away, his face starting to redden and his joke suddenly cold.

Tyler remained composed, his harsh jawline steady and his expression sober. "And you say he's been posing as me?"

"Yes."

"Why?"

"Because he's the killer, you dickhead," said Mark, putting his face in his hands.

"Oh," said Tyler. "Fuck."

"You didn't trust Jess, did you?" I asked. "Either of you. That's how he's been able to take this so far. If you —" I pointed at Tyler — "hadn't run away because you thought Jess did it, he would never have been able to pose as you."

Mark regained his composure and they both shrugged.

"So where is she?" asked Tyler.

"I think she's in there," I said, pointing up at the school. "Probably in whatever room this all started."

They both stood still, looking at me. I could see Sarah approaching over Mark's shoulder. She waved at me and broke into a run.

"What's happening?" she asked when she caught up to us, winking at me and adding, "Nice dress, babe."

"Nothing, yet," I said, smiling back at her. "We've all just got here. I was waiting for you before I did anything."

"Great," she said briskly, getting a camera out of her shoulder bag. "I'll just get a shot of these two . . ."

The side door that I'd been sitting by was locked, of course, and boarded. I kicked it a couple of times frustratedly, while Sarah started to quiz Tyler and Mark about their sordid past. I wished they would stop messing around. There was a woman trapped in there, and we didn't know whether she was dead or alive.

"We can't get in this way," I observed after a couple more kicks.

"Hang on," said Mark, breaking away and leaving Sarah in rapt concentration, listening to Tyler speak. "There's another way that they probably won't have bothered to board up."

We set off round the building, calling out to the others to hurry up.

"What's the matter with Tyler?" I asked Mark. "You'd have thought he'd be breaking down doors to get to his girlfriend."

"That's Tyler," he said, shrugging. "He's always been like this. Don't forget this is the bloke who reckoned Jess was a murderer and ran off the instant he thought there might be trouble."

"Poor Jess."

Mark looked at me and pushed his glasses up his nose. "Don't feel sorry for either of them. They absolutely deserve each other."

Sarah and Tyler had caught up by now, and we all found ourselves walking towards a small side door.

"We should be able to get in over here," said Mark.

In a way, I almost hoped we wouldn't; that the building would really be impenetrable and that Jess wouldn't be in there. But I knew beyond a shadow of a doubt that it had all been a lie now. Sure, *Tyler* had told me (and the police) that she was away. The problem had been that it wasn't Tyler.

All at once it became clear: Tyler's moodiness, his uncertain Scottish accent (the real Tyler's was softer, more distinct) and the fact that he was never in when I rang him — how could he have been, when he was busy following me? That had started just after I'd met him. *Of course*. And his alibi was great: posing as someone else who had a real alibi (of course, the real Tyler had been to the gym that morning) had been very clever: much better than inventing one of his own. Not that he'd needed one, since there was no connection between him and either the magazine or the women.

And the goodbye note. No one had left it; Elvis must have written it quickly himself when he'd left the room for those few minutes. I'd wondered at the time why the police hadn't taken it and now I knew. He'd written it specially for me, because I was the one asking too many questions; I was the one who hadn't been convinced by Jess's disappearance, because she'd asked me to come.

The door opened after a few hard shoves and led into what would have been the kitchens. Mark walked in first, with me following him and Sarah and Tyler behind us. It still surprised me that Tyler wasn't surging forward, racing on ahead, calling out her name. It surprised me — but not much. Like Mark had said, he'd thought she was capable of murder.

We made our way up a semicircular staircase that groaned at every step. Then through corridor after corridor in a maze that I felt certain I wouldn't be able to remember if I had to. Then, finally it seemed, we turned off into a thin, creaky passage.

"This is Maids'," hissed Mark. "Where the sixth-form studies used to be."

"And is the room down here?" I asked.

"Yeah. It's at the end. Seventh on the left."

"My old room," said Tyler softly.

"It's a bit dark," Sarah pointed out.

"Hang on," said Mark, rustling in his pockets. "I've got a lighter in here somewhere."

As he flicked it on the state of the devastation of the school really became evident. It was a good thing we hadn't walked down the passage in the dark: several floorboards had been removed, leaving gaping black holes to goodness knew where. The place was so dusty I had to keep my hand over my mouth as we picked our way carefully down towards the room. Spiders' webs caught and snagged on my bare legs, and the now greying white dress.

We were only two doors down when we heard it. A faint banging, which grew more insistent, and the sound of a girl crying.

"Is that you, Elvis?" called a girl's voice, cracked and weak. "Come and let me out. I'm ill — *please!*"

"Jess?" called Tyler uncertainly.

"Please let me out," cried the voice pitifully.

We all moved forward rather more quickly to the door of the seventh room. It was locked, but Mark and Tyler kicked it down. We were in.

The sight inside the room was unbelievably grim. A cereal packet and water bottle lay empty by the side of the room, their edges chewed as if by rats. The room itself was entirely dark, save for the thinnest sliver of light penetrating the boarded window. It picked out a notebook on which the word SORRY was written in large capital letters. In a foetal position next to the notebook was a figure which was unmistakbably Jess, naked, pale and shivering.

"Lily," she said, ignoring Tyler, Mark and Sarah. "You *did* it. Thank God. Help me out of here."

And then she passed out.

And then you asked your first question: How did you kill them?

So I suppose this is it. Interview over. Time to die.

Sarah only managed to snap a couple of shots of Jess before Tyler swept her subject up in his arms and carried her out of there. Mark hurried after them.

"Could you call Addenbrookes and tell them we're on our way?" he shouted to me.

"Who?"

"The hospital," called Tyler, almost dropping Jess as he stumbled in his haste to get out.

"Hmm," said Sarah, getting out her mobile phone. "I'll send a photographer as well." She looked at me excitedly, her face contorted in the dark so it was one big smiling shadow. "Now all we have to do is find the murderer."

"Well, the last time I sensed his presence he was outside my house," I said, wryly, watching Sarah's eyes widen. "But, then again, he may be back in Deptford, still posing as Tyler."

"You are something else," she said.

Sarah came back to London with me in Henri's car, so she could listen while I called the police and told them who their man was. Then she interviewed me (or so it felt) at great length about how exactly all this had been resolved. We were in good spirits by the time we reached Camden. It was only a matter of time before Elvis Wilson was picked up and charged with the murders of Sasha, Tam and Rebecca.

Then we saw all the police cars outside Henri's house, along with an ambulance. The front door was wide open and there were police and paramedics everywhere.

I'd seen this scene often on TV. But nothing had prepared me for what it really felt like to arrive home and realise that something awful had happened while you were out: awful enough for at least six police cars to be waiting for you, blocking the road and holding up the traffic. I felt a volcanic blast of bile in my throat; my heart became almost silent in my chest.

"Oh, fuck," I whispered, digging my fingernails into my legs. "Not Star. Please God, not Star."

Sarah looked at me as though she was going to say something and then thought better of it. Jumping out of the car, we pushed our way through the police officers and tape now surrounding the house. My head was full of images of Elvis getting in there and attacking Star. I felt sick. It was all my fault: getting her to dress up as me and then leaving her here as a sitting duck while I went off to be a hero at the school. I could honestly say I had never felt so bad in my entire life. Henri's lovely new girlfriend; my great new friend, Star. Not dead. Not my fault. *Please*.

I was vaguely aware of Sarah pushing aside more policemen, saying *She lives here* in that authoritative way of hers. Then I saw Tyler, or rather Elvis, being driven away in a police car. Hate twisted inside me: for the murders of the three poor, innocent women, for Jess and now for Star. I wanted to run after the car and shout at him; break the window; punch him. My face felt wet and only then did I notice the hot tears of hate and anger pouring out of my eyes. Brushing the tears away, vaguely wondering how long I'd been crying, I walked into the house, Sarah steadying me as we went.

CHAPTER TWENTY-THREE

TO THE END

INSIDE IT WAS A MESS. The door mat was scrunched up against the wall in the hallway, and two pictures and a vase lay smashed by the stairs. With an ever-increasing feeling of dread I picked my way through the debris to the sitting room, not knowing what I would find there.

We found Star sitting on the sofa with her feet up and a blanket wrapped around her, drinking a steaming mug of tea. Opposite her sat Jon, looking like he'd come out of a war zone. Sarah took one look at the scene and disappeared into the kitchen to make some more tea, breathing an audible sigh.

I sat down next to Star, shaking with relief, and wrapped my arms around her protectively.

"Star," I gulped. "I was so frightened. I can't believe you're all right. What on earth happened?"

"Your friend," she said, smiling at Jon, "has been very brave."

"I was going to ask what he was doing here."

"Sexy dress, babe," he said, grinning lopsidedly at me.

"Never mind that. What's going on? And what happened to your shirt?" His shirt was covered in blood, and his arm was freshly bandaged. He looked like he'd been through some kind of mangle.

"I had a bit of a tussle with your psycho killer." He opened his blue eyes innocently. "I only popped round to see if you fancied another, um . . ."

"Yeah, we get the picture," I said quickly.

"What happened?" said Sarah, coming back in with a fresh pot of tea, having been listening from the kitchen. "Did you just knock at the door and disturb him, or what?"

"Nah, since I'd already been *intimate* with Lily I thought it would be all right to come round the back. I looked through the window and saw this other woman tied to a chair in the kitchen. I didn't know who she was. At first I thought I was walking in on something private, then I saw that bloke wandering around the kitchen with this massive fucking knife. That's when I started to get suspicious."

"I thought that was going to be the end of me," said Star hoarsely. "I'd kept Elvis occupied by doing an interview with him, but we'd just finished and he said he was going to kill me. I was terrified."

"I called the Old Bill on my mobile," said Jon. "But I got the feeling they weren't going to get here quick enough . . ."

"So the next thing I knew," continued Star, "the back door was opening slowly and this other guy I'd never seen before was coming into the kitchen. At first I thought to myself, *What's going on? I can't be having two murderers breaking into the house in one day.* Then I realised he was coming to help. He put his finger to his lips and started creeping over. Elvis's back was to him, and so I tried to help by keeping his attention focused on me, pretending that the rope was getting too tight. Jon took something from the draining board, I think it was a frying pan, and kept walking over, really slowly. Elvis was still facing me, pressing the knife to my throat. He still couldn't see Jon, but I knew he was about to cut me. I think Jon realised too, because at that moment he kind of screamed, got Elvis's attention and swung for him with the frying pan."

"I hit him really hard around the face," said Jon, demonstrating all his movements with his hands. "But he just kept coming. He slashed at me with the knife, and ripped half my fucking arm off with it. That made me really pissed off, so I picked up one of the chairs and charged him with it, knocking the knife out of his hands.

He kept going backwards until he fell over. Then I got down and hit him in the face. I think I broke his nose — it started bleeding everywhere — but that didn't stop him head-butting me. I'm not sure what happened after that." He shrugged, obviously realising he was losing his cool a bit. "Just a fight, really."

"You really let him have it," said Star admiringly. "You definitely had the upper hand."

"Course I did, babe," he said, smiling weakly.

"So did the police turn up, then?" I asked.

"Yeah," said Jon. "Luckily for whatshisname. I was on the verge of liquidising him."

"It was all over very quickly then," said Star. "They just kind of swooped in and grabbed Elvis, let me go and sat us down in here with hot sweet tea. I think they're going to come and take us off to give statements soon, once we're over the shock."

"But how . . ." I began. There were so many questions I wanted to ask. "How did he — Elvis — get in here?"

"He doorstepped me," she said, "thinking I was you. He'd seen the box of letters through the window and got frightened that you knew more than he'd expected you would. He'd come in here to kill you."

"Very intelligent," I said, trying to sound tough but feeling my insides fold in on themselves. No one had ever wanted to kill me before, not seriously.

"What did he do when he discovered you weren't Lily?" Sarah asked.

"It threw him," said Star. "I think he'd lost it completely by that point. He was delusional. He thought that he was in control of the whole situation; posing as Tyler, being interviewed by the police, convincing everyone that Jess had just 'gone away' and following Lily around. He was getting some kind of kick out of watching you," she said, looking at me. "He never thought you'd make any sense of what he'd done."

"Was he angry?" asked Sarah, slipping a Dictaphone out of her bag and placing it on the coffee table.

"He was at first, but I played on his weird God-complex and convinced him that it would be a real honour for me to interview him, what with him being such an exceptional and rare case and so on. I thought it was best to keep him talking — which I did for absolutely hours — but I was so glad when Jon turned up. Mind you, it was the best interview I've ever done."

"You're not serious?" I said.

"Mmm. He's a funny case. Quite mad on one level, but in a way, not at all. He had a strange childhood full of all kinds of bizarre incidents. I think the most disturbing thing was when his best friend was murdered. I remember the case — it was quite famous. Elvis actually discovered his friend's dead body in a park. The interesting thing was that he'd obviously completely repressed it. He kept saying that the worst thing that had happened to him was what Jess did. It quite clearly wasn't, but I think what was important was that it was the *last* thing. Like the last straw."

"I see," I said. "So she really picked the wrong victim, then?"

"Absolutely. By the time he ended up at Ivy Lane he was already obsessional and completely damaged. I think the worst thing about it was that she was the first girl who'd ever given him any attention. And for all that to have been put on as part of a silly prank. It just . . . *destroyed* him. No one had ever loved him, really, but at least there'd been no pretence. Jess just pushed him too far."

"Sounds like a right bitch," said Jon.

"What exactly did she do to him?" asked Star. "That was the one thing he didn't really elaborate on."

"Pretended to be his girlfriend and got him to pose naked for pictures which she distributed around his school," I explained. "Because he'd seen her in bed with Tyler and Mark and they were worried he'd spread the rumour."

"What a cow," said Jon. "She was the journalist, right?"

Sarah laughed. "If you can call it that."

"She made up all the stories," I explained. "The ones in *Smile!* magazine, about the women. They were never stalked, she just got them to pose for her so she could get up there on the first rung of the media ladder."

"Did this Elvis character know that?" he asked.

"No," I said. "If he had, then he would have done the whole thing differently."

I lit a cigarette and offered one to Star which she took. I noticed her hands were still shaking.

"Well, at least I've had the chance to apply some of my theory," she said. "It's so important not to show fear. I mean, I'm shaking now, but you should have seen me when he was in here. I was as cool as a cucumber — until right at the end, that is."

"Like in *Peeping Tom*," I said.

"Exactly."

"It was Elvis Wilson himself who led me into that particular cul-de-sac," I mused. "I wonder why he did it. I suppose it was just a way of keeping me busy, sending me off down the wrong track and giving Mark a bit of a hard time as well."

"He's a clever bloke," said Star. "He knew what he was doing. He'd planned it so he wouldn't get caught and it would have worked if . . ."

"Yes," I said, "I was thinking about that. *If* the whole thing hadn't been based on a scam no one had known about. And because of that, Jess won again. It's a good job Tam broke the rules and had the magazine cover in her room."

"Mmm." Star closed her eyes and rubbed her temples slowly.

"Are you sure you're all right?" I asked.

"I am now," she said, opening her eyes again and smiling at us all.

"Do you think he would have killed you if Jon hadn't turned up?" asked Sarah.

"No," said Star, "I don't think he would have done." Looking at our disbelieving expressions she tried to explain. "I think he would have done me some damage, no doubt about that. But he didn't have anything to gain from it, and we'd been talking for so long I think he almost saw me as a friend. You know, it's easier to kill a stranger, and all that. Still, I'm glad I didn't have to test out that theory. I would hate to have been proved wrong."

Jon looked like he didn't know how to deal with all the hero stuff, his eyes moving this way and that like he was embarrassed. But he'd rescued Star, and, just for that moment, I loved him for it.

"Come and get out of that shirt," I said, pulling him up from the chair and leading him by the hand into the kitchen.

"Okay," he said, grinning again and raising an eyebrow as I sat him down at the table and kissed him.

"What was that for?"

"For saving Star," I said, smiling broadly.

246

That was the last moment of calm for the rest of the day.

Jon and Star were whisked off to the hospital eventually for check-ups, while the police took statements from Sarah and me at the local police station. Jon needed a couple of stitches to his arm, but Star was fine apart from some rope-burn. After that they were taken to the police station to give their statements. Sarah disappeared eventually looking ecstatic, almost incoherent with the shock of getting such an amazing story. By the time she left she had it all: pictures and details of Jess's rescue; interviews with me, with Star and with Jon; and even, it seemed, a picture of Elvis being driven off in the police car, which I'd been too sick with dread to notice her taking.

At some point I managed to give the house the once-over, itemising the damage for the insurance people, rehearsing in my head what I would say to Henri when he came home, trying to find a euphemistic way of saying *Sorry your house has been trashed, but the good news is that Star's alive despite being tied up and held by a crazed murderer all afternoon.*

The next few days were a blur. There was a press conference, during which Jon was at first very bashful, very sexy and later very drunk. I still hadn't quite forgiven him for broadcasting the fact that we'd been "intimate," a fact that had also appeared in Sarah's five-page exclusive, but that didn't stop me going home with him that night. I eventually listened to the tapes Star had made of Elvis, which were disturbing and fascinating at the same time.

Epilogue

My decision to take a holiday was inspired mostly by Jon. We spent the majority of our two weeks in Paris indoors having fantastic sex; not talking, not analysing, just doing. This represented something of a departure for me. For most of my life I'd been obsessed with relationships of the lasting variety. But Jon wasn't relationship material, and we both knew that. He didn't have any social skills for one thing (like telling my father we were going away for a "shagfest"), neither did he have any real intention to settle down. I had a good time because none of this bothered me, and of course because he was fantastic in bed. Each morning we woke up in crumpled, cool sheets and just sort of melted into one another. Every night we danced together in our underwear in the moonlight on our balcony; slow almost-sex dances ending in real sex on the floor of the rented apartment.

But as we said goodbye back in London, I knew I'd never forget him. Not only had he rescued Star, he'd rescued me. I knew I wasn't hung up on Fenn any more; it was clear in my mind that I was going to devote more of my life to having fun. Pleasure wasn't something to be ashamed of. Jon had helped me realise that.

So it was with some reservations that I answered the call on the train going home. The number showing was Fenn's mobile. I'd been enjoying the journey so far: the train going fast, the carriage almost empty and me just sitting there thinking about the future. My life was only going to get better. I was going to make appointments to go and look at cottages to rent this week. I wanted something on the water. Near the sea, or possibly by the river. My new car was ready to be picked up, and even the stack of marking in my cupboard hadn't dampened my spirits.

I answered the phone.

"Lily Pascale," I said into the handset, pretending I didn't know who was on the other end.

"Lily," said Fenn's voice, "we need to talk."

"Do we?" I replied brightly. "What about?"

"Don't be like that."

"Like what?"

"I saw you in the paper."

"Yeah. You and the rest of the country," I said. "Anyway, how was the honeymoon?"

"Shit." He sounded bitter. His voice was all wrong.

"Sorry?" A few weeks ago this would have been what I wanted to hear. Now it just annoyed me. All his frustrating-but-compelling confusion from before the wedding had now turned into something less interesting: the mawkish resignation of a man who knew he'd made a mistake. Well, I'd told him so.

"It was awful. I spent the whole time wanting to be with you."

"Oh," was all I could think of to say. What the hell was he talking about? I needed to focus on something other than him, so I looked out the window. We'd just passed Teignmouth and the tide was in. Ducks, scores of them, gathered under the bridge. I watched a water-skier bobbing in the water, waiting to be picked up by a circling boat. We'd be arriving in Totnes in under half an hour and Mum would be waiting to pick me up. Then we were going to collect my new car. Then I was going to think about my cottage. My life was going to go on without Fenn, I reminded myself firmly.

"I just wanted to tell you something," he said after a long pause.

I stayed silent for a minute, then said: "What?"

"I love you," he said.

I love you. I *love* you?

"Um," I said, trying to sound cool while my heart tried to break out of my chest. This was surprise, I told myself, not anything else. The surprise turned to anger. I didn't know what to say. "That's, um . . ."

"I shouldn't have said that," he said. "But the thing is, I just keep bottling out. I deleted that message from your mobile the other week, by the way. I just . . . I had to be honest some time."

"Yeah, but why now? Does the concept of timing not mean anything to you? This is like the end of a story, Fenn, not the beginning. You got married. It's over. Anything that there was between us is finished."

"You're angry. I thought you'd be pleased."

"Maybe once," I said firmly. "But not any more. You get on with your cosy life which, don't forget, *you* chose, and just leave me out of it."

"I didn't have a choice," he said bitterly.

"Everyone has a choice. And you've made yours. I'll see you next term."

"But—"

"Goodbye, Fenn," I said firmly.

I switched off the phone and went back to watching the ducks on the water.

M THOMA
Thomas, Scarlett
In Your Face /